MOJO

ALSO BY TIM THARP

Badd

The Spectacular Now

Knights of the Hill Country

MOJO

Alfred A. Knopf

New York

TIM THARP

THIS IS A BORZOI BOOK PUBLISHED BY ALFRED A. KNOPF

Text copyright © 2013 by Tim Tharp
Jacket art copyright © Yakov Stavchansky for Shutterstock

Grateful acknowledgment is made to Hal Leonard for permission to reprint lyrics from "Peggy Sue," words and music by Jerry Allison, Norman Petty, and Buddy Holly, copyright © 1957 (Renewed) by MPL Music Publishing, Inc., and Wren Music Co. All Rights Reserved. Reprinted with permission of Hal Leonard Corporation.

Published in the United States by Alfred A. Knopf, an imprint of Random House Children's Books, a division of Random House, Inc., New York.

Knopf, Borzoi Books, and the colophon are registered trademarks of Random House, Inc.

Visit us on the Web! randomhouse.com/teens

Educators and librarians, for a variety of teaching tools, visit us at RHTeachersLibrarians.com

Library of Congress Cataloging-in-Publication Data
Tharp, Tim.
Mojo / Tim Tharp.
p.   cm.
Summary: A boy who feels powerless in his own life sets out to investigate the mystery of a missing high school girl in his town, who attends an elite private high school very unlike his own.
ISBN 978-0-375-86445-2 (trade) — ISBN 978-0-375-96445-9 (lib. bdg.)
ISBN 978-0-375-89580-7 (ebook)
[1. Self-realization—Fiction. 2. Missing children—Fiction. 3. High schools—Fiction. 4. Schools—Fiction. 5. Secret societies—Fiction. 6. Mystery and detective stories.]   I. Title.
PZ7.T32724Moj 2013
[Fic]—dc23
2012023886

The text of this book is set in 15.5-point Adobe Garamond Pro.

Printed in the United States of America
April 2013
10 9 8 7 6 5 4 3 2 1

First Edition

CHAPTER 1

I never set out to look for Hector Maldonado. I was just minding my own business, walking home from my part-time grocery-sacking job. This was fall of my junior year, and I was one of the carless crew. So my skinny little work buddy Randy Skivens and I were plodding down the side of one of the busier streets in our Oklahoma City suburb, not far from the high school, having our usual conversation about nothing.

Randy's like, "In my opinion Death Race is the best racing video game of all time."

I wasn't exactly the world's biggest fan of racing games, but just for the sake of argument, I told him I thought Adrenaline Monster was the all-time best.

He gaped at me for a second. "Are you kidding, Dylan? Even Supercharger Pro is better than Adrenaline Monster."

I'm like, "No way. That red car in Adrenaline Monster is the coolest car ever."

"You mean that classic '69 Mustang?"

"Yeah, I love that car. Matter of fact, as soon as I get enough paychecks put away, I'm going to buy one just like it."

"No you're not."

"Sure I am. It's going to be the fastest thing anybody's ever

1

seen. I'll pull into the high school parking lot and everybody'll be like, 'Check that out. I've never seen anything so awesome.'"

"No they won't."

"You don't think people are going to be impressed by a '69 Mustang?"

"Oh, they'd be impressed all right, but you're never going to get one."

"Why do you say that?"

"Because you don't know anything about cars, and you're never going to save enough money to afford a '69 Mustang."

And that was when these two ape men in an orange Camaro drove by, and the guy on the passenger side unloaded a half-full beer can that hit Randy right in the crotch.

Randy wasn't a big guy, but he did have a big mouth and wasn't exactly a genius, so he screamed one of his favorite obscenities and, in the direction of the Camaro, launched the single-finger salute, a.k.a. the "F" sign. As in "F" for *fool*. Because that's what you have to be to flip off a couple of nineteen- or twenty-year-old vo-tech-dropout gearheads on a weeknight bender.

The Camaro squealed to a stop.

Randy and I looked at each other, bug-eyed. "You are an idiot," I informed him.

And Randy's like, "Ruuuuuun!"

So away we ran. Over the curb. Around our high school field house. Past the practice field. Onto the senior parking lot. Here, I have to admit I carry a few extra pounds, so I'm not exactly a track star. And it didn't help when Randy stopped all of a sudden.

"Wait a second," he said.

"What the hell are you doing?"

He bent over and plucked something up from the ground. "I found a dollar." He held up the bill like it was a winning lottery ticket or something.

"Are you kidding me?" I said. "Come on!"

Luckily, the Camaro couldn't follow us directly but had to take the road to the east. Still, they'd hit the entrance to the parking lot just ahead of us, and doom would hammer us straight in the face if we didn't do something.

"Split up," I hollered. "They can't follow us both."

Without bothering to check which direction Randy took, I headed west and around the high school to the back of the building—behind the cafeteria where they dump the spoiled milk and the leftover rubbery Salisbury steaks.

The slamming of car doors echoed through the cool fall-of-junior-year evening, so I knew the ape men were close at hand. There was nothing to do but hide, and with the streetlight glaring down, I didn't have any shadows to duck into. So, reluctantly, I flipped back the lid of the nearest Dumpster, hoisted myself over the side, and plummeted into the dank refuse of high school. With the lid closed, it was pretty much pitch black, and the stench was enough to cause a dude to almost puke. But that's not all. As I tried to make myself at least a little comfortable, I leaned against what, for all the world, felt like somebody's arm.

I'm like, "Jesus, Randy, how did you get in here already?"

No reply.

"Randy?" I gave the arm a nudge, but still no response. I was like, *Hmmm, this is strange. Maybe it's just a garbage bag or something.* But I never knew a garbage bag to have arms.

I reached over and gave whatever it was a squeeze. It felt like an arm all right, though it was somewhat on the rigid side. Not good. Either this guy was frozen stiff with fear or he was frozen stiff with a whole bunch of dead.

Outside the Dumpster, the voices of the ape men piped up. "Hey, you little high school wussies, come out and face the music."

"Yeah," added the other one. "We're gonna play the bongos on your skulls, that's what kind of music we're gonna play."

"Heh, heh," the other one snickered. "Bongos. That's good."

That was the IQ level of what I was dealing with here. Stephen Hawking they were not. But cuddling up to what might be a corpse wasn't so cool either. Unless—an idea suddenly hit me—maybe this wasn't a corpse after all. Maybe it was a dummy, like the kind they practice CPR on. Sure, I told myself, that had to be it. Somebody got a little too rambunctious during first-aid lessons and busted the dummy, and the Dumpster was now its final resting place.

I reached up toward the head area and copped a feel. Hair. That was strange. Since when did they start making CPR dummies with hair? But it wasn't impossible, you know? If they can make bomb-detecting robots these days, why not a dummy with lifelike hair? A wonder of modern technology. And now here it was hiding in the Dumpster with me so Ape Man 1 and Ape Man 2 couldn't get their paws on us.

"You ain't got a chance," said Ape Man 1. "You might as well give up. We saw you run back here."

And then Ape Man 2's like, "Hey, I got an idea."

An *idea*? That seemed unlikely coming from one of these knuckleheads, but there was always a first time for everything.

Their footsteps headed in my direction. Loud footsteps. These guys must be wearing boots. All the better to kick my butt with.

4

One of them banged on the side of the Dumpster. "Come on, little wussies. Don't make us come in there and get you."

"You're just gonna make it worse on yourself," the other one said.

At this point, my choices were severely limited:

1. I could try to scrunch down in the trash, but that was likely to make too much noise.

2. I could try to hide behind the CPR dummy, but it probably wasn't big enough. Like I say, I carry a little extra weight.

3. I could sit there as quietly as possible and hope they went away.

But of course they weren't going anywhere. The lid to the Dumpster sprang open and the streetlight's glare flooded in.

"Gotcha," said Ape Man 1.

"You ain't gonna have any fingers left to flip people off with now, boys," added Ape Man 2.

Their fat white faces loomed over me like two evil moons. Then something happened—their snarling mouths went horror-struck.

Ape Man 1's like, "What the hell?"

And Ape Man 2 goes, "Jesus, what did you do, kid?"

They looked at each other, and then it was like, both at the same time, they go, "Shiiiiiiiittt!" And bolted. I stood up just in time to see them fighting for the inside lane as they galloped around the corner of the building.

I'm like, "Wow. What got into them?"

Then I looked down. It was no CPR dummy stowed away with me in that pile of trash. No. It was Hector Maldonado.

CHAPTER 2

ector Maldonado. Dead as a plank. You better believe I couldn't clamber out of that Dumpster fast enough. It was like just touching the same trash might make me catch whatever it was that killed him. But once I was out, despite a case of the cold shivers, I couldn't help gawking back in. I don't know why, but there's something about death that makes you want to stare at it. Maybe it's just because you're glad it's not you.

Hector was my age. I had him in Western Cultures. His father laid tile or something like that. I didn't know about his mother. Hector and I weren't friends, but he seemed like an okay guy. Smart, didn't play sports, not in a bunch of clubs, didn't crack jokes in class or bully anyone in the halls. I guess he was kind of a good-looking guy—not to sound gay or anything—but he was really quiet. Maybe in some other universe, he could've been cool, but not in the one at our high school. At our school he was just kind of *there*. Like desks, and water fountains, and vice principals.

Now here he was, stiffly leaning against one side of the Dumpster, chest-deep in garbage, his eyes staring blankly at the sky, a candy-bar wrapper sticking to the side of his face. A strange coldness seeped into my stomach, my elbows, my knees, like some kind of poison. This was real. Final. Foreclosed on.

"What's going on?" It was Randy sauntering up from the east side of the building. "Are those guys gone?"

"They're gone."

"What are you looking at?"

"You have your cell phone on you?"

"Yeah, why?"

"We have to call the police."

"What for?"

"Look." I nodded toward the Dumpster.

Randy had to stand on his tiptoes. "Holy crap. Dude's dead."

An argument about whether we should actually call the police followed. Randy was against it. Finally I persuaded him that we might find ourselves in plenty of hot water if the cops discovered we'd been here and didn't report Hector's condition. "Okay," he said. "But call on your own phone."

Things got involved from there. The cops don't want you calling in about a dead body and then leaving the scene. We had to stay and answer a bunch of questions:

"Name?"

"Dylan Jones."

"Age?"

"Sixteen and a half."

"Occupation?"

"Grocery-sacker-slash-student."

"Relationship with the deceased?"

"We go to the same school."

"And why were you enemies with the deceased?"

"What? We weren't enemies. I hardly knew him."

"Just a routine question."

I couldn't believe it. Apparently, we were actually suspects, which was really a pisser. I was like, "Look, I'm on the school newspaper. My dad's a teacher and my mom's a nurse," but they didn't care. Somehow we still looked unsavory to them.

At first, it was just a uniformed cop, but then a couple of detectives showed up along with some forensics people. The detectives were even bigger assholes than the uniforms. There was a huge one with a forehead like a cinder block and then a wiry cool-guy type who was too in love with his hair gel. It wasn't hard to see what their routine was. Detective Forehead's job was to intimidate you physically, and Detective Hair Gel was there to throw in a few zingers to deflate your self-esteem.

They were convinced Hector had OD'd on some drug or other and seemed to have their minds made up that Randy and I were involved somehow. Which was stupid—we obviously weren't on drugs at the moment—but once a cop gets an idea in his head, he has a hard time shaking it out.

"We'll need you to come down to the station," Detective Forehead told us.

"Just routine," added Detective Hair Gel.

Just routine. I'm thinking, *What? Is that the cop rationale for everything?*

At the station house, they split me and Randy up, I guess so they could try to poke holes in our stories. Relieved us of our phones too. *Just routine.* Lucky me—I was the first one they decided to mess with. They took me into an office—not one of those cop-show interrogation rooms where they beam the bright light in your face—and I ran through the story about the ape men again, but it didn't take long to find out I wasn't there to fill in some minor details.

"Dylan, we see this kind of thing all the time," Detective Hair Gel started out. "Kids out partying, trying new ways to get a buzz. Next thing you know, one guy goes too far, and then that's it." He snapped his fingers, his way of summing up the death of Hector Maldonado.

"We can tell you're a party boy," said Detective Forehead. He was standing behind his partner's chair, looming you could say, so as to keep up the intimidation.

I was like, "What? I'm not a party boy."

But Detective Hair Gel was unconvinced. "Sure you are. You got the hipster-style glasses, the baggy jeans, the rocker-boy black T-shirt. Shaggy hair. I'd say you probably like a taste of the ecstasy."

For the record, my jeans were baggy because I don't like pants pinching my gut too much, and the shirt was a retro Black Sabbath T-shirt that I only wear because I think Ozzy Osbourne is hilarious.

Anyway, I'm like, "Ecstasy? Is that still a drug? I don't even know anyone who's done ecstasy."

Detective Forehead leaned forward and glowered. "Oh, it's still a drug all right. And you know it."

This was getting ridiculous. You can live your whole life a certain way and what good does it do when the law clamps down on you? I mean, I'm no goody-goody, but I probably hadn't missed a day of school since I had the flu in seventh grade. Made mostly low B's but could've bagged some A's if I really cared that much and turned all my stuff in. The only time I ever got sent to the principal's office since I got to high school was for wearing a T-shirt that said F***K BIGOTS on the front. Now, just because I happened to stumble over a dead body, all of a sudden the cops were treating me like I was some kind of terrorist with a bomb in my underwear or something.

They kept at me for about an hour. Didn't matter that I told them I'd better call my parents so they'd know where I was. They just said it was early yet and I could call them in a little bit. Then they came back at me, wanting me to tell the story again and again until finally they got sick of hearing the same answer over and over.

"Why don't you call the place where I work? They'll tell you I was there and not out snorting crystal meth and ecstasy or whatever."

"Hey," said Detective Forehead. "You don't make the rules around here. We do."

"Dylan, just sit here and think about your predicament for a while," Detective Hair Gel said. "We'll see what your buddy has to say. And it'll be too bad for you if he rolls over first."

Then they swaggered out the door to put the screws to Randy.

So now I was alone, but it wasn't much of a relief. Hanging at the police station is weird. There's this air about the place that makes you feel guilty even if you didn't do anything. It's like you can't move or even think the way you normally do. Chances are, they have a camera trained on you and are analyzing every move you make. There was a phone right there on the desk. I could've called my parents, but I didn't. It was stupid, but it was like even doing that might make me look bad, like I was a criminal because the powers that be thought I was. So I just sat there staring at the floor.

I don't even know how long it was before the dynamic duo waltzed back in to tell me how Randy just confessed. Usually, I would find that funny. After all, I was the king of watching

TV crime shows, true-life and fictional, so I knew it was pretty much standard procedure to trick one guy into spilling the beans by saying his partner already did. But knowing Randy, I wasn't so sure he wouldn't cough out a confession. I could just imagine the exchange:

Detective Hair Gel: I'll bet you'd like a Coke right about now, huh?

Randy: I wouldn't mind a Dr Pepper.

Detective Hair Gel: Well, you tell us what we need to know, and I'll see you get one.

Randy (*unable to sacrifice immediate satisfaction in order to keep out of the big house*): Okay, yeah, we did it. We pumped Hector Maldonado full of ecstasy, heroin, and a little jet fuel just to see what would happen. Now, how about that Dr Pepper?

No, I didn't feel so good about my chances. "I want to call my parents," I said.

"Dylan wants to call his parents," Detective Forehead told his partner, in a mocking, playground-bully way.

"Do you really?" Detective Hair Gel asked. "I doubt that. I mean, what are you going to tell them, that you're down at the police station because you were out doing drugs and killed your best buddy? Because that's what we've got on you right now. The only question is whether it was an accident or intentional. And let me tell you, we're a lot more likely to lean toward the accidental side of the situation if you just come clean about what you were up to tonight."

It was starting to look like I'd never get home. At least not until I'd served a good twenty years in maximum security. I wondered what I'd done to deserve this kind of trouble. Obviously, I didn't kill Hector, but maybe I'd done something else the universe was paying me back for.

Just then, the door opened and a lady cop motioned for the detectives to come into the hall. "Sit tight, kid," Detective Forehead told me. "We'll be back to have you sign a confession in a minute."

They didn't have anything for me to sign when they came back, though. Instead, they did something I never would've expected in a million years. They told me to go home.

I'm like, "What? Just like that?"

"Just like that," Detective Forehead said as he studied the contents of some kind of paperwork.

"Don't worry, Dylan," added Detective Hair Gel. "We'll be in touch. Don't leave the city."

Don't leave the city. Like maybe I had a private jet waiting to fly me off to Acapulco.

CHAPTER 3

Waiting for my parents to come pick us up, Randy and I sat on the edge of the concrete planter in front of the station trading interrogation stories as we simultaneously texted the news to whoever came to mind. Turned out Randy didn't crack under pressure after all. In fact, he had a better strategy than I did—playing dumb ass. He acted like he couldn't even understand the questions, getting the cops to restate them over and over, then acting like he understood, only to come up with an answer that made no sense at all.

"I think those guys chasing us might have been Wiccans," he told them when they asked him how long he'd known Hector.

Not bad. Maybe Randy was some kind of weird genius after all. He wore them out way before they could wear him out, so they came back at me.

"But why do you think they let us go all of a sudden like that?" he asked, the streetlight shining on his oily brown hair.

"Simple," I said. "They probably finally called the grocery store and found out we were at work all evening. Idiots."

"Yeah," he said. "Kind of hard to get loaded up on ecstasy with your buddies when you're standing around catching salami coming down a conveyor belt and packing it into paper or plastic. They should've called the store before hauling us to the station."

"Nazis."

Driving us home, my parents also got pissed about the cops giving us the third degree, but did they do anything about it? No. They just rattled on about civil rights until it finally dawned on my mom that finding a dead kid in a Dumpster might be traumatic for our tender teenage minds. Then she and Dad both started in with their TV-talk-show psychotherapy. Randy and I traded exasperated looks like, *Parents—how can they be so clueless?*

At home, I passed on their offer to sit around the kitchen table with some cold leftovers and discuss my feelings about what happened. They meant well, but how could I talk about Hector Maldonado while Mom and Dad stared back at me like I was still their five-year-old little teddy bear? No, I accepted the cold meat loaf all right, but I took it back to my room, where I could call my all-time best friend and confidante, Audrey Hoffman.

I'd known Audrey since the days of the little inflatable backyard swimming pool—me in my Tiki-head swim trunks and her in the frilly pink one-piece that I never let her forget. I mean, you should see her now—she's definitely not frilly or pink. Mostly she does her hair in pigtails and wears plaid shirts, baggy black pants, and some kind of hat, mainly a black Kangol 504. Artsy garb. She's the photographer on the school paper but plans on doing high-art photography later on.

Audrey used to live across the street, so we did everything together. We read the same books, watched horror movies on late-summer nights, even shot two-character videos in the backyard. The best had to be the one about two Martians try-ing to figure out how to eat spaghetti. It was pretty hilarious.

When she found out her parents were getting divorced and she would have to move across town with her mother, she came straight to me. Same with when she decided she was a lesbian in seventh grade. Turned out we had similar tastes in girls. Not that either one of us was exactly successful in that department. At least not by the start of junior year.

So, anyway, there was no way I could go to bed without talking to her voice-to-voice about this latest ordeal. In a way, she was kind of like my conscience sometimes. I could talk to her, and she'd help me figure out what was really impor-tant. This time she didn't seem to totally get what I was going through, though. I tried to explain how the cops had ham-mered away at me, making me feel like a total nobody loser, but she kept pulling the conversation back in Hector's direction.

Why didn't I haul him out of the Dumpster? she wanted to know. Give him a little dignity. And she couldn't understand how the cops could be so sure Hector had OD'd. Guys like Hector don't OD, not in her opinion. She even wanted to know when his funeral was going to be. Like I could possibly know that already.

I'm like, "Look, I'm trying to explain how these cops go at you like everything you ever were doesn't matter."

And she goes, "Well, I just thought you'd care a little more about Hector."

"I care, but nobody can do anything to him anymore. Me, I'm not so sure about."

Maybe talking about the thing wasn't such a good idea after all. When I got into bed, every time I closed my eyes I saw Hector's face, staring blankly, the candy-bar wrapper stuck to his cheek. I felt his arm next to mine and his hair against my fingers. Dead-kid hair. And in the background I heard Detectives Forehead and Hair Gel drilling me with questions, trying to beat me down. What if I hadn't had an alibi? Would I be in jail right now? It was enough to make you feel like a beetle on the sidewalk with a boot raised right over your head.

CHAPTER 4

The next morning there wasn't much in the news about Hector, just the basics about where he went to school and who his family was. Body in the Dumpster. Cause of death: suspected drug overdose. Discovered by two teenagers. Names not released because of their ages.

Really? It was okay to tell Hector's name but not Randy's and mine? No wonder the local news wasn't barraging us with phone calls.

My parents offered to let me stay home, like finding a dead body was some kind of stomach bug. I passed. No, I had to go somewhere. If the newspapers weren't going to call, I could hang with Audrey and rehash the ordeal with Randy. Funny thing, though. As I walked down the hall to first hour, kids started calling to me.

"Hey, dude! Way to go!"

"Dylan! That is, like, so surreal, man!"

"Hey, Dylan, what was it like?"

Some of these people I didn't even think knew my name. Obviously, the story had blazed its way across the text-message universe like a renegade asteroid. Nothing so perfect to prick up the curiosity of the high school populace like the death of a classmate.

So there I was, surrounded by eager faces, some of them even belonging to some pretty decent-looking girls. They all wanted to know what it was like, sitting in a Dumpster with a dead body. Hector and I were suddenly famous. Too bad Hector wasn't there to enjoy it.

I don't know how many times I told the story that day. First in one hall, then another. At the beginning of class, at the end of class. In the cafeteria, the library, the parking lot. Everybody wanted to hear it. This one guy, the baggy-black-clothes-and-silver-chain-wearing Corman Rogers, kept coming back for more. I'm like, "Dude, morbid much?"

I got better with each telling. By lunch, it started to seem more like a movie I'd seen than something real that'd happened to me. And Hector, I guess, became more like a movie character than a kid who had walked those same high school halls. Maybe that was what I needed him to be at the time.

After lunch, my teacher sent me to the front office to have a talk with this special grief counselor they called in to deal with the student population's feelings about the death. There wasn't exactly a line waiting to get in. Apparently, Principal Chrome Dome, or whoever, thought if anyone needed to talk about it, Randy and I were it. But I didn't have much to say. Nobody likes having someone they don't know picking at their brain.

I was okay, I told the counselor lady, but she insisted I had some feelings I needed to sort through. Maybe she was right. Later, at night, when I was in bed in the dark, Hector's face came back again, and the detectives came back, and it wasn't like a movie. It was like doom itself had infiltrated my brain.

CHAPTER 5

A couple days later, Hector's family threw him a funeral. I thought it would be weird to go—maybe they didn't want to be reminded of the condition I'd found him in—but Audrey was like, "No, you have to go. We'll both go. It'd just be too sad for his family if, like, nobody from school shows up. Besides, don't you want to remember him at peace instead of how you found him?"

So there we were on Thursday afternoon at St. Andrew Avellino, and what do you know—the place was actually pretty full. Sure, there were only a couple of kids from school—that's all the friends Hector had—but apparently he had a pretty big extended family. By far most of the people there looked Hispanic to some degree. Audrey and I had to grab a seat in back, which was fine. I didn't want to stick out as the guy who only spent time with Hector in the Dumpster after he was already dead.

I'd never been to a Catholic funeral before. My parents aren't exactly into organized religion. On Facebook, under *Religion,* they entered *spiritual.* But I have to say this for the Catholics—they really know how to put on a show. And I don't mean that in any kind of disrespectful way. I don't usually call clothes *garments,* but the priest running the program had some mega-cool garments going on. The hat alone made you feel like, *This is going to be serious.*

And then there was the light filtering through the stained-glass saints, and the praying, and the Latin, and the rituals. Even some Mexican songs. And on top of that, this huge crucifix staring down at you from the front of the sanctuary, all kind of sad and beat and worn out with humanity but forgiving you anyway. I'm telling you—as the thing wound down, I couldn't help but feel Hector's ghost or spirit or whatever was a long way from the high school trash bin.

It made me wonder what my funeral might be like. I'd probably have about the same number of friends from school show up but a whole lot less family, since I was an only child and our nearest relatives lived in Dallas. No fancy garments or elaborate rituals either. No big accomplishments to reel off in the eulogy. After all, my most noteworthy act so far was finding Hector. That wasn't exactly eulogy material.

I'd be lucky to get a half-dozen flowers around my casket. The school probably wouldn't even hire a special grief counselor to come in. Outside of Audrey and Randy, my other so-called friends would probably forget me in a week. I felt like Scrooge from *A Christmas Carol* when the Ghost of Christmas Yet to Come showed him his own gravestone. The good thing was Scrooge had a second chance to do something, so maybe I did too.

After the service, we hung around so Audrey could snap some photos of the church and the crowd coming out for the school paper. I should mention that I submitted a story about Hector in the Dumpster to the paper, but Ms. Jansen, my journalism teacher, wouldn't accept it. She said my writing style was too informal and the Dumpster stuff was too undignified. She thought a simple obituary would do.

Anyway, several of the mourners were standing around staring in our direction. I didn't know whether they were staring at Audrey, this picture-taking chick with pink, blue, and green streaks wound into her brown pigtails, or if they figured out I was the guy who'd found Hector.

Then, on the way to the parking lot, this minivan of a guy in a black suit and a black hat with a red feather tucked into the hatband walked up and grabbed my arm.

"Your name is Dylan Jones?" he asked. He was probably nineteen or so—his goatee made it hard to tell. He was a good couple inches shorter than me but was so square and solid, you knew he could run you over and leave nothing but a dark spot on the road.

"That's my name," I said.

"Do you know the North Side Monarchs?" he asked, his eyes digging deep into mine.

I'm like, "The what?"

"One of my boys told me you're the one who found Hector when he died."

"Uh, yeah."

"And you don't know who the North Side Monarchs are?"

"No, I don't have any idea."

His face relaxed, and he almost smiled. "I guess it was just fate, then, that you found him."

"Fate, yeah, that's right."

He put out his hand for me to shake. "My name's Alberto Hernandez. Everyone calls me Beto. I'm Hector's cousin. Thanks for coming to the funeral."

I'm like, "That's all right," and introduced him to Audrey.

"You know," he said, "it's not like the cops and the news said—Hector didn't take no overdose. If he had drugs in him, someone else must've dosed him."

"I never thought he took any drugs," Audrey said, and I go, "Me either," though truthfully I wasn't so sure. I mean, yes, he didn't seem like a druggie type, but then you can't really be sure what goes on with people after the last school bell rings.

Beto stared into my eyes again. "You be careful."

"Never anything but."

As he walked away, Audrey goes, "Wow, that guy was good-looking. I mean, if I liked guys, that's the kind of guy I'd like."

"I don't know," I said. "He kind of weirded me out the way he just came up out of the blue like that."

Audrey nudged her shoulder against my arm. "Well, that's just the cost of being famous, I guess."

CHAPTER 6

Famous. Yeah, right. Fame is fleeting, they say, and they know what they're talking about. In my case, it lasted less than a week. And to be even more specific, it changed within five seconds. On Friday, I walked into first hour, and Jason "The Growth" Groethe—who's a big loser idiot—called out, "Hey, check it out, here comes Body Bag."

Body Bag. What was that even supposed to mean? I didn't put Hector into a bag. But the whole class erupted into laughter. Ha ha ha. How lame. But by the end of the day, that was all I heard—*Here comes Body Bag.* Even from girls.

It was all over then. A major rule of high school is that once you get a nickname, you're stuck with it no matter if it makes sense or not. Maybe Jason figured he had to get even with somebody for his getting tagged as The Growth, but, hey, I never called him that. At least not before he came up with the Body Bag deal.

By the next week, I'd given up on getting a decent article about Hector in the school paper. Instead, I decided to interview Haley Pressler, the cheerleader's cheerleader. Okay, yes, some people did call her "The Pretzel," but apparently being super-hot is a pretty effective inoculation against the full-time nickname curse. Anyway, I had this idea for an article about how new kids could adjust to school, and Haley seemed like a good expert to get tips from. Besides, like I said, she was ultra-hot.

So I met her by her locker right before lunch, thinking just maybe I'd talk her into doing the interview over a burger and some fries. But no, she wanted to do it right there in the hall. So I'm like, "Okay. I mean, it's not the most comfortable way to do an interview, but I guess it's cool," and just then I heard footsteps and a rustling sound behind me. Before I could turn around, some of Haley's stupid jock friends grabbed me and yanked a big plastic trash bag over my head and shoulders.

It was the worst. You cannot see when you're stuffed inside a Hefty bag. I couldn't move my arms, and I was stumbling around the hall yelling, "Get this thing off me! Get this thing off me!"

All the while these idiots were chanting, "Body Bag! Body Bag! Body Bag!"

And the worst part was knowing that The Pretzel had set me up for it. No, that's not true. The worst part was that somebody caught a video of it and pasted it all over the Internet within probably fifteen minutes.

That was the last straw. I had to do something.

CHAPTER 7

A couple days later Audrey and I were cruising to Topper's for burgers. Like I said, I didn't have a car, but it wasn't so bad since Audrey had this pretty sweet champagne-colored Ford Focus, and we were together most of the time anyway, so it was cool. As we drove, I got the idea she might be getting a little tired of me complaining about the whole Body Bag situation because she's like, "You know what? You need to stop focusing on that so much. Let it go."

"How can I let it go? Next time I walk back into school, it's going to be there again. 'Here comes Body Bag. Let's shove him in a sack and roll him down the stairs.'"

"You know why I think it bothers you so much?"

"Why? Pray tell, Dr. Freud."

"Because it hits a little too close to home. Let's face it. You're built kind of like a bag. A bag with arms and legs."

"What?" I glared at her. Sometimes her blunt-and-to-the-point act could get on your nerves. "How would you like it if I said you were built a little bit like a fireplug with pigtails and a Kangol 504?"

That didn't faze her. "I wouldn't care. I am built a little like a fireplug. I'm short and solid. Only a fireplug has two arms and just one breast, so I guess I come out ahead on that part. I don't care what anyone else thinks."

So I'm like, "Okay, you can be a double-breasted fireplug, but me, I don't want to be Body Bag anymore. Anyway, the bag-with-arms-and-legs deal's not the worst part of it. The worst part is it's like when I was at the police station—they take your identity away. They strip you of that, and all you have left is a stupid nickname."

"So, you know what they say?" She smiled at me. "The best revenge is living well."

"Really? *They* must not have been in high school when they said that."

When we pulled into Topper's, Rockin' Rhonda was out front as usual. You might think Stan, the owner, would chase off a weird homeless character like Rhonda, but he didn't. Instead, Rhonda became part of the Topper's experience.

She was probably in her forties or so and huge, not only for a woman but for anyone. In fact, I thought she was a man the first time I got a look at her. You'd always see her out there in her faded army jacket, pants, and boots—with a frizzed-out pink scarf. The color of her hair I don't know. Maybe she didn't have any. She always covered her head with an orange stocking cap, even in the summer.

She got the name Rockin' Rhonda because she played a beat-up guitar that had no strings and pretty much nonstop sang one golden oldie after another—or at least as much as she could remember of them.

As we walked up to the front door, it's like:

Me: Hey, Rhonda, how's it going?

Rockin' Rhonda (*singing*): Peggy, my Peggy Sue-hoo-hoo-hoo.

Me: I'll catch you with some coin on the way out.

Rockin' Rhonda: I love you, gal. Yes, I love you, Peggy Sue-hoo-hoo.

Audrey: Rock on, Rhonda.

Rockin' Rhonda (*nodding*): Yeah, I love you, gal, and I want you, Peggy Sue. Hoo-huh-hoo-hoo. Hoo.

So, yes, having Rhonda out front was a definite bonus, but the real draw to Topper's was the burgers. The thing is, I'm pretty much an authority when it comes to hamburgers—a real connoisseur of the ground beef and bun—and Topper's has the best burgers south of Twenty-Third Street. Not that I've tried every burger place in the metroplex, but I'll bet I've been to most of the good ones. My personal menu involved about three burgers a week, more when I got lucky, and sometimes I wrote reviews about them for the school paper. The best place I'd tried was actually in Dallas, a place called the Stackhouse, but it's not like I could make the three-hour drive down there every day. No, Topper's was easily the best place within fifteen to twenty minutes of my house.

Audrey and I took our usual booth in the corner and looked over the menu. Of course, we knew everything on there, but it's always fun to look at the selections anyway, especially since they have pictures of the food. Usually, I got the Number 11, which has pepper-jack cheese, bacon, jalapeños, and anything else you want. In my case, I went for lettuce, tomato, onions, and mustard. Mustard is key. Mayonnaise might be all right for a turkey sandwich, but please leave it off the burgers. Also, Topper's asks how you want your meat cooked, which is a must for a really good hamburger, and I go for the medium well. No blood for me. Just a light touch of pink so I don't feel like I'm going to come down with *E. coli* poisoning or something, but not so overcooked that they burn the succulent juices out of it either.

As for Audrey—here's a major difference between us—she's been a vegetarian since eighth grade, so she always ordered the Number 2 with both Swiss and sharp cheddar cheese, lettuce, tomato, onion, mustard, AND mayonnaise—hold the meat! That's right—HOLD THE MEAT! I told her that a little piece of me died every time I heard that order.

So, we're sitting there perusing the menus when who comes out of the restroom? Corman Rogers in all his black-and-silver-chain glory—the same guy who seemed a little too interested in the morbid details of Hector's death. He's like, "Hey, hey, Body Bag, found any more good corpses lately?"

"Don't call him that," Audrey warned him. "He doesn't like it."

But Corman just snickered and headed for the door with a couple of his buddies, their silver chains jingling from their oversized belt loops.

I shook my head. Even a vampire like Corman was going with the Body Bag moniker. You might think that would dampen my appetite, but actually it just made me feel like eating two Number 11s.

I'm like, "Jesus, I have to do something about my life. And it's not just the Body Bag thing either. It's feeling like you're a zero in the scheme of the universe. If I died five years out of high school, I probably wouldn't have a single person at my funeral. If someone found me dead in a Dumpster, they might as well just leave me there. It'd save the city money for having to bury me."

"Is this about Hector? Just because he died young doesn't mean you're going to."

"I'm talking about this whole process we're caught in. I mean, think about grade school—there was just a small number of kids. It was manageable. And you get to fifth grade and you're totally on top. There's these puny first graders walking around with their cartoon-character backpacks, and you just—you know—you feel huge. Then comes middle school and there's like ten times more kids, and you don't even get to know who they are before they ship you to high school and there's even more kids. You're fourteen and there's guys in the halls with full-grown beards. Girls with giant boobs. And it's not like I'm a bottom-feeder or anything, but I'm sure not at the top, and the middle is so vast you might as well be nobody. So think about what college will be like. And then you get spewed out of that into this churning ocean of life. What then? Am I going to be like this little speck of plankton for these humongous stupid cop sharks to gobble up and crap out their other end?"

"Wow, you really let those cops do a number on you." Audrey's expression of concern turned into a mischievous smile. "But think of it this way—at least then you could go to prison. That ought to be pretty manageable. Who knows, you might even be prom queen."

But I'm like, "That's not funny. I mean, listen, you have no idea what it was like sitting in that police station having a couple of cops trying to hound you into confessing to something you didn't do, treating you like everything you ever did doesn't matter. I guarantee there's nothing more depressing than knowing morons have complete power over you."

"Really, Dylan? What do you think it's like being gay? I have the whole legal system telling me I'm not good enough to fall in love and get married, but that's because they're losers, not me."

"Yeah, well, good for you."

Brenda, the waitress, walked up to take our order, and when she left, I'm like, "My problem is I don't have any *mojo*. That's what I need. I need to get some mojo."

"Some what?"

"Mojo. You know, power."

"I don't think that's what mojo is."

"Of course that's what it is. Mojo. Juice. Pull. Clout. Respect."

"No." Audrey shook her head. "I don't think that's it. I don't think you know what you want."

"Why do you always have to disagree with me so much?"

"Because you're wrong so much?"

"Really? Think about this—what if Hector had been some rich dude? Things would be different now. The cops would do a whole lot more investigating into what happened instead of just rubber-stamping it as an accidental overdose. And on top of that, I'd get a lot more respect for finding him that night. That's mojo."

"And you think that'd change everything?"

"It'd be a start."

"Then why don't you go looking for Ashton Browning?"

"Ashton who?"

"Browning. Ashton Browning. The missing girl who's all over the news."

"What missing girl? I haven't heard anything about it."

"Of course you haven't. And that's exactly why you'll never be the editor of the school paper—because you never actually pay attention to the news."

Audrey was always trying to goad me into taking the paper more seriously.

Acting all exasperated, she pulled out her phone—which I'd like to point out was a lot more expensive than mine—and started looking up the news story online. "Here it is. Come here."

I moved over to her side of the booth. Sure enough, it was a big story. There was even a video about it from the local news. Apparently, this Ashton Browning girl was the daughter of a banking big shot. I don't even think he was president of the bank—he was more like the boss of the president. Anyway, Ashton told her friends she was going jogging at the nature park north of town, where you can go hiking or running if that's what you're into, among the squirrels and foxes and lizards and whatnot. She never came home. Officials—whoever they were—found her car there but no trace of her.

I stared at her photo—seventeen, blond, blue-eyed, rich. It's funny—some people you can tell they're rich just by looking at them, and she was definitely one of those people. But there was something else about her too, a certain mystery in those blue eyes. It made a weird contrast to her little thin smile. I felt like she was looking straight into me, asking, "Can't you help me?"

I guess maybe I fell a little bit in love with her right then.

"There you go," Audrey said. "Made to order. You find her, and you've got your mojo—or whatever."

"Yeah, but how am I going to find her?"

"I don't know, Dylan. You're the detective-show junkie."

Then I'm like, "Wait a minute. Look at this. They're asking for volunteers to come out to the nature park tomorrow to help search the place, I guess for clues or who knows—maybe her body."

"Well, you've got experience with that."

"You're right. I do." That's when it hit me, the whole

31

investigative-journalist thing and all the mojo that went with it. Sure, I didn't know Ashton like I knew Hector, but in a weird way I felt like if I could find her, it'd be like making things up to Hector. "This is it," I said. "This is what I was meant to do. We have to go out there."

"What do you mean, *we*? I'm not going out there. I was just kidding you. They have all the cops they need to find her. You'd just get in the way."

"I won't get in the way. It says right here they need volunteers. I'd make as good a volunteer as anyone. Besides, I could write about it for the school newspaper, and you could take the pictures. After all, you're the one always telling me I need to take on some more hard-hitting topics."

I had her there. She sat staring at the phone for a second. "You know, you're actually right for once. This would make a great story. And I could get some seriously kick-ass photos."

"I'm telling you."

Brenda came back with our order and I moved back to my side of the booth. The Number 11 sat there on the table, gazing up at me with all its fat-packed goodness, like a reward for coming up with the best idea since the invention of the emoticon.

"There's just one problem," Audrey said as she lifted her meatless Number 2 from the dish. "Tomorrow's Saturday. Don't you work Saturday?"

My heart sank. "Crap. That's right."

"You could quit."

"I can't just quit. I'm saving up for a car—the '69 Mustang."

"Then you're just going to have to decide what's more important. You can't really keep working there and expect to do much for the paper anyway. If you want to be the guy who does more than get a piddling article about flu season or something in every third issue, then you're going to have to put in time after school. It's up to you. You can work on the all-time best story that's ever been in the paper, or you can sack groceries."

"And don't forget I'm also going to find this missing girl."

"Whatever. The real thing—the important thing—is working on this story."

I looked back at the Number 11. It was definitely on the side of finding Ashton Browning. "Okay," I said. "I'm out of the grocery business and on to being a full-time investigative reporter. With emphasis on *investigative.*"

Audrey wiped her mouth with her paper napkin. "I'm so proud of my boy. He's getting all grown up."

After we finished eating, I stopped out front to give Rockin' Rhonda the change I got from paying for my meal.

"Thank you," she said, Elvis-like. "Thank you very much."

"Rhonda," I said, "you've heard of mojo, right?"

With what you might call the classic faraway look in her eyes, she's like, "Mojo? Sure. 'Mojo Hand,' by Lightnin' Hopkins. 'Got My Mojo Workin',' by Muddy Waters, 'Mr. Mojo Risin' '—Jim Morrison and the Doors. Oh yeah, man. *Mojo.*"

"So what does it mean? It's like power, right?"

"Oh yeah, it's the special power. It's the magic power."

I looked at Audrey. "See, I told you."

She gave me the *whatever* eyebrow shrug.

"You want to see my mojo?" Rhonda asked.

I'm like, "Uh. Okay?"

I admit I was a little afraid of what she was going to show us, but she just held up her stringless guitar and goes, "This is it, man. This is my mojo." And then she made a big windmill pantomime strum and launched into song: "Mr. Mojo risin', Mr. Mojo risin', gotta keep on risin'—"

CHAPTER 8

Saturday morning I woke up feeling guilty about quitting my job. Don, my boss, wasn't happy about it, considering I gave less than a day's notice. I explained that I had to do it for my future as an investigative journalist, but that didn't help much. He seemed to think doing anything outside the grocery business was stupid. So I told him my parents and my journalism teacher were making me do it, which wasn't exactly true. I still hadn't told my parents about quitting, and Ms. Jansen never did act like I had much potential. She always said my stuff was too *informal,* which was a load of crap as far as I was concerned.

Anyway, I started to think I'd made a mistake, so I turned over in bed to consider the prospect a little more and ended up drifting back to sleep instead. I woke up again later with Audrey yanking on my covers, going, "I should've known you wouldn't be ready. Come on, let's go."

"I have to take a shower."

"We don't have time for that. The search party starts at ten o'clock."

"Well, I at least have to eat breakfast."

"We'll get it on the way. I'm going out to the kitchen

34

and talk to your parents. You'd better be ready to go in five minutes."

"I don't know if I want to do it anymore."

"Oh, you're doing it all right." She popped me on top of the head with the flat of her hand. "I'm not letting you back out now."

When she left the room, I dragged myself out of bed and pulled on my favorite jeans and sneakers and my Chuck Norris T-shirt. Here, let me point out that I am a huge fan of Chuck Norris and his show *Walker, Texas Ranger*. I watch the reruns religiously. I mean, nobody can kick someone in the neck like Walker—bikers, drug dealers, crooked corporate tycoons, you name it. Walker is the man. I know about ten people I wouldn't mind kicking in the neck like that.

Anyway, after I got dressed, there was nothing to be done with my hair, so I shoved my black porkpie hat down over it. Not that I'm big into hats like Audrey, but six months ago I had a weak moment and thought it'd be cool to go with the porkpie. Now it was the only hat I owned.

About fifteen minutes later we were on the road, and Audrey's like, "So I had this idea about what happens to Harry Potter in ten years. He dies and comes back as Edward from *Twilight*, but the catch is Hermione has also died and come back as this moody chick who is actually a lesbian now and is in love with Sookie from *True Blood*."

And I go, "Yeah, but then it turns out that in the meantime, Sookie died and has come back as Jacob the werewolf."

"So that would mean that Jacob is actually now an awesome she-wolf."

Usually, we could have gone on like this for twenty minutes, but I was still feeling the guilt over the job situation and switched the topic over to how everyone at work probably hated me now.

"Quit worrying what other people think of you so much," Audrey said. "You're starting a new phase in life. You never know what might happen if you apply yourself."

"You sound like my parents."

"Well, you should listen to them."

We stopped for breakfast burritos, which I am also something of an expert on, but I won't go into that right now. With Audrey speeding pretty much the whole way, it still took us almost forty minutes to get to the nature park. We weren't late, but a ton of cars were already parked in the lot and overflowing down the shoulders of the road.

We fell in with the rest of the crowd heading to the check-in area at the far end of the parking lot, but this redheaded girl stopped us. According to her, we wouldn't be allowed to take our bags on the search. I had a backpack and Audrey had a big bag that also carried her camera.

I'm like, "But we have our snacks in here," and the redhead goes, "Sorry, they said no bags. I guess they don't want people smuggling anything in or out. Besides, they're going to provide hamburgers for lunch."

I'm like, "Hamburgers? Cool." And that was it for the guilt over quitting my job. Hamburgers for lunch—that had to be some kind of sign that I was doing the right thing.

I ran the bags back to the car while Audrey stayed and chatted up the redhead. I was only gone for about two minutes, but they seemed like buddies already by the time I got back.

Turned out the girl's name was Trix Westwood. Trix was short for Beatrix, she said, an explanation that she'd obviously tossed off so many times before it was practically part of her name by now. It wasn't hard to see why Audrey was grinning at her. Trix had the artsy flair Audrey would be attracted to— her red hair wound into pigtails just like Audrey's, blue lipstick, black top, short black skirt with black-and-white-striped tights underneath, and clunky black shoes—a cool look but not really great hiking attire. "Trix goes to Hollister," Audrey informed me. Hollister is the rich-kid private school Ashton Browning also attended.

"Where do you guys go?" Trix asked.

I'm like, "How do you know we don't go to Hollister too?"

"Oh, please," she says. "You guys are much too cool to go to Hollister."

She didn't follow up on where we went to school, and I didn't volunteer the information either. Not that I was ashamed of our high school, but it's quite a few cuts below a place like Hollister.

"You don't like Hollister much?" I asked.

She rolled her eyes. "Are you kidding?" Which obviously meant that she didn't. "So, you guys just decided out of the goodness of your hearts to help find Ashton Browning?" she asked.

"That and we're doing a story for our school paper," I told her.

"I'm the photographer," Audrey said. "Guess since I had to put my bag back in the car, I'll have to use my phone."

Trix goes, "A story for the paper, huh? That's cool. Stick with me. I've done this before."

I'm like, "Really? You've gone on a missing-girl search before?"

She nodded. "Yeah. When I lived in California. A missing twelve-year-old. It didn't turn out well."

That seemed like an odd coincidence, that Trix would be around when two different girls in two different states went missing. I glanced at Audrey to see if she might be thinking what I was, but no—she just grinned at Trix, obviously with other things on her mind.

At the check-in area, we signed our names and gave our phone numbers and addresses, both real-world and virtual. A huge cop asked us a few questions, which needless to say jangled my nerves a bit. What if he looked me up on the computer and found out a couple of his cop brethren once suspected me in the death of Hector Maldonado? Maybe he'd think I was somehow involved with the disappearance of Ashton Browning too.

I didn't like the looks of him, and he didn't like the looks of me either. He stared at my hat like it was a suspect all by itself. He didn't arrest me or anything, though, and we squeezed through into the big blue-and-white tent where the cop in charge was about to give instructions for the search.

The place was nearly full—the local news was even there—so we had to stand in the back. The crowd wasn't what I would call diverse. By far most people looked like rich kids or rich kids' parents or maybe the rich kids' parents' employees. There was little doubt that, except for maybe the cameramen and some of the cops, Audrey and I were the only ones who came up from south of Tenth Street.

The cop in charge—Captain Lewis—looked pretty smooth with his starched white shirt, crisp gray suit, and high-dollar haircut. Everything about him said, *Check out my authority— it's awesome.*

He explained how the police had already scoured the nature park with their dogs, but now they wanted to cover more ground in case they'd missed something. According to him,

Ashton was last seen by another visitor to the area about four p.m. Wednesday as she put some of her things into the trunk of her car. She was wearing a blue running outfit with blue running shoes and probably a blue hair clip, one of her usual exercise getups. Her jewelry included a gold necklace and two gold rings. It was pretty clear to me that finding any of this stuff would mean that whatever happened to Ashton wasn't going to be good.

Before explaining the search routine, Captain Lewis asked Ashton's dad to say a few words, I guess to pump us up for our mission. Eliot Browning looked to be in his early fifties—a square cowboy-hero chin, the kind of complexion that looked like he probably paid someone else to take care of it for him, and salt-and-pepper hair that swooped back behind his ears, more like what you'd expect from a movie director than a banker. And, of course, he had the expensive, perfect-fit suit, and I'm sure a pair of thousand-dollar shoes, though I couldn't see them from where I was. Talk about mojo—this guy was probably born with it.

He started in about how all of us had daughters or sons or brothers or sisters and asked us to imagine how we'd feel if one of them disappeared. In my opinion, this was a pretty good way of engaging the crowd, including those who'd be watching on TV. Me, I didn't have any siblings, but Audrey had an older sister who'd moved away to college this year, and I missed her every once in a while.

Anyway, Mr. Browning went on to talk about how great Ashton was, how she excelled at tennis, won awards for her civic involvement, and how her smile could set a whole room aglow. You had to hand it to him—he was a good public speaker and never let his emotions get the better of him.

Toward the end, he waved for his wife and son to step

forward. Julia Browning was probably about ten years younger than her husband. She was the kind of woman you would rate as attractive but you'd never call hot—too stiff and formal, kind of like she was trying to hold a fart in all the time. But there was a hollow look about her face, especially in her eyes, that let you know she wasn't taking the disappearance as calmly as her husband.

The son they called Tres—pronounced "Trace"—but his real name was Eliot Browning III. He was my age, really pale and skinny, and had a bit of a turtle face. There wasn't anything majestic about him. Sure, his forest-green shirt and dark brown trousers had the big-money sheen going, but if you put him in a hoodie and old jeans, he'd look more like a prime target for bullies in my high school cafeteria than a big-shot banker's son.

He and his mom didn't say anything. They were just there for emotional impact. Mr. Browning went on about how empty the house had been the last few days and how he wouldn't rest until his daughter was back to fill it with her smiles and laughter. Then he pulled out the big guns.

"That is why," he said, stepping back to loop his arms awkwardly around the shoulders of his wife on one side and son on the other, "the Browning family has decided to offer a one-hundred-thousand-dollar reward for information leading to the safe return of Ashton."

You better believe that sent a murmur through the crowd. Me, I was thinking about all the mojo a hundred thousand bucks could buy. Plus, the '69 Mustang was back in the picture.

"So, please," he added, "as you set off on this search today, keep Ashton in your hearts"—I wanted to add *and wallets*—"and don't pass over any detail. You never know. It could be the key to finding my daughter."

All in all, Mr. Browning was impressive, though that last part came off a little bit too much like a coach telling us to get out there and win the big game for the old alma mater. Still, I'd watched enough true-crime shows to know the cops usually assume parents or boyfriends are the most obvious suspects in cases like this. So you'd think that would've landed Mr. Browning right at the top of my list, except I also knew from watching all my fictional detective shows that the culprit is never the most obvious suspect. So that would rule him out. It was a real conundrum.

Then I had a stroke of brilliance—if the dad is the *most* obvious suspect and the real culprit is never supposed to be the most obvious suspect, then doesn't that really make him the *least* obvious suspect? Therefore, if he's the least obvious suspect, then he must be guilty.

Case solved. Now all I had to do was prove it. And hope that his wife would still make good on the hundred-thousand-dollar promise.

CHAPTER 9

Outside the tent, officers came around and assigned everybody to search different sectors of the nature park, so Audrey and I and Trix got lumped into the same group, along with two uniformed officers and about thirty other people, mostly teenagers. Unfortunately, we had to walk in a line through a hilly field way to the east of the prime location for clues—the woods where the hiking and jogging paths were.

"This is crap," I said as we headed into the field. "How am I supposed to find any clues out here? I want to go where Ashton went, see what she saw, hear what she heard. I have to get into her mind."

"Oh God," Audrey said. "He's kicking into TV-detective mode."

So I'm like, "Well, it's true—you have to know your victim first to figure anything out." I turned to Trix. "You must've known Ashton pretty well, right? What kind of girl was she?"

Trix brushed a pigtail back over her shoulder. "I knew her, but I can't say I knew her *well*. This is just my first year here. But I guess she seemed okay. Bad taste in music, but she was cooler than most of the androids at Hollister."

"Androids?"

"Yeah, you know." She made a stiff motion with her arms like a robot. "Like sixty percent of the student body has been programmed to act the same way—like they're better than everyone else. I can't believe how many people around here think everyone from California is some kind of freaky hippie driving around in an electric car and eating kelp or something. Like the world would be better off if the big earthquake hit California and it sank into the ocean."

Actually, being from Oklahoma, that viewpoint didn't sound so strange to me, but I'm just like, "Right. So what was different about Ashton?"

"I don't know. At first she seemed like a lot of the other people around here who like to think they're *high society*." She put on a snooty voice for the *high-society* part. "But the thing is the real society types in New York or someplace like that might let them in the door, but they'd make fun of them after they left. It's pathetic, really. But then this one time in class Ashton gave a speech about helping to feed the poor. That was different. She was definitely more likable than her little brother."

"Tres? Isn't that his name?"

"Yeah, Tres. You saw him up there with his dad and mom. He's a little on the wimpy side. I think he was born prematurely or something and never quite got caught up."

"So it's not like she was the type people would hate and want to get out of the way?"

Trix laughed. "Hey, around here, people don't necessarily have to hate you to want you out of the way."

"Why's that?"

"What I mean is they don't have to *hate* you. You just have to be in their way."

43

I'm like, *Hmmm—interesting. Maybe Ashton's dad's not the only suspect around here. Maybe she just got in the way of the wrong person.* But out loud, I go, "See, that's why I don't think we're doing much good in this field. We'd be better off interviewing her friends. All we'll find out here is anthills and rabbits."

"I don't know," Trix said. "Think of it this way—the police and their dogs have probably already done a good job of combing the trails. We may be the first ones paying much attention to this area."

That was a good point, a very good point, and it reminded me of how Trix had *coincidentally* been through this kind of thing before. "So," I said, keeping my tone nonchalant like I was just asking about the weather, "that twelve-year-old girl in California, did you find anything when you went looking for her?"

"No, we came up empty," she answered, totally unaware that I might have my suspicions about her too. "They found her body six months later in the desert about a hundred and twenty miles from where we searched."

"I'm so sorry," Audrey offered. "That's terrible. Was it someone you knew?"

"A friend of mine's little sister. They arrested the pool guy for it. He's in prison now, but I never thought he did it."

"Really?" I said. "Did they ever look at the parents?"

"How did you know?"

"He watches all the murder shows on TV," Audrey said.

"Well," Trix said, "her mom was a bitch. I wouldn't have put it past her. But you know how it is when you've got money."

Audrey's like, "No, but I can imagine."

"When you got the money, you got the mojo," I said.

And Trix's like, "The what?"

44

"The mojo."

"Don't get him started on that," Audrey said.

After that, Audrey took over the conversation. It was kind of embarrassing. I'd never actually watched her try to flirt with a girl so obviously. Still, I kept my ears open. Sure, Trix seemed cool and everything, but I couldn't rule her out as a suspect.

It turned out her dad was what she called a "corporate gunslinger," which she explained was a high-powered lawyer who keeps one company from getting busted for screwing over another company. She didn't sound like she admired him much. He'd moved her here from California after his wife—Trix's mom—left them for, of all things, a Broadway choreographer. That was just the kind of exotic touch that was sure to intrigue Audrey even more. But I figured it could also be something that would trigger an already-troubled girl into acting out in some kind of bizarro way. You didn't even have to be a Californian for that to happen.

Our group's assignment was to trudge to the end of the field, then move over and trudge back, then do the same thing all over again until we'd covered the whole area. Since we had to stay in a single line, the pace was excruciatingly slow. Also, the yellow-brown grass was knee-high and getting higher as we went, so the chances of us finding any hot evidence seemed less and less likely. I occupied my mind by working on kidnapping theories. Obviously, the basic motive for kidnapping was collecting a ransom, but so far no ransom note had appeared. As far as I was concerned, that fact put a big bold check mark next to Mr. Browning's name on the suspect list.

So, if it wasn't ransom, what could it be? Maybe she hadn't been kidnapped at all. Maybe she'd been murdered. I hated to be Mr. Negative, but I had to at least consider the possibility. A crazy sex-maniac serial killer could've been hiding behind a tree and when she jogged by—well, *goodbye, Ashton*. But I didn't like that theory. A crazy sex-maniac serial killer would probably just leave her body out here. It'd be too much trouble to lug her all the way back to his creepy serial-killing van. Someone would've seen him. That brought me back to Mr. Browning again.

But if he killed his daughter, why would he come out here to do it? Then my mind started clicking—maybe he didn't. Maybe he killed her somewhere else and just planted her car here. But no, that couldn't be it. A witness saw her putting something in the trunk of her car in the parking lot. At least the witness saw *someone*. Maybe it wasn't Ashton at all. Maybe Mr. Browning hired a look-alike to pretend to be Ashton.

That theory sounded pretty good. I'd seen something close to it on my favorite detective show, *Andromeda Man*. In case you haven't seen it, *Andromeda Man* is about a Minneapolis, Minnesota, homicide detective who is actually a space alien. He's semi-telepathic. He couldn't be all the way telepathic or he'd solve the cases too easily, but he can really read people. It's pretty awesome.

Anyway, on one episode, this woman, who is like a local theater diva, gets murdered via a curling-iron attack backstage before the opening-night performance, and everyone thinks the understudy did it. Or the director. Or the leading man. Or the playwright. Everyone except Magnusson, who is actually the Andromeda Man. He has another suspect in mind. It's weird because his cranky boss and his own partner, the super-hot Detective Carin Svendsen, keep arguing with him about it, even though he solves every case week after week. Turns out he's right, of course. It was the diva's own daughter who killed her. And here's the thing—the daughter had disguised herself as her mother so people *thought* they saw the diva walking around backstage while she was actually already dead.

So, yes, I decided it was pretty likely that Mr. Browning paid someone to dress up as his daughter while he disposed of Ashton's body, not backstage at a play or anything, but maybe in the basement of one of the properties his bank foreclosed on. I didn't have any proof, but I figured it wouldn't hurt to at least run my theory by one of the cops in our search party. I didn't get the chance, though.

I had just broken ranks and started to walk down the line to where the first cop was when I stepped on something in the deep grass. It made my ankle do that thing where it turns sideways real fast and hurts like you've just been shot by a crossbow. I'm like, "Arrrrgh!" and buckled to the ground. That's when I found it. What I'd stepped on was a shoe. A blue running shoe.

CHAPTER 10

They never told us what to shout if we found a clue. Probably it should've been something official-sounding, but all I could get out was, "Holy crap, I found her shoe! I found her shoe!"

Immediately, the cops rushed over. I was holding the shoe up by the loose shoestring, and the first cop goes, "Weren't you listening? You weren't supposed to touch anything!"

So I dropped it back into the grass, which pissed him off all over again. The second cop was already on his walkie-talkie. He's like, "Captain, I found a blue running shoe in sector four."

For real. That's what he said: "*I* found a blue running shoe." Completely stealing the credit. I mean, this was a big discovery. If this really was Ashton's shoe, it didn't look good for her. Unless, of course, someone else came out here disguised as her.

Everybody had to stay perfectly still—like we were playing freeze tag—until the captain and his entourage showed up. He wanted to know exactly where the shoe was found, so the uniformed cop had to give it up that I was really the one who found it. Then I got reamed all over again for moving it from its original place. You'd think they'd be grateful.

I showed the captain the exact spot where I stepped on the

shoe, and he's like, "It was probably transported to this location by an animal"—not to me but to his flunkies. Still, this seemed like a pretty good time to offer up my theory, so I'm like, "Captain, it might be good to test that shoe for DNA in case someone else might have come out here disguised as Ashton Browning as a trick."

"What are you talking about?" He looked at me kind of like a teacher will when you say the exact wrong answer in class, only more so. Then he looked at the uniformed cop next to him. "What's this kid talking about—a disguise?"

The uniform shook his head.

But I didn't think I should give up that easy. "Have you seen that show *Andromeda Man*?"

Captain Lewis looked at me again, this time like he couldn't figure out why I hadn't disappeared yet. "Everybody, stand back," he shouted. And the next thing you know, he was on the walkie-talkie, and a few minutes later our search party got replaced by the first team.

Audrey's like, "Really? *Andromeda Man*? Are you kidding me?"

"Hey, at least I found the shoe. What'd you do?"

Trix stepped over and goes, "That really was pretty cool. You're quite the detective."

"Yeah, right," said Audrey, but I was thinking, *Hmmm, maybe I should be the one flirting with Trix.*

Then, after about a half hour of watching the police and their dogs scour our sector without finding anything else, Trix came up with a superb suggestion: "You know what? Since they took over our job, why don't we head back to the tent and see if they've started on those burgers."

Yes, all of a sudden I had a whole new outlook on her.

CHAPTER 11

Only one other search party had returned to the tent by the time we got there, so we nabbed some good seats. Green plastic chairs and tables with white tablecloths had been set up while we were gone. It was weirdly festive considering the circumstances. As for the burgers, all I can say is they were a revelation.

First we filed past a long table where all the fixings were: warm whole-wheat buns, cheeses I'd never heard of, crisp leaves of rich green lettuce, deep red tomatoes, crunchy onion circles, three kinds of pickles, five kinds of mustard, four kinds of mayonnaise, and gourmet barbecue sauce.

I admit I put one kind of mustard on the top bun and another on the bottom. Then, along with the Camembert cheese, lettuce, tomato, and onion, I went with all three kinds of pickles. And of course, *zero* mayonnaise. I won't go into all the side dishes, except to point out they had no French fries, so I chose the fancy macaroni and cheese, which, by the way, was white, not yellow, and had jalapeños in it.

Now, I'm not going to declare the meat was grilled better than anyplace else, but I can guarantee this—the ingredients were mind-blowing. The freshness of the produce, the texture of the Kobe beef, everything was amazing. It dawned on me that this must be how it was for rich people every day—the best of everything. I could just imagine what Topper's could do with ingredients like this.

Sitting at our table, I guess I must have been going on about all this a little too much because Trix's like: "What's with him? Hasn't he ever had a hamburger before?"

"Oh yeah," Audrey said. "He's had a few in his time."

Trix turned to me and goes, "God, I thought you were going to have an orgasm."

I was just thinking how sexy it was, the way she said the word *orgasm,* when this tall blond guy—obviously a Hollister student—stopped next to our table. "Hey, Trix," he said with a smile like the white cliffs of Dover. "Mind if we sit with you guys?"

With him was a fine looker who also sported an orthodontic miracle for a smile. Actually, she was absolutely striking—black hair and blue eyes, a completely killer combination.

"Why?" Trix said. The tone of her voice switched to bored.

"Just wanted to get to know the man who found the big clue," he said, setting his tray of food on the table. He clapped me on the back and then sat next to me while Blue Eyes sat on the other side next to Audrey. He reached over to shake my hand. "I'm Nash Pierce," he said. "This is Brett Seagreaves."

Brett. A girl named Brett. So here I was at the table with Beatrix, Nash, and Brett, thinking, *Don't rich people ever have regular names?* It was like their names were fancy brand names, you know? Like brands of clothes I couldn't afford.

I introduced myself and Audrey, and Nash asked the inevitable where-do-you-go-to-school question. I admitted the whole truth, and surprisingly he's like, "That's cool. I've always wanted to know someone who went there. You guys have a badass reputation."

I'm like, "Really? We do?"

And he's, "Sure. Everyone at Hollister thinks that. So how did you happen to come all the way up here to join the search party?"

"We're working on a story for the school paper," Audrey said. "He's a reporter, and I'm the photographer."

"That's interesting," Nash said. Then he looked me in the eyes. "So, how did you do it? How did you find her shoe? Did you have some kind of system for searching for it?"

"He's just an amazing detective, that's all," Trix cut in.

"He must be awesome," Nash said. "Maybe you'll be the one who finds Ashton. I hope so. We're really worried about her."

Usually, I have a pretty strong irony detector—you can't love *Walker, Texas Ranger* like I do without having a good sense of irony—but I wasn't sure whether Nash was putting me on or whether he really did think I was awesome. Maybe it was the hamburgers. I have to admit they left me feeling a little intimidated. You have to assume these Hollister kids are mega-smart. I mean, if they're going to use only the best ingredients in their burgers, you can just imagine what they put into their education.

Anyway, I figured the best strategy for dredging up some scoop from these people would be to play humble, so I'm like, "Oh, I'm just trying to be of whatever help I can. Maybe if I knew a little more about Ashton, I could contribute some little something or other. How well did you two know her, Nash?"

Before he could answer, Brett cut in: "Nash and Ashton used to date."

"That was a year ago," Nash said.

Very interesting—Nash seemed cool, but the ex-boyfriend

52

has to rank pretty high on the suspect list. Maybe he was just playing friendly with me to find out how much I knew.

So I asked him what happened with him and Ashton, and he's like, "I don't know. She's a sweetheart, but, well, we were just juniors, you know?"

"And then Ashton started to get this whole save-the-world thing going," Brett added.

"Like that's supposed to be a bad thing?" Trix cut in.

"That was a long time after I dated her," Nash said. "I just can't wrap my mind around the fact she's missing."

"Was she dating anyone else?" I asked. "You know, more recently?"

"Yeah," Brett said. "As a matter of fact, she dated Rowan Adams up until the end of summer."

Another suspect for my list. This was getting good.

I asked if this Rowan guy was around anywhere, and Nash goes, "I'm sure he is," but before he could point him out, a voice came from over my shoulder.

"Hey, Nash, you saving this empty seat for anyone?"

I looked around to see Tres Browning standing behind me, a gloomy expression on his pale turtle face. Nash told him we were saving the seat for him and introduced me as the guy who found Ashton's shoe.

"I heard about that," Tres said as he sat next to Brett. He had kind of a queasy air about him, like, as rich as he was, he still wasn't quite in the same league with Brett and Nash. "I was wondering," he said, looking at me without raising his head all the way. "Can you tell me what the shoe looked like or if you happened to see what brand it was?"

I felt stupid for not checking the brand. I guess I was too excited. Not that I'm much of an expert on running shoes.

"Well, it wasn't a Nike. I can tell you that much." Nike being the only logo I would probably recognize. "But I can tell you it had a logo that was sort of a sideways triangle with a line sticking out of it."

"That sounds like her shoe all right," Tres said, looking solemnly down at his plate.

"Why?" I asked. "Were you thinking maybe someone came out here disguised as her?"

"What?" He looked up. "Did the police say they thought that's what happened?"

"No," Audrey volunteered. "That's just one of his crazy theories."

A crazy theory. That's what Detective Svendsen said to the Andromeda Man too.

But then Nash's like, "I don't think it's so crazy. What if someone did come out here disguised as her to throw everybody off?"

I looked at him but still couldn't tell if he was being sarcastic or not. Just then, *sploosh!* Tres dropped his soda cup smack into the middle of his plate. His hand was trembling.

"Hey, Tres, what's the problem?" Nash asked.

"Sorry," Tres said. "I guess my nerves are kind of frazzled."

For a second, Brett looked at him like he was some kind of mental defective, but she covered it quickly, patted him on the arm, and went, "We know you miss her, but things will be all right. They'll find her."

I wasn't sure—I hadn't been around a lot of rich kids—but her sympathy seemed kind of fake.

"I keep thinking about her," Tres said, mopping up the spilled soda with his napkin. "We had a fight just the other day. I called her—well, something I shouldn't have."

"Hey, brothers and sisters have fights," Nash told him. "It's natural. When you get her back safe at home, she won't even remember it."

Staring at the table, Tres goes, "When we were kids, this one time I got lost and she—" He stopped. His head was bowed, so I couldn't tell if he was crying, but it seemed likely.

"I know it's hard," Nash said. "But think of it this way, Tres—we have Dylan on our side. He's already doing a better job than the police."

"I don't know about that," I said.

And Nash's like, "As a matter of fact, Dylan, you need to friend us on Facebook so we can keep in touch. What do you think about that?"

"Uh, sure."

"Maybe we'll get together and talk some more about the case for your newspaper article."

"Really?"

"You bet. And it'd be great if maybe you could send me copies of your articles. That way I could spread them around at school to keep everyone up to date."

"I could do that," I said, flattered to think of my writing circulating among the Hollister elite.

"We might even have a party," Brett said, flashing me that brilliant smile. Before I could follow up on that, she excused herself, saying she had to go talk to somebody on the other side of the tent, but as she stood, she looked down at me and goes, "Nice hat, by the way."

I watched her walk through the crowd. Maybe she did really like the hat or maybe she thought it was the lamest thing she'd ever seen—I just couldn't be sure.

CHAPTER 12

After I got home from the search, I had to come clean to my parents about quitting the grocery-store job. They didn't care so much that I quit the job, but they definitely weren't happy that I did it on such short notice. Dad was all about how you never knew when you might need a job reference sometime down the line, and Mom was all, "That's not how we taught you to treat people. You have to have more respect for others than that."

They were right, of course, and I did feel bad about the job, but I explained how I had to make a choice between sacking groceries and devoting myself to my investigative journalism. The kids who became editors and got all sorts of articles published had to stay after school, I told them. Sure, it was great to make money for right now, but I also had my future career to think about.

That calmed them down. They were glad to see I was taking something seriously for a change. So they switched the lecture over to explaining how all my other school subjects were also important for a journalist, and then, when they started listing the classes I should take in college, my mind drifted off into a mental movie of me cruising up and down in front of my high school in a red '69 Mustang.

Next Monday at school, I found out my buddy Randy was even less happy with me for quitting the grocery store, and he wasn't at all impressed with my new emphasis on being an investigative journalist. Seems that since I left, the store was shorthanded, and the extra workload fell on him. That was something I hadn't thought about. To make it up, I invited him over to help research the Ashton Browning case with me and Audrey.

We congregated in my bedroom, and like a good host I cracked open some Dr Peppers and laid out a bowl of Chex Mix, the Traditional blend. I really like the Bold Party Blend, except the drawback is it lingers on your breath the rest of the day. No amount of teeth-brushing, mouth-washing, or mint-eating can destroy that taste. It's nuclear.

Now, when the Andromeda Man did research, he had access to all sorts of records—bank accounts, rap sheets, tax files, even parking-ticket info—but me, I had Facebook. So the three of us sat on the floor with our backs against the bed and began poring over the Facebook profiles of some of the Hollister kids I'd hooked up with. I halfway expected Nash, Brett, and Tres to have forgotten who I was already, but no, they friended me right back when I sent in the request. Trix friended me and Audrey both.

Then I used their friends lists to hook up with quite a few people who'd never met me, including Rowan Adams, Ashton's latest boyfriend. Every one of them friended me right back too. Really, these Hollisterites seemed to be just like kids at my school. They didn't care if they knew you or not. They just wanted to add as many names as they could to jack up their friends total.

There wasn't a whole lot to find out from their profiles, just the usual stuff about music, movies, books, that kind of thing. But there were a few interesting tidbits like how Nash was a hotshot wide receiver on the football team, Brett was class treasurer, Tres played the oboe, and Trix didn't say anything about only being interested in girls. That didn't deter Audrey, though. Right off, she jotted down a list of books and movies Trix liked, I guess so she could work them into their next conversation.

Randy's like, "This is boring. I thought we were going to scope out some hot rich babes, not a lesbian girlfriend for Audrey."

"Who are you trying to kid, Randy?" Audrey said. "I'll bet you've had more secret gay sex than a Republican senator."

To which Randy responded with an extended fart, his usual comeback to anything he didn't like.

"Real mature," Audrey said.

But Randy was right. We weren't getting anywhere with the profiles, especially since we didn't have access to the most important one—Ashton Browning's. So we moved on to check out the Hollister kids' photos instead. It was pretty interesting looking at their sweet rides and houses and bedrooms and whatnot, but that really wasn't getting us anywhere either. I was after some photos of Ashton and finally found some. Nash had quite a few of him and her, and some of the older ones looked pretty cozy. I couldn't help imagining myself in his situation— her head leaning against mine, her fingers touching my face, the two of us with our arms around each other.

Maybe someday it'll be like that, I thought. *After I find her and bring her home, how could she resist me and my hundred-thousand-dollar reward and my awesome '69 Mustang?*

Surprisingly, Rowan Adams had no pictures of him and Ashton. That was weird. Why wouldn't you keep her photos? Obviously, Nash did, which meant they must've stayed friendly after the breakup. But Rowan and Ashton? Apparently, not so much.

Looking at the photos of him, I couldn't figure out what she saw in him in the first place. For one thing, he was a little too flamboyant in the attire department. Definitely a hat guy. And an ironic-blazer wearer. By that, I mean these blazers were outrageous—red, orange, even chartreuse—so you had to figure they were some kind of joke.

But that was nothing. The real thing that irritated me was his eyes and smile. It was like he had small dark eyes and a good-sized beak that made them look even smaller. Not that he was ugly, but he had this smug expression in almost every picture that told you he thought he was hot stuff. You've seen that little smirk. It made you want slap him in the face with a cold fish.

Audrey's like, "Put a blond wig on that kid and he's Draco Malfoy all over again."

"Definitely prime Slytherin material," Randy added.

Next we moved on to eyeball the posts and comments, hoping they might reveal some tasty clues and that Ashton might have some stuff on there too. Like the profiles, though, the posts weren't much different from the tidbits kids at my school cluttered their walls with.

It's weird—reading posts like that, you only get one small side of people's personalities. One's always griping, another's impossibly upbeat, and yet another's always coming with the jokes. You could get the idea that's how they are all the time if you don't know them outside of cyberspace.

One word that kept coming up did spark my interest, though—*Gangland*. As in: *Gangland this Saturday*. Or: *Gangland, baby, Gangland*. Or simply: *Gangland!* What that meant was anybody's guess.

There were no comments from Ashton since her disappearance, of course, and in fact, we had to go back a couple of weeks before we found anything from her at all. Nothing looked suspicious. Actually, she seemed like a pretty positive supportive-type friend. Except for one comment she made in response to Rowan's post.

Rowan Adams: Another glorious Gangland extravaganza!

Ashton Browning: :(

That was her only response, just the frowny face.

Audrey's like, "Maybe that has something to do with why they broke up."

"Maybe," I said.

"Yeah," Randy added. "He probably broke up with her because he didn't like her putting a frowny face on everything he said."

"You would blame the girl," Audrey said. "I bet she broke up with him because she couldn't stand his little smirk."

I started to scroll back even further into the past, but just then a private message showed up. It was from Nash. Admittedly, I felt a little rush. I mean, this guy was top-of-the-heap material, and here he was sending me a private message.

He's like, *Hey, master detective! Good to meet you the other day! We should hang out and talk about the case! I have a game going on at my favorite pool hall this Saturday! You should come!*

Besides the correct grammar and overuse of exclamation points, there was something else odd about the message—the address of his favorite pool hall was smack-dab in the middle of the Asian District, not at all the kind of high-rent place you'd expect a Hollister kid to hang out in. But that was okay. This was just the kind of opportunity a good investigator needed to take advantage of. Maybe I could even find out what Gangland was. Plus, it would be pretty cool getting to hang with a guy like Nash.

"Hmmm," Audrey said. "This is interesting. Very interesting. I wonder what he wants out of this."

I'm like, "Hey, is it so impossible that the guy just wants to hang out with me?"

She shrugged.

Randy goes, "But *pool*? Who plays pool anymore?"

And I'm like, "I guess I do."

CHAPTER 13

Saturday night I put on my newest old jeans and my retro Iron Maiden T-shirt. I'm not sure I'd ever heard an Iron Maiden song, but the shirt was pretty awesome, and besides, they say black is supposed to be slimming. Audrey picked me up about seven, and then we swung by to get Randy. He was wearing a cheesy collared shirt that was unbuttoned far enough to expose his pale bony chest. I should also point out that he'd been trying to grow a mustache for about a month, but it only had about twenty whiskers—twelve on one side and eight on the other—which had the texture of armpit hair. Apparently, he thought it was suave. I wasn't so sure I wanted him along on this mission, but I still owed him for the tough spot I'd put him in at the grocery store.

As we headed into the city, he started asking about Trix, wondering if maybe she'd be at the pool hall. That possibility was the main reason Audrey wanted to go, but Randy, always up for meeting a new girl—any new girl—figured if Trix turned out not to be a lesbian, he might have a shot at her.

I'm like, "No way. If she's not a lesbian, then I'm first in line in front of you."

"Forget that, Dylan," Audrey said. "You can't ever ask her out."

"Why not? If she's not into girls, why would you care?"

"Because we're best friends, and you don't ask out somebody your best friend already likes. The gay thing doesn't make any difference."

I hadn't thought of it that way, but she was right. It wouldn't feel so good to see her going around with some girl I liked. And I would never—never—in a million years want to make Audrey feel like that. Besides, I didn't think it was a good idea to date a suspect.

Anyway, the Asian district is a cool part of town. There's a healthy Vietnamese population in Oklahoma City, and they've opened up all kinds of interesting restaurants and shops. If you've never tried *pho,* which is this super-hearty Vietnamese noodle soup, then you need to. They have whole restaurants devoted to it. In fact, even though I'd already had dinner, I voted to stop in for a quick bowl, but Audrey and Randy vetoed me.

Trang's, the Vietnamese pool hall, was on a little out-of-the-way side street in a building that I think used to be a carpet store. Although a lot of the Vietnamese places were all spruced up, Trang's was pretty dingy on the outside, not a total dump, but not exactly welcoming either. I was pretty sure we weren't going to fit in.

"Are you guys sure you want to go in here?" I asked.

"Why not?" Randy said. "My dad used to take me into worse places than this when he was still around."

I looked at Audrey.

"We're here," she said. "We might as well check it out. Besides, how bad can it be if a Hollister boy hangs out here?"

I'm like, "It's times like this I wish I had a derringer or something."

"Oh, sure," said Randy. "Someone would take that away from you in about five seconds and let the air out of your big belly with it. Now come on, let's go in."

That Randy. He sure knew how to reassure a guy.

My hope was that the owners had put all their money into decorating the inside. I pictured gold Buddha statues, fake exotic plants, a couple of big-screen TVs, maybe even a snack bar made out of bamboo. No luck. I guess all their money went into used pool tables. There were ten of them, each with plastic-shaded lamps, which were pretty much the only sources of light in the room. The walls might have been another color at some time, but now they were pretty much a shabby slate gray, except for the cue racks and a few signs with Vietnamese writing on them. Cigarette smoke hung over everything. Either this place was exempt from smoking laws or nobody bothered to enforce them here.

It wasn't hard to spot Nash, being tall and blond and all. He and a buddy of his were the only non-Vietnamese guys in the room. Emphasis on the word *guys*. Not a single female in sight, except for Audrey. Nash looked up from the pool table where he was playing and waved. "Hey, Dylan, my man, I'm glad you could make it."

He introduced me to his playing partner, another blond-statue Hollisterite, whose name was Holt, and to the two Vietnamese guys they were playing against, Huy and Tommy. I thought that was pretty gentlemanly of him to introduce everybody like that, so I introduced them all to Randy and Audrey.

Nash chalked the end of his cue and leaned over the table to take a shot. "Five in the side," he said. He made the shot and looked up at me. "Ahhh, I'm on a hot roll."

He missed the next shot, and Huy and Tommy laughed.

"Can't make 'em all," Nash said, smiling. He walked around the table and stood next to me. It was weird. In the dingy atmosphere, he seemed almost to glow. But I wasn't so sure it would be a good idea for him to win the match. The regulars around here might not like that.

"So I guess these two are your detecting partners, huh?" He nodded toward Audrey and Randy.

"Something like that."

"What's the word? You found out anything new?"

"Not really. I was hoping maybe you had something to tell us."

"Need a little info for your newspaper articles, huh? How about the one you were going to write about the search party? I thought you were going to send me a copy."

"Yeah, I'll send it to you. It doesn't come out in the school paper till next week. The teacher liked it. Said maybe I might make an investigative reporter after all."

"Oh, I have no doubt you will. That's what I like about you—you have a passion for something interesting. *Investigative journalism.*" He said it like it was the title of something grand. "Too many people are bland, but not you."

I have to admit I swelled a little at that. It felt good to have somebody of Nash's stature recognize that I wasn't just another member of the herd.

Randy poked his head around to get into the conversation. "Where's all the girls?"

"We're not here for girls," Nash said. "Girls come later."

"There's a couple things I was wondering about," I said. "You dated Ashton, and it seems like you two stayed friends—how did she get along with her dad?"

"Her dad? You know the story—at the office twelve-hour

days, flying around the country, never there for her recitals, or plays, or anything like that. Bought her everything she wanted, though. You don't think he had something to do with it, do you?"

"You never know. A lot of times in cases like this it's the parents or the spouse or something—crimes of passion and all."

"You really know a lot about this kind of stuff."

"I do my homework."

"Well, I'd say her mom caused more problems than her dad."

"Why's that?"

"Her mom's what you might call the nervous type. A real pill popper."

"Her mom, huh?" I had a hard time picturing her as a suspect. She didn't look like she could get the lid off a jar of pickles—or a jar of caviar—much less do bodily harm to someone.

"Well, what about that Rowan Adams guy?" Audrey asked. "Didn't he and Ashton break up a month or so ago?"

"Something like that," he replied. "But Rowan wouldn't be involved. I mean, he's a douche, but he's still my friend from way back. No, a lot of girls break up with Rowan. He's used to it."

That was interesting. *She* broke up with him. Despite Nash's opinion, that sounded like a pretty good motive to me.

"Hold on," Nash said. His turn was up at the pool table. He made one shot and missed one. When he came back, Randy asked him if there was anything to drink around the place, and Nash said they had Vietnamese soda. "It's weird, but it's good."

"Get a couple for me and Audrey," I told Randy, and he's like, "Give me some money."

When Randy left, Nash goes, "What's that thing on your buddy's upper lip?"

"He thinks it's a mustache," I explained.

"Yeah?" Nash raised an eyebrow. "Well, he's wrong."

I had to laugh. It was good to share an inside joke with Nash, even if it was at Randy's expense. Or maybe *because* it was at Randy's expense.

"So anyway," Nash said, "to tell you the truth, I wasn't really thinking about someone getting violent with Ashton. You know, killing her or something. I was figuring more along the lines of kidnapping. Something she could come back from safe and sound."

"But nobody ever said anything about a ransom," Audrey pointed out.

"There's still time."

"That's true," I said. "I wonder who might want to kidnap her."

Nash thought about that for a moment and even looked like he might have an idea, but if he did, he wasn't sharing anything specific. "Who knows? Anyone who wants a bundle of money the easy way, I guess. You haven't heard of any real hard evidence that something violent might have happened to her, have you?"

I wanted to mention that blue running shoes didn't just take themselves off, but he looked too genuinely worried, so I said, "No, I haven't heard anything like that. Just have to take all the scenarios into consideration, you know? You're probably right. A ransom note will probably show up, and she'll get back home just fine."

"I hope so."

"But there's one other thing I was wondering about," I said.

"What's up with this Gangland deal? You know anything about that?"

"Gangland? Where did you hear about that?"

"Oh, I hear things. That's part of my job."

"Hey, Nash," his buddy Holt called from the other side of the pool table. "It's your turn."

"Already?" Nash stepped over and eyed the remaining balls, then proceeded to run the table.

"Oh yeah," he roared. "Yeah, baby, yeah, baby."

I looked around to see if his celebration pissed off the regulars, but no one seemed to care. Huy and Tommy only shook their heads and took out their wallets. I couldn't see how much money they paid off on the bet, but it wasn't small change.

"You give us a chance to get some of that money back, right, Nash?" Tommy asked.

Nash slapped him on the back. "You know it."

I was finishing off my Vietnamese lemon drink when he came back over. It wasn't bad.

"So, you want to know about Gangland?" he asked. "I'll do better than tell you about it. I'll show it to you."

CHAPTER 14

According to Nash, it wouldn't take us fifteen minutes—depending on the traffic lights—to get where we were going. "There's one rule," he said. "You can't write about this in your paper."

"You mean *nothing* about it?"

"Well, I don't care if you mention something vague like that you went to a party, but you can't say where it is or even mention the word *Gangland*."

"Why not?"

"Because it's special. It won't be special if everyone knows about it. Besides, it doesn't have anything to do with Ashton."

"Okay, sure," I told him. "I guess that's fair." And I really did figure it was fair—as long as he was telling the truth about the connection, or lack thereof, to Ashton Browning.

We rode in his Lexus SUV along with Holt while Audrey and Randy followed us. And I wouldn't be lying to say this vehicle was *ripped*. Black inside and out. Leather seats. A console that looked like it belonged in a flying saucer. I was like, *Who needs a '69 Mustang? I'm a Lexus man now.*

Nash had good taste in music, but he blasted it a little too loud. He pulled a half-roasted joint from the ashtray, lit it, and took a deep drag before offering it to me.

"No thanks," I said. "Have to keep my wits sharp when I'm on a case, you know."

"Probably all for the best," he said, then passed the joint back to Holt.

This was unexpected. Somehow you just don't figure on a rich-kid wide receiver also being a stoner.

"You know," I said as the weed smoke billowed around me, "I would've thought the cops would question you—you being one of the ex-boyfriends and all."

"Who says they didn't?"

"This weed has an evergreen-like, almost sweet taste to it," Holt said. "Not too sweet and not too harsh. A decent pre-party blend." He sounded like a wine connoisseur.

"You mean the cops did talk to you?" I asked Nash.

"Sure. They talked to a lot of people."

"What'd they ask?"

"Oh, you know, the usual—*Why did you and Ashton break up? Did she have any enemies? Where were you when she went missing?* That kind of thing."

Of course, I'd thought of asking him where he was when Ashton disappeared, but I didn't want to come across as so obvious. My theory was you don't want people thinking you suspect them of anything. That way they're likely to be less guarded. But now that he'd mentioned it, I had my opening.

"So, what did you tell them about where you were?"

"The truth—I was at football practice."

That sounded like a strong alibi to me. Which was a relief. I was starting to really like Nash. I'd never had a cool friend like him, and I didn't want anything to spoil that—like him being guilty of kidnapping or murder.

A little east of the heart of downtown and north of the

entertainment district, we turned down an alley next to what looked like an abandoned warehouse. You wouldn't expect an alley like this to be lined by high-dollar luxury cars, but there they were. And more were parked in the small lot by the loading dock at the back of the warehouse. One spot was left open and Nash pulled into it. I mentioned that he was lucky to get the spot, but he said luck had nothing to do with it. The spot was reserved for him. Too bad there was no reserved parking for Audrey and Randy. They had to park a block away and hoof it back to where we waited next to the Lexus.

The warehouse was a solid squat thing made out of red brick. The few small windows had been sealed and painted black, and the metal sliding door on the loading dock was shut. As we stepped onto the dock, Randy's like, "What the hell are we doing here?"

And Nash goes, "This is it, brother. This is Gangland."

Next to the big sliding door was a smaller one, also made of metal. Nash banged on it a couple of times and a narrow slot, about at eye level, clicked to the side. A second later the door opened. Nash looked back at us with a smile. *"Après vous,"* he said, which I figured meant something like "Go on in."

Unlike the pool hall, the inside of the warehouse was way different from the outside. Yes, the inside walls were also red brick, but they'd been polished to a shine. Gold-framed movie posters hung on one wall, all of them from one gangster movie or another—*Juice, Scarface, The Godfather, GoodFellas, American Gangster,* even some from old black-and-white movies like ones I used to watch with my dad—*White Heat, The Roaring Twenties,* and *Little Caesar.* On the opposite wall hung posters of all the great gangsta rappers like Ice-T, Tupac Shakur, Notorious B.I.G., Insidious, and on and on.

The glow of red neon lights hung over everything like the atmosphere of some foreign planet. A mirrored disco ball swayed above a stage at the far end of the spacious warehouse, and on the stage sat a drum kit, keyboards, and a couple of racks with electric guitars in them. No band yet, though. The rest of the room was filled with teenagers, mingling, talking, laughing, apparently from Hollister and maybe some of the other hoity-toity schools in the area. And the biggest difference between Gangland and Trang's? Loads of girls.

Randy's like, "Wow, this place has more perfect female bodies than a mannequin factory."

"You can put your tongue back in your mouth now," Audrey told him. "You're starting to drool."

As we made our way along the gangster-movie wall, Nash goes, "Pretty cool place, huh?"

And I'm like, "Yeah, this is the greatest. Who owns it?"

"Rowan Adams and I. Well, we don't actually own it—we just run it. Rowan's dad owns the warehouse. He owns property all over the city, but real estate being what it is these days, he's just holding on to it till he can get a better price. Meantime, he let us fix it up for our extracurricular activities."

"Must be nice," I said. "What's with the name *Gangland*?"

"Just a little game we have going. Over the summer Rowan and I were kicking around ideas about how to make our senior year monumental, and we decided to start our own gangs."

"Your own *gangs*?"

"Yeah. He's the godfather of one and I'm the godfather of the other. Only instead of having turf battles and drug wars and whatnot, we have these different contests, and the gang that loses the most by the end of the school year has to pay for the biggest graduation party in the history of graduation parties."

"And Gangland is your headquarters?"

"Something like that. We call it our 'rec hall.' That's what we tell our parents, anyway."

"So what kind of contests do you have?"

"Oh, a little of this, a little of that. Crazy stuff, that's all. Like this battle-of-the-bands thing we have going. Tonight, Rowan has a band competing against the one I hired last week." He stopped walking and looked me in the eye. "Remember, this is completely confidential. I'm just telling you because you seem like a really good guy, and you're helping out with Ashton and everything."

"Don't worry," I said. "All I'm interested in is writing about the case." I couldn't help regretting the confidentiality clause, though. I mean, the kids at my high school would eat up a story about something like Gangland, even if they never would get to be a part of the gangs. But what could I do? I was a journalist, and journalists were supposed to have ethics about this kind of thing. Plus, I'd never get invited back.

Just then, a spotlight shone down on the stage, and a tall thin guy stepped into it. I recognized him immediately from his Facebook photos, mostly because of the red blazer he was wearing—Rowan Adams.

In addition to the blazer, he wore a mauve shirt with ruffles down the button line and these crazy green-and-yellow-striped pants. His face was long and lean, and his brown hair fell down over his ears and swooped over one eyebrow in front. To top off the look, he waved a cigarette in one of those long black cigarette holders in his right hand. Altogether, he looked like some kind of fairy-tale duke.

"Ladies and gentlemen," he said into a handheld microphone. "Welcome once again to Gangland, where all of your foulest dreams can come true. As you remember, last week our poor unfortunate and most terrible wide receiver almost-friend Nash Pierce attempted to introduce us to what he thought was a memorable band—the totally unworthy Rat Finks."

The crowd seemed about evenly split between those who cheered the Rat Finks and those who jeered.

"Yes, it was a pathetic attempt, Nash. But tonight, it's my turn to invigorate your musical senses, so without further ado, ladies and gentlemen, please welcome Colonoscopy!"

With that, the band scrambled onto the stage, took up their instruments, and began thrashing away. It was nothing but noise, and not good noise. Those guys looked like eighth- or ninth-grade fake juvenile delinquents. The bassist and lead guitarist even had tattoos that had obviously been drawn on with Magic Markers. The keyboardist twisted his face into a snarl, but you could tell, by day, he was really a band nerd. Still, the crowd cheered as if the all-time greatest dead rock stars had risen from their graves just to play a gig at Gangland.

"Hey, I like these guys," said Randy, and Audrey's like, "Are you kidding me? They're the most terrible band that ever existed."

"Damn, you're right," Nash said, thoughtfully rubbing his chin. "They are the most terrible band ever. That Rowan has one-upped me again."

Audrey pulled her camera out of her bag, but Nash clamped his hand on her arm. "No pictures," he said.

"Why not?" she asked.

"You know I like you," Nash said. "But we're trying to keep this place on the down-low."

Audrey looked at the crowd. Several people were taking pictures of the band with their cell-phone cameras. "What about them?"

"They're members."

"Members, huh? Okay." Audrey slid the camera back into her bag, but I could tell she didn't like it.

By the middle of the band's second tune, Rowan walked up to Nash, slapped him on the back, and said, "So, Nash, are you ready to admit defeat?"

"Not yet. They still have to play a whole set. They might be better than the Rat Finks yet."

"Let me get this straight," I said. "You guys are having a contest to see who can find the *crappiest* band?"

"Pretty much," Nash said.

Rowan looked at me like I was some kind of specimen he wasn't familiar with. "What do we have here?" he asked Nash.

Nash introduced me, along with Randy and Audrey.

"Glad to meet you," Rowan said, and then looking at Audrey: "How you doing, little guy?"

"I'm a girl," she said.

Rowan cocked an eyebrow. "Hey, I took a wild guess."

"Don't pay attention to him," Nash said. "He thinks being a douche is funny. He doesn't mean anything by it."

Rowan asked something that Nash had to ask him to repeat. We had to talk pretty loud to be heard over the *squink-squawnk* of the band.

"I said"—Rowan raised his voice—"are these some of your newest prospects?"

And Nash's like, "No, this is the guy I told you about, the investigative reporter who's helping find Ashton."

Rowan inspected me more closely. "Right. You're the one who found Ashton's shoe. I guess you want to ask me some questions."

"Well," I said, "you *were* the one who dated her most recently."

"I dated her all right, but I don't know if I dated her most recently."

"What do you mean? I haven't heard about anyone else dating her."

"I can't tell you anything for sure." Rowan fixed another cigarette into the black holder and lit it. "There were just some rumors she was maybe seeing someone from another school. A *South Side* school, no less."

He said the phrase *South Side* like it was a cheap cut of meat he had to spit out before he tasted too much of it.

"I never believed those rumors," Nash said.

Rowan blew out a puff of smoke. "Well, something was keeping her from dating anyone at Hollister. I mean, it's not like she didn't have plenty of guys asking her out."

"Surely, someone would know," I suggested. "Are any of her best girlfriends here?"

Rowan glanced at the crowd. "Some of her *ex*–best friends are here."

"Ex–best friends?"

"Yeah, she started hanging out with a different crowd."

That was an intriguing morsel of news. If she'd had a falling-out with her friends, maybe they were the ones starting rumors about her. And maybe—just maybe—they did something worse than that. But I could check on that later. Right now I wanted to delve into Rowan's relationship with Ashton a little more.

"I guess you weren't too happy about some of those rumors," I said. "If it was me, I'd be pretty mad."

"I'm sure *you* would be," he said. "I, on the other hand, have plenty of other interests to keep me occupied."

"Is that right?" I said. It was a lame comeback, but it's kind of hard to be snappy when you're talking to a guy who looks like a mad aristocrat from a Brothers Grimm story. Audrey came to my rescue, though.

"What about the day Ashton went missing?" she asked, stepping into Rowan's personal space. "Were you pursuing one of those other interests, or don't you have an alibi?"

"An alibi?" He laughed and looked at Nash. "Really, Nash, these people are too funny. I'll have to give you points for finding them."

"Yeah, we're real funny," I said. "We're the kind of comedians who don't like it when an ex-boyfriend goes looking for revenge against the girl who dumped him. So maybe you can just answer a simple question and tell us where you were."

"That's a good one," Rowan said. He took a drag from his cigarette and blew the smoke into my face. "You *are* a comedian. Apparently, you've mistaken me for the kind of people you're used to hanging out with, running around in their sweaty muscle shirts, getting into arguments over welfare checks, hitting each other in the face with toasters, and chasing women around the apartment complex with steak knives."

"Hey," Randy interrupted. "We're not on welfare." As if that was the worst part of Rowan's picture of us.

"Come on, Rowan." Nash stepped up, pressed his hand to Rowan's chest, and eased him back. "These people are my guests. They aren't accusing you of anything. They just want to help find Ashton. I know you want that too."

"Yeah, they're just routine questions," I said, and immediately realized I sounded like the cops who quizzed me about the Hector Maldonado case. Whether that was a good thing, I wasn't sure.

Rowan looked away, then back. "You're right, Nash." He

turned to me. "My apologies. I'm not really the asshole you might think I am. I have my role to play. But you're wrong if you think I'm not worried about Ashton. Everyone here is. You may think these little recreational activities of ours are in poor taste with Ashton missing, but we have to do something. You can't just sit around feeling black. If you hurt, you have to take some kind of medicine, you know?"

"I never said otherwise." Suddenly, I felt bad about using the cop routine on him. It was probably true—he probably really was hurting. Maybe he still loved her.

"So," he said, patting my shoulder, "no hard feelings. I hope you three musketeers will mingle and have fun until ten o'clock."

"Ten o'clock?"

"Uh, yeah," Nash said. "It's a Gangland members-only thing after ten."

"Now, if you'll excuse me." Rowan made a slight bow with his head. "I have to make the rounds and see to it that everyone's having a good time."

When he was gone, Randy goes, "That guy's a real dick."

"I feel sorry for him," Audrey said. "I'd hate to have to put on that act all the time."

"I got the impression that, underneath, he really is pretty broken up about Ashton," I said. But at the same time I realized he'd left without ever answering the most important question: Where was he when Ashton Browning disappeared?

CHAPTER 15

Nash left us to try out our mingling skills on our own, but Audrey and I weren't exactly advanced in that department—especially around an upscale crowd like this—so since there weren't any tables or chairs, we lagged back by the wall, sizing everyone up. Audrey even snuck in a few photos with her cell phone. Randy, on the other hand, poured himself right into the mix, his idea being that "these rich girls would love to hang with a *real* guy instead of the snakes they're used to."

Most of the crowd had broken into small groups that paid no attention to the band, but a couple rows' worth of people actually crammed together near the front of the stage, I guess judging whether Colonoscopy was worse than Nash's band the Rat Finks. Everyone looked like they were having a good time without putting out much effort. Kids at my school had to strain to have a good time. They had to grab a good time by the hind legs and wrestle it down. There was that kind of desperation to it. Not here. Fun floated on the air like a light fog, despite the Ashton Browning situation.

"You know," I said to Audrey, "I'm not so sure about what that jerk Rowan said. These people don't look like they're partying down to forget about their good friend Ashton. They look more like they already forgot about her."

"Yeah," Audrey said, looking at the crowd. "I just wonder what Rowan meant when he asked Nash if we were his *newest prospects.*"

"I don't know. Maybe they bring in new prospects to nominate for gang membership."

"Maybe. But I'm not so sure their gangs are as innocent as Nash was making out."

"What do you mean? You think a bunch of Hollister kids are going around robbing banks or selling crack?"

"No. I just think it's a little weird that they chose to be gangs instead of, say, teams or families or something."

"*Families?* Are you kidding? Gangs are just a more fun concept. Besides, maybe they already had the posters."

"Well, I'd be a little worried about someone who was obsessed with gang posters."

"That's because you're a girl," I said. "It's a guy thing." And that was the truth. Besides, I couldn't see Nash getting up to anything too nefarious. Rowan, maybe, but not Nash.

For me, a more important line of investigation concerned the girl gangsters in the room. Which ones were Ashton's ex–best friends? Everyone knows that when it comes to certain things, girls can be a ton more evil than guys, so I couldn't help wondering if her old clique hadn't come up with a way to wreak some vengeance on her for ditching them. None of them looked evil, though. In fact, if I'd had as much nerve—or stupidity—as Randy, I wouldn't have minded talking to about a dozen of them.

"Why don't you go over there?" Audrey said. "You know you want to."

She'd caught me staring at a cute blonde who was dressed in a white tuxedo, of all things.

"Yeah, sure."

"Dylan, you're never going to get a girlfriend just by standing around staring."

"You really think that girl and me might make a good match?"

"No, but at least you could get some practice in."

"Yeah, at getting rejected. No thanks. I think I'll hold out for Ashton Browning."

"Really? Even if she ever does show back up, how are you going to talk to her when you can't go up and talk to any of the girls here?"

"Hey." I threw her my best one-eyebrow-raised suave expression. "When you save somebody's life, you don't have to have a good opening line."

Audrey looked past me. "Well, maybe you're not going to need an opening line tonight."

At that point I turned to see, coming straight at me, none other than Brett Seagreaves, the tasty black-haired, blue-eyed hottie from the search-party hamburger cookout. "Hey, Dylan," she said, nudging me with her shoulder. I couldn't believe she actually remembered my name. "Where's your cool hat?"

"My hat? Oh, it's probably at home under the bed, hiding—as it should be."

She laughed. "I like your T-shirt. Iron Maiden—scary."

"Not as scary as this band that's playing," Audrey said.

Brett glanced toward the stage. "They're pretty bad all right. Poor Nash. He had such high hopes for the Rat Finks."

"More like *low* hopes," I said.

She touched my arm and laughed again. "How do you like our little recreation center?"

"It's cool," was all I could muster at the moment. The

touching and laughing threw me off balance, this not being the usual hot-girl reaction to my humor.

"So," she said. "Nash tells me you were interrogating Rowan for your news articles about Ashton."

"I wouldn't call it interrogating. Just trying to clear some things up. He did say something I found interesting. Apparently, Ashton was kind of on the outs with a lot of her old friends. You know anything about that?"

She brushed her black hair back from her face. "Oh, I don't know if I'd say she was on the *outs* with any of us. We just kind of went our separate ways."

"Separate ways?"

"You know—we had different interests. Lately, she got so involved with her charity work. Not that we don't all do our parts for charity. I can't count all the luncheons, dinners, and galas I've been to, but I draw the line when it comes to delivering free meals to people at their homes. Those neighborhoods are scary. I understand some people have it hard, but you'd think they could at least drive over to someplace nice to get their food instead of having it delivered."

"You mean like drive over in their Rolls-Royces?" Audrey asked.

"You sound like Ashton," Brett said.

"Did she work for some kind of charity organization we could check into?" I asked.

Brett thought for a second, then shook her head. "I'm not sure, but I know someone who could tell you. Wait right here."

When she left, Audrey's like, "You realize she was flirting with you, don't you?"

"No way."

"Sure she was—complimenting your shirt, laughing at your little joke, touching your arm. That's what flirting is."

"But why?"

"Good question."

Before I could figure out an answer, Brett was back with none other than the cute blonde in the tuxedo. Introductions went around and it shook out that her name was Aisling Collins.

"Love the Iron Maiden shirt," she said, and reached over and touched my arm.

I glanced at Audrey, and she gave me this look like, *Something is up, but I don't know what it is.*

Brett explained to Aisling how I was out to help find Ashton by doing some articles for the school paper about her disappearance. "He was wondering if you knew the name of the charity she worked for delivering meals and whatnot."

Aisling pressed a finger to her bottom lip. She really was incredibly cute, and the tuxedo just added to it. "Let's see, I think it's called FOKC."

I'm like, "Did you say *Fock?*"

She giggled. "No, FOKC. F-O-K-C. Feed Oklahoma City."

"Wow, that's some acronym," I said. "So, you used to be pretty close with Ashton?"

"Oh my God, yes. We were practically like sisters. Brett too."

"I guess it was kind of—I don't know—*awkward* when she stopped making time for you."

"I don't know about awkward," Brett said. "Actually, it kind of pissed us off. I wouldn't put it past her to get all involved with that charity just to have something else to put on her college application."

And Aisling's like, "Don't say that, Brett. Ashton wouldn't do that. Anyway, I wasn't mad. It was just that we missed her."

"Sure, we missed her," Brett agreed. "But she had a way of making you feel guilty for wanting to have fun instead of driving down to some high-crime ghetto where you could get your throat cut just to deliver ham sandwiches."

"Well, there was *that*," Aisling said.

"Yeah, that'd be annoying," I said. "Was there any particular person she pissed off more than anyone else?"

"You mean besides Rowan?" Aisling asked.

"Rowan?"

"Yeah, he didn't like it that she spent more time on her charity stuff than at Gangland and everything."

"So Ashton used to come here?"

"Sure," Brett said. "But then she decided it was too—I guess—frivolous."

I wanted to dig into this Rowan thing a little more, but just then Randy showed up.

"Hey, girls," he said, grinning. "Either of you want to dance?"

Brett and Aisling glanced at each other. "Uh, no," they said in unison.

"Oh, come on. Why not?" Randy insisted, keeping the grin burning.

"Because no one's dancing?" replied Aisling.

"And because the band is atrocious?" added Brett.

Randy's grin fizzled.

"Look," Brett said to Aisling. "There's Tres. Let's go see how he's holding up." She reached over and touched my arm again. "Talk to you more later?"

"Sure." I watched her wind through the crowd to catch up with Tres. She had a whole different walk from the sexy girls at my school—a little less lubricated in the hip area—but it was sexy just the same.

When she latched onto Tres, she gave him a tight hug and leaned her head on his shoulder in a consoling way. He looked like he enjoyed it. I thought it was strange, though, that he'd showed up here, with his sister missing and all. I mean, I could understand that the rest of the kids needed to blow off a little steam, but Tres? You'd think his parents would order him to stay home and hide or something.

A moment later, Nash stepped up next to him and shook his hand. Then with Brett and Aisling, they formed a line and snaked through the crowd and past the stage, Nash in the lead. I had to hand it to Nash—he moved with such easy confidence, like it was something he was born with along with his blond hair and blue eyes. A guy like that—he had plenty of mojo.

They disappeared into a corridor to the right of the stage, and I'm like, "I wonder what goes on back there," and Audrey's like, "Probably plotting their gang activities."

"The chicks here must already have boyfriends," Randy observed. "I couldn't get a tumble out of a single one."

"Did you ever think it might be your mustache?" Audrey said. "You really do need to get rid of that thing. It looks like a caterpillar with mange."

"Hey," he said. "Show a little respect for the 'stache. It's working as hard as it can."

"Well," Audrey said, "Dylan's already had two girls flirting with him."

"Those two hotties you were talking to? Give me a break. They were probably just high."

"Yeah," I said. "High on Dylan Jones." But I couldn't help thinking Randy might have a point. Both of them very well could've partaken of some chemical appetizers on their way to Gangland. And maybe they were going back for seconds with Nash somewhere down that dark corridor into the bowels of Gangland. A good investigator, I told myself, wouldn't leave before checking out where that corridor led.

CHAPTER 16

Colonoscopy plowed through a couple more songs before taking a break. At that point, Rowan hopped onto the stage again, and after a few sarcastic remarks about how great the band was, he turned serious, basically repeating the same spiel he handed me about how everyone needed to break up the darkness that Ashton Browning's disappearance had cast over them. "But make no mistake," he said. "This isn't lighthearted fun tonight. It's heavyhearted. This is serious fun, the kind that's required to bring us together so we can make it through the hard times until Ashton's back with us, safe and sound."

It sounded good, as if he really meant it. But, with a guy like Rowan, there was about a 70–30 chance he was putting on an act.

While he was still on the stage, I noticed Tres emerge from the corridor where he'd disappeared earlier. This seemed like a good time to get a word in with him, but before I could make it over there, he veered away and took the stage next to Rowan.

Everyone cheered as Rowan handed him the microphone. The two of them whispered something to each other, and then

Tres looked down and nervously brushed the top of his head. None of that easy confidence for him. He appeared almost scared as he gathered his thoughts. Finally, he looked up at the crowd—kind of—and started to speak, but the microphone squawked with feedback. Rowan stepped over and nudged his hand to move the mike back from his mouth.

"Good evening, everybody," Tres said softly. "Um, you know I'm not good at speeches, so I'll just say thank you for coming out to show your support for Ashton. I know she would appreciate it." There was an awkward silence as he looked toward Rowan, then back at the audience. "So, um, that's it. Just, thank you."

He handed the microphone back to Rowan, and everyone applauded politely, the energy of the room momentarily drained. Then Rowan started in about how there was much more entertainment to come and zapped some electricity back into the place. Just like that, Ashton's shadow disappeared.

"Before Colonoscopy comes back for more sweet indie rock-'n'-roll action," Rowan announced, "I want to mention some special guests who came all the way up from the South Side." He looked straight at me. "And the word is they have something very tasty planned to help us celebrate."

"What's he talking about?" Audrey asked, and I'm like, "I have no idea. But I think it's time to pay Nash a visit and find out exactly what goes on down that side corridor."

As Rowan rambled on about how talent was everywhere— you just needed to know how to find it—Audrey and Randy followed me through the crowd. We didn't make it into the corridor, though. Big blond Holt blocked our way. "You can't go back there," he said, clamping his hand onto my shoulder. "VIPs only."

Randy stepped up next to me. "Hey, dude, in case you forgot, we're guests of the main VIP."

Holt looked down at him. "All that means is you're just lucky to get in the front door."

"Yeah?" said Randy. "But how do I know the front door isn't down that hall?"

"What?" Holt said, consternated.

"All I'm saying is it looked to me like I came in the back door, so if I'm supposed to come in the front door, maybe I need to go down that hall, where the front door really is, and come back in through it."

"That's ridiculous," Holt told him.

"Is it? You're the one who said we were only supposed to come in through the front door. I'm just trying to be official here."

Holt was getting exasperated, and that was the point, of course. In one of his rare strokes of brilliance, Randy was running the same dumb-ass routine he'd used on Detectives Forehead and Hair Gel. It was perfect. All I had to do now was ease away and sneak down the hall.

The only light was a vague hint of neon that seeped in from the main room, so I had to feel my way along the wall until I came to an open doorway. Running my hand up the wall inside, I found the light switch and flicked it on. The room was about twice the size of my living room at home and appeared to be a combination storage area and dressing room—big cardboard boxes, spare decorations, metal benches and chairs, a long table, empty guitar cases, and backpacks. Nothing mysterious about the place. But I admit I took a little bit of offense over how Colonoscopy could be considered VIP enough to come back here while I wasn't.

I turned off the light and crept further into the darkness,

passing a couple of closed doors along the way until I noticed, at the far end of the corridor, a sliver of light showing beneath what I could just make out as the black shape of a final door. As I crept nearer, I noticed a sign hanging on the door and held up my phone for a light. The sign was obviously hand-painted, and someone had really gone to a lot of trouble with the calligraphy-style lettering:

O-TOWN ELITES & NORTH SIDE MONARCHS ONLY.

ALL OTHERS WILL BE SHOT AT DAWN.

North Side Monarchs? It took me a moment to place where I'd heard that before, but it was the name Hector Maldonado's cousin Beto dropped on me that day at the funeral. *How would he know about that?* I wondered. *And why did he think I might be involved with them?*

Then it hit me—maybe, just maybe, Hector's death was somehow connected to Ashton's disappearance. But how? It didn't seem likely they'd know each other, much less have the same enemies. Unless he was the South Side boyfriend Rowan had mentioned. The image of Hector in the Dumpster flickered in my head along with what Beto had said: *If Hector had drugs in him, someone else must've dosed him.* I couldn't help Hector then, but this little clue gave me hope that I might be able to help him now. But what could I do, call Detective Hair Gel and get myself placed back on the suspect list? No. There was still too much I had to find out.

Voices burbled vaguely behind the door, but no matter how hard I pressed my ear against the cool wood, I couldn't understand a word. Then a sliding lock clacked from inside, and I'm like, *Holy crap! They're going to catch me!*

It wasn't like I was breaking into a sacred crypt or anything, but for some reason my heart felt like it was trying to claw its way out backward through my shoulder blades. At first I backed away, then I turned to run, then I turned again and froze. *Just act natural,* I told myself. *No need to freak out. These aren't vampires you're dealing with.*

Then someone shouted from the other end of the hall: "Hey, I told you not to come down here."

It was Holt. Audrey and Randy followed as he strode toward me. Then the door opened and I was double busted.

Nash, Brett, and Aisling walked out, all three of them grinning in the wash of light from the back room. I wasn't sure, but my guess was they'd been indulging in some more of the sweet yet evergreeny weed.

Holt's like, "Sorry, Nash, this character sneaked back here," and Nash's all, "Don't worry about it. That's cool. Dylan's my man." He slapped me on the back. "Isn't that right, Dylan?"

And I'm like, "Yeah?"

"But really," Nash said, his arm now around my shoulders, guiding me away from the room he just came out of. "What are you doing back here? You guys should be out there schmoozing. Ten o'clock isn't too far away—you have to cram in the fun."

"I know," I said. "That's why I wanted to come back here. I just wanted to get your ideas on my investigations so far."

"That's cool," Nash said. "But nothing needs investigating back here."

The girls laughed.

"Seriously, though," Nash said, "before you head out, I was wondering if you'd do me a little favor."

"Um, okay," I said. "What is it?"

"Well, until the band comes back, we're going to have a

little karaoke action, and I thought you three might want to represent the O-Town Elites."

"O-Town Elites?"

"Yeah, that's my gang."

That meant Rowan's gang must be the North Side Monarchs. Could it be that Hector's cousin actually thought the Monarchs were a *real* gang? Could Hector have told him they were? Before I could muster any answers, Audrey stepped up.

"Wait a minute," she said. "You want us to do this because you think we'll be terrible and you can win some bet?"

"Not exactly," Nash replied. "I was hoping you'd be terrible on purpose so I can win a bet."

"But everyone will think we're idiots," I said.

"No they won't." Brett gave my arm a squeeze. "They'll think you're *notorious.*"

"And I would love it," added Aisling.

"I'm in," Randy piped up from behind Holt.

I looked at Audrey, and she's like, "It might be kind of funny. Like that time we did the comedy version of 'Bullet Head' by Insidious at the journalism fund-raiser."

" 'Bullet Head'!" Nash sounded thrilled. "That's perfect. I know we have that one on the machine."

Brett aimed her brilliant blues at me. "Besides, you have to contribute something for getting into Gangland free tonight."

I didn't really like the sound of it. After all, I figured an investigator should remain more low-key than that. You'd never see Walker, Texas Ranger, or the Andromeda Man doing karaoke. But I had to make up for getting caught in the forbidden corridor. Besides, what are you going to do when you have a black-haired, blue-eyed rich girl standing so close you can smell the mint on her breath?

CHAPTER 17

agreed to go through with the bad karaoke under one condition—that they didn't announce us by our real names. Nash said that was all right by him, and after some discussion, we ended up with me as Nitro, Randy as TNT, and Audrey as Lil' Dynamite. But there was no time to rehearse. The Hollisterites herded us out of the corridor, and we squeezed our way to the front of the stage, where Rowan was already rambling off a long, overblown introduction to the first act, a tall, lanky brunette by the name of Paige Harrison.

That was her first mistake, I thought. No cool alias.

As the opening notes of one of those horrible generic girl-pop songs started up, she slunk across the stage to the microphone, popping her eyes wide and licking her lips in what appeared to be a caricature of your typical teen diva. Now, I'm no *American Idol* judge, but even I could tell she was way off-key, and I'm not sure that part was intended. She was pretty funny, though. She had to strain her eyes to read the lyrics, and with her awkward bumping and grinding, she had all the grace of an ostrich with its tail feathers on fire.

I knew she was supposed to be bad, but as I listened to the boos and jeers and laughter of the crowd, I couldn't help feeling sorry for her. There were so many gorgeous girls around, and she was so obviously not gorgeous I found myself hoping she'd drop the act and end up being great after all. No such luck, though. She was horrible from start to finish.

"That's going to be hard to beat," I told Audrey.

"Yeah," she said. "We'd better start off with our big guns. Let Randy go first."

Nash introduced us as if we actually were three badasses from the wrong side of town, even going so far as listing our supposed crimes: barbecuing a baby, killing a hobo with a pitchfork, and stealing all the stuffed animals out of the game machine in the lobby of Pizzalicious.

The karaoke machine cranked up the beat as soon as we took the stage, and Nash handed off the microphone to Randy. The crowd cheered and booed at the same time. Randy wasn't involved in our journalism fund-raiser performance, so he had a hard time with the lyrics, but he made up for it with his god-awful dancing. Moving to the very edge of the stage, he grimaced, twisted, threw up his version of gang signals, and grabbed his crotch. At times, he looked like he was being riddled by machine-gun fire. It was pretty hilarious, except I knew he thought he was phenomenal.

When his part was done, he pranced back and handed the microphone off to Lil' Dynamite. Rocking her shoulders in perfect time to the beat, she launched into the lyrics of "Bullet Head" with a vengeance. No pretending to be bad for her—she ruled. But about halfway through, she veered away from Insidious's rhymes and started freestyling her own. I'd seen her do this before—the girl could seriously throw down:

Boys in the hallway putting up a cockfight.

Losers and winners, they both the same at midnight.

Girlie-girls with satin gloves twirling in their ball gowns.

Everyone bleeds red every time they fall down.

Flashing cash creeps they never see the real me.

And all of you straight fits don't know how to feel me.

Then it was back to the "Bullet Head" chorus, and for the first time, the crowd was neither cheering nor booing. I don't think they quite knew how to process what just blew at them.

Then it was my turn. Lil' Dynamite handed off the microphone, and I knew I couldn't stick to the script either. After a couple of lines, I started in about how I was a real investigator who wouldn't stop digging till I found the perpetrator. Didn't matter if they were rich or if they were poor, they'd better look out 'cause I'd be knocking at their front door.

But I was a journalist, not a rapper, and the rhymes came unraveled pretty quickly. The boos roared after that, and I doubt many people heard the rest. Before I wrapped it up, though, I caught a glimpse of Tres standing in the front row. He had this weird expression on his face like he was angry or worried or both. Or maybe it was just sweet but evergreeny weed paranoia. Whatever it was, it seemed personal and aimed at me.

After our performance, we remained on the stage, and Paige Harrison joined us for the award—or anti-award—presentation. Rowan took the mike first and crowed about how awesome Paige was, heavy on the sarcasm. Then Nash grabbed the mike away and argued that Nitro, TNT, and Lil' Dynamite were way awesomer than anyone who had ever done karaoke in the history of the art form.

Now it was time to vote by popular decree. First, Rowan

held his hand above Paige's head and called for the audience to voice their support. Boos rolled toward the stage like a huge dark wave, and Rowan smiled. Apparently boos were a good thing in this kind of contest. Next, Nash held his hand over my head, and again the boos rose up—only this time they came crashing like a tsunami.

We won by being bigger losers than probably the biggest loser girl at Gangland. I wasn't really sure how I should take that, but Audrey seemed proud, and Nash was obviously thrilled. He was going to fail in the battle of the bad bands, but at least he pulled out a win at lousy karaoke.

CHAPTER 18

I t was ten till ten by the time the contest wrapped up—time for us loser non-Gangland members to scurry out of there. Nash thanked us for giving him his victory, and even Rowan congratulated us. Brett gave me a hug and a kiss on the cheek. I don't know if it was the kiss or the shampoo smell from her hair, but I felt a little light-headed when she pulled away.

As we made our way to the door, Tres came up and shook all of our hands, though when he spoke, he looked only at me. "I'm glad you're doing so much to help with Ashton," he said. "You seem pretty determined." That earlier weird expression on his face had been replaced by his trademark shyness. Which was a relief. I was afraid I offended him by bringing up his sister's situation in my rap.

"I am determined," I told him, but I didn't say why. A rich kid probably couldn't understand how important reaching for a little extra mojo was to a guy like me.

At the door, Nash shook my hand. "Glad you made it out tonight," he said. "You were awesome up there onstage, but I knew you would be. Too bad you have to leave, but those are the rules. We'll have to do it again, though."

"Sure," I said. "I'd love to."

On our way to Audrey's car, we passed quite a few people heading the other direction. That made sense—probably the best part of the night at Gangland was just getting ready to crank up. But something else didn't make sense. Two of the people we passed were Huy and Tommy from the Vietnamese pool hall. They grinned and waved. I stopped and watched them, and sure enough they got in the door.

"That's weird," I said. "How do those guys rate getting to go in while we got kicked out?"

Audrey and Randy agreed that it was weird, but they didn't think it was any of our business. We'd done our time in Gangland, and they were ready to head home. I wasn't about to let it go that quickly, though.

"Come on," I said. "I have an idea."

We snuck around to the far side of the building, the side away from the street. There were several windows set high in the wall, all sealed and coated with black paint, just like the windows on the other side.

"What do you think you can do back here?" Randy asked.

"Give me a second."

As I studied the windows, it occurred to me I might be able to scratch a little peephole into the black paint and maybe cop a view of what kind of shenanigans went on inside after ten o'clock. The problem? The windows were too high to reach—without help, that is.

I had Audrey and Randy make stirrups with their hands so they could boost me up a couple of feet. Unfortunately, this didn't work so well—me being the heaviest one in the group—and I ended up crashing down on my butt in the gravel. There was nothing to do but change course—Randy and I lifted Audrey up while she scratched at the black paint with her car key.

"Can you see anything yet?" I whispered.

"Not yet. This paint's pretty thick."

"Well, hurry up," Randy said. "You're not exactly a feather, you know."

"Hey, I think I can see a little light starting to come through," she said, but as she leaned forward to get a better look, Randy's grip loosened, and we almost dropped her.

"Look out," she said. "Are you trying to break my neck or something?"

Just then, a voice boomed behind us. "What are you kids doing back here?"

That was it. Randy lost his grip altogether, and as Audrey started to topple over I lost my balance trying to hold on to her, and we all three crashed onto the gravel.

Sitting there, the gravel dust puffing up around us, we looked up to see a very wide, almost-square man in a dark suit glaring down. His gray hair was thinning on top, and he had a big, bushy swooping cowboy mustache.

"Get up from there," he growled. "And let me see your IDs." He wasn't as tall as me, but his gut was bigger.

I pulled my ID out of my wallet and handed it to him, but Audrey wasn't so ready to comply. "Hold on a minute," she said. "Are you the police?"

"Never mind who I am." He studied my ID, then returned it. "What are you doing back here?"

The idea crossed my mind that Nash and Rowan hired him to do security for Gangland.

"We were just in there," Randy said. "We're practically members of the place."

"Shut up, Randy," Audrey snapped. "We don't have to talk to him."

"Practically members, huh?" the man said. "Then maybe

you don't mind if we go around to the door and ask them about that."

"That won't be necessary," I said, not wanting Nash or Rowan to know we were snooping around. "We were just getting ready to leave and got curious about what was going on in there, that's all."

"That's all, is it?" Mr. Mustache said. "How well do you know Rowan Adams?"

"We know he's a douche," Randy said.

The bushy mustache raised a notch, and I suspected its owner was smiling underneath it. Maybe he didn't like Rowan either. "Let me give you some advice," he said. "You should steer clear of this place. There's an investigation going on, and it's not something you want to get caught up in."

"An investigation?" I said. "You mean into Ashton Browning's disappearance?"

"What do you know about that?" Mr. Mustache was serious again.

"Just what we saw on the news," Audrey told him.

"Well, that's none of your business," Mr. Mustache said. "You got that? None of your business."

"Yeah, we got it." I didn't see any reason to get into an argument at this point.

"All right, then. You three get on your way. And I don't want to see you skulking around anymore."

"We were just leaving anyway," I said.

As we walked away, I glanced back over my shoulder to see he was still standing there watching us.

"That was creepy," Audrey said. "What do you think that guy's deal is?"

"I don't know," I said. "But I wouldn't be surprised if we run into him again somewhere down the Ashton Browning trail."

CHAPTER 19

Writing the next installment of my series on Ashton wasn't easy. Sure, I had my suspicions about Rowan Adams, Mr. and Mrs. Browning, the girls who Ashton unfriended, and those scary neighborhoods where Ashton delivered meals—plus there was the connection between the North Side Monarchs and Hector—but what could I say about any of that? All I really had were hunches, and you can't start putting people's names in newspaper articles based on hunches. Well, I guess you can—you see it all the time in the media these days—but the so-called newspeople who do that have some deep pockets behind them. Me, I'd probably get sued out of existence.

Then there was also the problem of writing about Gangland and the O-Town Elites and North Side Monarchs. For sheer reader interest it was a hard topic to beat. I'd come out looking like a star just for having been to a cool place like Gangland. But I wasn't sure how it tied in with Ashton. Or Hector. Plus, I couldn't break my promise to Nash. He'd been a good guy to me, and besides, as a journalist, I had the obligation to protect my sources. How could I get anyone else to talk to me if I didn't do that?

So I decided to focus completely on showing who Ashton Browning really was. I described her blond hair and her perfect nose and most of all her blue eyes. I wrote about how broken up her brother was about her disappearance and how her friends didn't always understand her charity work but admired her anyway. By the end I felt like I'd written a love letter to her.

I almost deleted the whole thing. I mean, how much crap would I catch if the kids at school knew I was falling in love with a rich missing girl from Hollister? But in the end I had to keep it pretty much like it was. I wanted people to care for her like I did. To see she was more than just a picture in the paper or a future candidate for a true-crime show on network TV.

And what do you know? When we got together after school to work on the next issue of the paper, Ms. Jansen said my piece was one of the best articles anyone had turned in that week. She thought it didn't really work as hard news, but it was a perfect human-interest piece to follow up my last article. Now, she said, I needed to dig into some of my leads and find a new slant for my next article on the case. I felt pretty good about that, like I'd made the right choice after all when I quit the grocery-store job. Things were really looking up for my investigative-journalism career.

I recruited Audrey to head to Topper's with me after school to discuss what my next move would be. On the way in, I said hello to Rockin' Rhonda, and she started singing her "Mr. Mojo" song at me. At least it was a better nickname than Body Bag.

To shake things up, I ordered the mushroom and Swiss burger. It's not as good as my usual, but having too much of the same thing all the time can kill the effect. We discussed staking out Rowan Adams's house or even the Brownings', but that sounded boring. Plus, you could probably get into some heavy trouble that way. Two teenagers sitting around a rich North Side neighborhood in a five-year-old Ford Focus? That's bound to draw some unwanted attention. Especially since neighborhoods like that are known to have their own special police forces.

Then I had the perfect idea. We could check into FOKC, the charity Ashton delivered meals for. It'd be easy. We'd just go down to their headquarters and pretend we wanted to get involved, say we wanted to do the same route Ashton usually delivered to. We were her friends, we'd tell them, and we knew Ashton would want to make sure her people were taken care of until she could come back and do it herself. Not that I actually wanted to deliver any meals. I just wanted a good excuse to find out who she delivered them to. It was an idea worthy of the Andromeda Man himself.

"How about we go Friday afternoon after school?" I suggested.

Audrey frowned. "Friday? I don't think I can do it Friday."

"Why not? What else could you possibly have going on?"

She didn't like that. "What?" she said. "You don't think I could have something going on? You think you're my only friend? I could have a date or something."

"Yeah, right. You could have a date. And I'm marrying Princess Leia."

"Hey, I could have a date."

"Well, do you?"

She looked away, then back. "I'm not sure exactly. It's just that Trix asked me if I wanted to get together this Friday for coffee."

"You're kidding. That's great. Why didn't you tell me?" I made a point to sound supportive even though the truth was I hadn't scratched Trix off my suspect list yet.

Audrey fiddled with one of her French fries for a moment.

"The thing is, I don't know if I really want to go. There's, like, a catch to it."

"Look, if you really like this girl, you shouldn't worry about some little catch."

"But it's kind of a weird catch."

"What is it?"

"Well, uh, she kind of said she wants you to come along too."

"Me?"

"Yeah."

This was awkward to say the least. It was just possible Trix was actually interested in me and not Audrey. But I'd already told Audrey—and myself—any kind of romantic deal between me and Trix was strictly taboo, so I had to walk a thin line here.

"You know what?" I said. "I'll bet she's not sure you're gay, so she didn't want to ask you out on an actual date. If I'm there, she can get to know you better without things getting weird, you know? It's the old 'Let's be friends so we can segue into a relationship' strategy."

"You really think so?"

"I'd say there's about a seventy-five percent possibility."

"So you'll come?"

"If you think I ought to."

"Yeah, I think you ought to."

"Okay. On one condition—we convince Trix to go to FOKC headquarters with us."

Audrey mulled on that for a moment. "That might work," she said finally. "That just might work."

I hoped it would work too, but I also couldn't help wondering if maybe Trix had some sinister ulterior motive for wanting to get together, a motive that had nothing to do with liking either one of us.

CHAPTER 20

On Friday afternoon, we met Trix in a coffee shop on her side of town, an upscale place with men and women in suits chatting or working on their laptops. As for Trix, she was wearing the exact same thing she wore the day we met her. Or the exact same look, I should say. She explained that she had a closet full of identical outfits. "When you find a look that's you," she said, "you might as well stick with it."

The coffees all had weird names, but I figured anything with the word *mocha* in the title couldn't be all bad, and it wasn't. Finding a place to sit was not a problem—the place was loaded with comfy chairs and little sofas gathered around coffee tables. I headed to one of the chairs, catching Audrey's eye and nodding toward the two-seater sofa so she'd have a chance to sit next to Trix. Unfortunately, another chair was left open and Trix sat there.

So far she seemed perfectly cool and all, but I had to consider the possibility that could just be an act to hide the fact she was the psychopath who killed her little friend in California. Maybe her dad even knew she was a psychopath and that's why he moved her to Oklahoma City. And this may sound paranoid, but sitting there, I even imagined a derringer tucked into her little black purse. Weirder things happen on *Andromeda Man* every week.

At first we traded some awkward small talk, but sooner or later the subject of Ashton Browning was bound to come up, and it did.

"So I guess you're still working on your articles about Ashton," Trix said after taking a sip of her cappuccino. "Word is you even showed up at one of those stupid Gangland parties."

"You know about that place?" I said. "I thought it was supposed to be secret."

"Everyone at Hollister knows about it," she said. "It's just that the people I hang with don't really care about it."

"We don't care about it either," Audrey said. "We just thought it'd be a good chance to get more of a feel for the crowd Ashton ran with. Or at least used to run with."

"I hope you didn't get the idea that just because I go to Hollister, I'm anything like Rowan Adams and Brett Seagreaves."

"We never thought that," Audrey assured her, although Trix didn't seem like the kind of person who needed much reassuring.

"Brett was all right," I said. "But Rowan's definitely on my suspect list."

Trix laughed. "Rowan? You know, as much as I'd like to see him get into trouble and bring his ego down in flames, I just don't see him being involved with anything that would actually take real balls to pull off. No, my guess is that nobody at Hollister had anything to do with Ashton missing."

"Why not?" I asked.

"Because probably some perv stalker grabbed her. Someone she never even knew."

So I'm like, "Is that what you think really happened to your friend's sister in California?"

But Audrey goes, "Dylan, don't bring that up. She probably doesn't want to talk about it."

"That's all right," Trix said. "Actually, Dylan's right. I met that pool guy they arrested for it. I just couldn't see him doing something like that. He was kind of dumb, but he was sweet. As far as I'm concerned, it was probably just some random guy. That's the way the world is, you know? It doesn't always make sense. It's just a bunch of randomness whirling around."

"Wow," Audrey said. "That's pretty deep." She looked so love struck I couldn't help feeling a little sorry for her. I'd been there before with Jennifer Roberts in ninth grade, to no avail.

"Well," I said, "we're not just looking at Hollister kids. We have some other leads too." I went on to explain about Ashton's charity work and how it took her to some pretty sleazalacious neighborhoods. "In fact, after coffee, we're planning on heading to FOKC headquarters to see if we can find out exactly where Ashton used to deliver meals. You want to come with?"

Trix's eyes brightened. "That sounds like an adventure," she said. "And I love adventures."

CHAPTER 21

For the drive to FOKC headquarters, we took Trix's sweet silver BMW. It wasn't as luxurious as Nash's Lexus, but it had its own kind of flair. I hated to be wishy-washy, but I had to seriously consider whether I was actually more of a BMW man after all. There was no doubt something like this would look tasty sitting in a parking spot in front of school next year. I wondered if they made them in red.

I rode in the backseat while Audrey sat up front with Trix. Mostly they chatted while I kept my mouth shut. They actually had quite a bit in common—musical artists, taste in fashion, books. Trix was even impressed that Audrey wanted to be a high-art-style photographer. She wished she could be an artist, but so far she hadn't found something she was that good at. I was glad they were getting along. You never want to see your friends put their hearts out there just to get trampled on.

We finally found the building we were looking for a couple blocks west of the bus station and not too far from the homeless shelter. The BMW definitely stood out in the middle of these dilapidated surroundings. If Ashton had to deliver meals in a neighborhood even worse than this, I wasn't sure I wanted to go there.

Inside, the place wasn't so bad. They'd fixed it up to look cheery and hopeful. Earlier in the week, I'd contacted FOKC and set up a time to come in and talk about delivering meals to the disadvantaged or whatever they go by these days. Nobody was there to greet us, though. I called out a hello, and shortly a woman in a pastel-blue pantsuit appeared from a hallway. At first she looked confused to see us, but when I explained about our appointment, her face burst into a sunny smile.

"You must have talked to Linda," she said. "Come on back."

We followed her to a small office where a little gray-haired lady sat behind a cluttered desk. The lady was talking on the phone and held up a finger, a signal for us to wait until she finished. When she hung up, the pantsuit lady explained who we were, and Linda smiled and asked us to sit down. There were only two chairs, so I stood while Audrey and Trix settled into their seats.

"I thought there were only going to be two of you," Linda said. "But the more the merrier." She tapped at her keyboard, bringing something up on the computer. "Let's see—you were the ones interested in taking over Ashton's route until she comes back." She looked up at us. "And we all know she will be coming back, don't we?"

"Definitely," I said. "No doubt. But—"

"Okay, then, we'll put you right to work."

What I was getting ready to say, before she cut me off, was that I never mentioned anything about actually taking over Ashton's route. I just wanted to talk about it. Maybe get a list of who she delivered to. But for a little five-foot-nothing lady with a slight hunchback, this Linda was a real go-getter. Never letting me get in a word, she popped up from her desk and led us to the back room where the meals were being prepared. Audrey and Trix gave me looks like, *What's going on?* But all I could do was shrug.

The back room was a regular meal factory—part kitchen and part assembly line. There were probably thirty people flocked around two long tables, putting sandwiches together and stuffing them into white foam containers. A lot of the volunteers looked to be retired, mostly old ladies, but there was also a sprinkling of old men, along with a few teenage girls. None of them looked like they came from the same kind of rich neighborhood that Ashton came from.

"We do three meals a week," Linda said. "Monday, Wednesday, and Friday. Hot meals are only on Wednesdays. Let's find you a place at the table so that you can start putting your meals together. Then I'll go over your route with you. Usually, we like to send teens out with an adult, but with a big boy like you, Dylan, I don't think we need to worry. Do you know the city streets pretty well?"

"We're experts," Trix said. She looked as if she thought the whole thing was highly amusing.

The assignment was to slap turkey sandwiches together, plop down a dollop of potato salad, and finish off with a handful of chips and a pickle spear. I was wedged in next to one of the old men, who introduced himself as Bernie and showed me the routine. Compared to the old ladies, who were real masters, he was pretty slow. Obviously, this was more of a social thing for him. He made the typical old-guy comment about how I was lucky to be the escort of two lovely ladies and kept up a running conversation about where I went to school and where he went to school and how things had changed since his day. I liked him. I also figured he might be a good source of information.

When the chance finally opened up to throw in a question of my own, I asked if he knew Ashton, and his eyes lit up. When Ashton first started working for FOKC, she had been teamed up with him to make deliveries, and he got to know her pretty well. Then her brother got involved too, at least in the delivery part. He didn't come in to help fix sandwiches because of some kind of school activity, but Ashton would go pick him up so she wouldn't be on the route alone, which was an FOKC no-no.

"Ashton Browning," Bernie concluded. "She's a real corker."

I didn't know what a *corker* was, but it sounded positive.

"They have to find that girl." A look of concern washed his smile away. "If they can find that Mormon girl in Utah, they can find Ashton."

I knew about the Mormon girl from one of my true-crime shows. She was abducted by a nut who thought he was some kind of prophet. It was quite a while back. The nut brainwashed her with his crazy-prophet act, but she finally got away. Things hadn't been good for her while he held her captive, but she seemed to deal with the whole thing in a heroic way. I admired her. Maybe she was a corker too.

I asked Bernie if he thought Ashton might've been kidnapped by some nut too, and he's like, "No, no, I wouldn't ever say that. But I just don't see how that girl could have any enemies. I pray she just ran away for a little while and that she'll come back as soon as she sees how much her parents really love her."

"Really? She didn't think her parents loved her?"

"Oh, I don't know. Young people—they can get on the outs with their families every now and then. It's normal. I tried to run away once, but I ended up down at the pool hall, playing pool all day long. When I got over being mad, I went back home, ate green beans and meat loaf for dinner, just like nothing ever happened."

"So, what was Ashton on the outs with her family about?"

Bernie picked up a slice of bread and scattered a healthy layer of turkey across it. "The usual thing, you know—didn't think her parents understood her. She had a boyfriend they didn't like. Or maybe they hadn't met him, but she just knew they wouldn't approve of him. Something like that."

"Interesting," I said. "Did this boyfriend happen to be named Rowan Adams?"

"She never did say. Why? You don't think the boyfriend had something to do with her going missing, do you?"

"I don't know." I snapped the lid shut on another meal. "But anything's possible."

CHAPTER 22

When we finished fixing the meals, it was time to load them up, which wasn't that easy. They don't really make BMWs like Trix's with hauling stuff around in mind. We figured the trunk would be too hot, so I ended up having to share the backseat with a whole pile of meal boxes. Linda explained our route, along with a few rules such as how we should greet the people, what we should do if they weren't home, and what topics of conversation to avoid. "Don't mention the word *charity*," she said. "Don't comment on their homes, no matter how bad they might be, and always smile." She supplied us with an example of the kind of smile she was talking about—cheery and wholesome. "We're not just in the business of feeding people," she added. "We're also in the business of spreading good cheer."

Ashton's route ran through a mostly Hispanic area south of the river. It wasn't really what I would call a *bad* neighborhood. Audrey and I had driven around there a couple of times before, checking out the cool flavor of the place—green buildings, orange buildings, lowriders, vendors pushing their tamale carts down the streets. It was a place where people sat on their front porches by the dozen. They even cooked out in the front yards. None of that hiding behind a stockade fence with the grill so neighbors couldn't horn in.

As we started handing out meals, though, it was strange—none of the folks on our route were actually Hispanic. Mostly they were ancient white people—old ladies or old men who lived alone. They'd probably bought their houses way before the Mexicans migrated in and just stayed, unlike the younger set. Maybe they liked their houses too much to move, or maybe they were too set in their ways for a change, or maybe they just weren't bigots. Of course, I didn't ask. Linda hadn't told us not to, but I figured she would have if she'd thought of it.

Another question was, *Why didn't any Hispanics want meals?* I thought it could be because they didn't like turkey sandwiches, but Audrey suggested they might be too proud to accept charity.

"Or maybe they just don't trust us," Trix said.

And I'm like, "Why wouldn't they trust us?"

"Because they might be here illegally," she said. "And they don't want us to turn them in."

"I wouldn't turn them in," I said. "They never did anything to me."

Another topic Linda hadn't told us to avoid with our customers, or whatever you call them, was the Ashton Browning thing. As we went from house to house, I always mentioned how we were filling in for Ashton and followed that up with a couple of questions about what they thought of her. Surprisingly enough, many of them didn't know she was missing. Either they didn't pay attention to the news or they never knew her whole name and couldn't see well enough to identify her picture on TV. But one thing was for sure—they all loved her.

"She had a real good sense of humor," said one old-timer who came to the door in his bathrobe. "I'm a pretty good one with a joke myself, but she always came right back with one of her own."

An old lady with lavender hair told us, "She was the only person who ever came up these front steps that my Mikey wouldn't bark at." Mikey was the homely dachshund who'd gone crazy barking at us when we knocked on the door.

"She used to go get my pills for me," said another lady. "One time she even ran down to the store to get me some toilet paper, and believe you me, I needed it."

I didn't follow up with any more questions about that.

A couple of old ladies got to know Ashton especially well. Apparently, they didn't like to go outside, not even onto the front porch. The first old lady, Miss Ockle, only cracked the front door to see who we were, but she was friendly enough and asked us to come in, unlike most of the others, who just grabbed their dinners and said goodbye before we could get much info.

"Yes, come on in, come on in," said Miss Ockle. "If you're friends of Ashton's, I know my mother would love to see you."

Her mother? This was a surprise since Miss Ockle appeared to be about a hundred years old herself. Her hair was dyed a faded gold, and her eyebrows were penciled on. She wore a shin-length flowered dress that could have doubled as a curtain. All in all, she looked like something from two universes away.

She led us into the cramped living room, where her mother sat hunched in an overstuffed chair, one of those walkers with tennis balls on the legs standing next to it. Her eyebrows matched her daughter's, but she'd given up the dye job in favor of a natural yellowish-white color and wore an old nightgown instead of a dress. She had tubes leading from an oxygen tank stuffed into her nostrils. Obviously, she had trouble breathing, but that didn't stop her from puffing on a cigarette.

After several tries, each louder than the one before, Miss Ockle got the idea across to Mrs. Ockle that we were friends of Ashton's. A little smile bloomed beneath the nose tubes. Although Mrs. Ockle was only about the size of an adult pelican, her voice was a deep nicotine croak. "Ashton made better sandwiches than my own mother," she said.

For a second, I feared that Mrs. Ockle's mother—Miss Ockle's grandmother—might be waiting somewhere in an even smaller room, but I remembered we only had two sandwiches for the household.

The subject of sandwiches propelled Mrs. Ockle into a story about peanut butter and jelly from her childhood, which threatened to throw us completely off schedule, so I cut in with a question about whether Ashton had ever talked about having any enemies.

"That girl?" Miss Ockle said. "Impossible."

"Who?" croaked Mrs. Ockle.

"Ashton, Mama. Ashton. The sandwich girl."

"That girl could sure make sandwiches."

"Well," I interrupted before the peanut-butter-and-jelly story cranked up again. "How about her brother? Did he have any enemies?"

Neither of the Ockle ladies seemed to know what I was talking about, so I explained that her brother had been the one helping her on her delivery route.

"Oh no," said Miss Ockle. "That wasn't her brother. He was her boyfriend."

"Who?" asked Mrs. Ockle.

115

"Ashton's boyfriend, Mama." Then louder: "Ashton's boyfriend."

"So handsome," Mrs. Ockle said dreamily. "He lived right next door."

"No, Mama. He didn't live next door. He just knew the people who lived next door."

"He didn't know the people who lived next door," Mrs. Ockle argued. "Ashton knew the people who lived next door."

"Oh, Mama. First you say her boyfriend lived next door, and then you say Ashton knew them. Make up your mind."

"Who?"

Miss Ockle turned to us. "I do know one thing—the children on the street loved Ashton. I used to peek out the window and watch them run up to her, grinning like she was the Holy Mother herself come back to earth."

By now it was pretty obvious we weren't going to get a whole lot more useful information from the Ockle ladies, so I made an excuse to get out of there. Miss Ockle saw us to the door, but before we left, she touched my arm and peered into my eyes. "He really was her boyfriend," she said. "I can tell those things. Just like I can tell that red-haired girl is your girlfriend."

"Uh, enjoy your meal," I said. That was all I could think of.

CHAPTER 23

On the front porch of the Ockle house, Trix burst out laughing. "I love those old ladies," she said. "I want to be just like that when I'm a hundred."

"I'll turn your oxygen on for you," Audrey said, and Trix was like, "Awesome."

And that's when I heard the kids laughing in the backyard next door.

"Listen," I said. "Hear that? We should go back there and check it out."

"What for?" Audrey asked.

"You heard what Miss Ockle said. The neighbor kids loved Ashton. Maybe we can find out something about this boyfriend of hers."

Trix laughed. "*Boyfriend?* You really think those old ladies knew what they were talking about?"

"Yeah," Audrey added. "I'll bet it was Ashton's brother all along."

And I'm like, "Maybe, but the Ockles seemed pretty certain. Besides, Mrs. Ockle said the guy with Ashton was handsome, and you have to admit that doesn't exactly fit Tres Browning."

"No," Trix said. "But when a woman gets to be Mrs. Ockle's age, she probably thinks every teenage boy is handsome."

Still, I didn't think it would hurt to go back and ask a couple of questions.

"Okay," Audrey said. "We'll wait in the car. Just make it quick. We still have dinners to deliver."

The house was on the corner, so I walked around the far side to talk to the kids over the chain-link fence. There were eight or nine of them, ranging in ages from around two to twelve, laughing and shouting as they played some kind of chaotic game, possibly tag except a ball was involved.

"Hey," I called to the oldest, a pretty Hispanic girl with long black hair parted on the side. "Can I talk to you for a second?"

She froze and stared at me for a moment but didn't answer.

"Tú y yo habla, por favor?" I asked, trying to piece together the little bit of Spanish I remembered from middle school.

She backed away.

I pointed to my chest. *"Amigo del Ashton."*

That didn't help. I wouldn't say she ran onto the porch and into the house, but she wasn't loafing around about it either. *Crap*, I thought, *now she thinks I'm some kind of skeevy child molester.*

"You're funny," said a boy of about nine, who was closer to the fence than the others. "You don't talk right."

"You got me there," I admitted. "But I'm just delivering meals to people around the area and thought it would be a good idea to get to know the neighbors."

The boy walked closer. "You deliver meals to the crazy ladies next door?"

"The Ockles? They're not crazy. They're just a little different. Actually, they're nice once you get to know them."

118

Then a brick hit me on the back of the head. Well, okay, it wasn't actually a brick—it was a fist—but it felt like a brick. My glasses flew off and my knees buckled a little, but I didn't fall down. "Holy crap," I said. I picked up my glasses and turned around to see this huge Hispanic dude standing there. He had a deep blue maze-like tattoo on his shaved head and a gold tooth that was about two shades warmer than Miss Ockle's dye job. And twice as shiny.

"Whatchoo doing back here, sick puppy?" he asked, both fists balled at his sides. He didn't look angry so much as happy to get the chance to beat someone to death.

"Dude, I'm just trying to be friendly. I'm in the neighborhood delivering meals to people."

"We don't need none of your meals here," he said.

"I know, but I was next door at the Ockles' and I just thought—"

He stepped closer. "That's your problem. You shouldn't go around thinking."

At this point, I was like, *This is it. My life's over. This is what it must be like for a pilot the split second before his plane crashes into the side of a mountain.*

But I never hit the mountain, and it never hit me. Just then another guy came striding up from behind Tattoo Head. "Hold on," he said. "Back off, Oscar. Dylan's all right."

And Oscar's like, "You know this *pendejo,* Beto?"

"Yeah, he's a good guy. He came to Hector's funeral."

Sure enough, that's who it was—Beto Hernandez, Hector Maldonado's cousin, only he'd traded in the black suit and hat he wore at the funeral for jeans, a black-and-white sport shirt, and a straw porkpie that put mine to shame.

He stepped over and shook my hand. "Good to see you," he said. "What brings you over to this neighborhood?"

I explained I was just doing some volunteer work, filling in for Ashton Browning after she went missing.

"Ashton who?" Beto said.

"Ashton Browning. She's been on the news. She disappeared from the nature park up on the North Side."

"Did you hear anything about that?" he asked Oscar.

Oscar shook his head. "I don't pay attention to what goes down on the North Side," he said.

"She used to deliver meals next door," I explained.

"To the crazy ladies?" Beto said. "Yeah, I think I do remember seeing a pretty blond girl over there sometimes."

"She was probably with her brother, a skinny little dude with brown hair and a pale turtle face?"

"Her brother? Do you remember seeing her brother, Oscar?"

"I don't remember nothing."

"Or it could've been a boyfriend. Miss Ockle said she thought it was her boyfriend."

Beto smiled. "Oh, them ladies is crazy. I never saw no boyfriend."

"We don't mess around with no blond girls," Oscar added.

"Besides, we don't live here. This is our grandmother's place. We just come by to check on her. She takes care of everybody's kids. You never seen anyone like my *abuelita*. She's a saint."

"A saint," Oscar confirmed.

"Well," I said. "I was just wondering about Ashton, that's all."

"Whatchoo care about some rich girl, anyway?" he asked.

"I don't know. She seems like a good person. It's weird a girl like that would just disappear into thin air."

"That is weird," Beto agreed. "But not as weird as what happened to Hector, and it don't seem like anyone's interested in finding out about that too much. I went down to the police station myself and talked to this fool detective who had so much gel in his hair he looked like he mopped up an oil leak with it, and he started acting like I had something to do with selling them drugs to Hector. They don't care what really happened to him."

I could definitely sympathize with him about that. "I wish I could've done more about Hector," I said. "But I told that same stupid detective everything I know, which isn't anything, really."

"Cops," Oscar said, practically spitting the word. "They don't care about nobody around here."

"That's okay, Dylan," Beto told me. "You did your best."

I wanted to ask him how he knew about the North Side Monarchs, but I didn't know how to bring it up without breaking my promise to Nash to keep mum on the Gangland deal. Besides, I was ready to get out of there before I said something that might spark another punch in the head from Oscar.

"Yeah, I did my best," I agreed, feeling a twinge of guilt. "Well, I guess I'd better take off. I have more food to deliver."

"Good to see you, man." Beto shook my hand again, but I couldn't walk away without at least some hope of getting more info from him later.

"Um, you know what?" I said, standing at a safe distance from Oscar. "Why don't I give you my phone number just in case you happen to see any rich blond girls hanging around the neighborhood?"

He grinned. "Sure, that's a good idea. Just tell it to me. I'll remember it."

I rattled off the number, and he nodded. "See you later, *amigo*."

Back in the car, I told Audrey and Trix what'd happened.

From where they were parked, they couldn't see how I almost got massacred.

"Wow," Trix said. "What are you, like a bizarre trouble magnet or something? You're always running into dead guys or missing girls' running shoes or dead guys' cousins."

"It is an odd coincidence," Audrey added.

"Maybe," I said. "Or maybe it's not such a coincidence."

"What do you mean?" Audrey asked.

I looked out the window at the run-down houses as we drove past. "I don't know. But I'm pretty sure Ashton and Hector are tied together. I'm thinking he might've even been the mysterious boyfriend."

"And someone didn't like it," Trix added, a gleam in her eye.

"Oh God," Audrey said. "Now he has you playing *Andromeda Man* too."

CHAPTER 24

I felt creepy calling Linda at FOKC to tell her we had to quit, but what could I do? We couldn't keep delivering meals three times a week just so they wouldn't suspect we were investigating the Ashton Browning deal. Linda sounded bummed but guaranteed we could always come back if we could find the time. That'd be great, I told her, but I doubted it would happen. Here I was—a big fat quitter all over again.

For my next newspaper article, I wrote about Ashton's FOKC connection and what the clientele had to say about her. So, yes, I'll admit it was a bit of a love letter again. How could it not be? The more I learned about her, the greater she sounded. Smart, funny, independent, socially conscious. The perfect match for an investigative reporter.

However, the part about Beto and Oscar didn't end up in the article. For one thing, admitting I got punched in the back of the head wasn't likely to charge up my mojo level, but more than that, I didn't want to go into the Hector Maldonado connection until I knew if there really was one.

I had a couple of theories. First, if Hector actually was Ashton Browning's boyfriend, that would fit with what the

Ockles said. Plus, Hector was a pretty good-looking guy, and rich girls have been known to fool around with poor bad boys for the thrill of it. If her dad found out, it'd probably be just like Trix suggested—he wouldn't like it one bit. Or maybe Rowan Adams was the one who didn't like it. That angle felt better. As certain as I'd once been that Mr. Browning was guilty, I now preferred seeing Rowan go down. Besides, he was the godfather of the North Side Monarchs, and undoubtedly there was some connection there.

One problem with that theory—Hector wasn't really poor and he definitely wasn't a bad boy. So in my second theory, I imagined Ashton falling for Beto. Sure, he was friendly to me, but he had a dangerous air about him. Definite bad-boy material. Was he the type to get violent with the girls? I didn't want to think so, but if he was, then maybe he went too far one night, and she ended up dead. How Hector and the Monarchs figured into that scenario, I didn't know, but I decided digging into Hector's life a little deeper might bring some answers.

I turned in my article to Ms. Jansen and sent a copy to Nash like I promised. Then, during lunch, I looked up Diron Moore, one of Hector's small circle of buddies. Diron was a lot like Hector actually—a quiet guy who sat in the back of class and turned in his homework on time. His clothes always looked brand new.

I latched onto him in the west hall and told him I'd been doing a lot of thinking and decided I wanted to know more about Hector so I could get over picturing him as the guy I found in the Dumpster. Diron looked a little suspicious, and I couldn't blame him—I had let quite a bit of time go by between then and now. Once he started talking, though, he poured out some pretty solid info.

Apparently, if you really got to know Hector, he wasn't the shy kid you might have expected. He was funny, smart, and interested in all sorts of things. That sounded like a pretty good match for Ashton. Also, he had his sights set on going to college somewhere East Coastwards, then wanted to come back here and get into politics, do something good for the Hispanic community. He had a lot of family all over the city, some who had lived here a long time, some who arrived more recently—Diron didn't say, but I took that to mean some of them might be illegals.

That was all interesting, but what I really wanted to know was whether Hector had had a rich blond girlfriend. Or if his cousin Beto did. Diron didn't know about that, though. It seemed Hector hadn't hung out with his friends so much after school hours this fall. Yes, he did have a girlfriend over the summer, but she was black-haired—Mexican American—and went to a different South Side school. They broke up, though, and afterward Hector kept making excuses not to hang around with his old crew at our school.

"I just figured he was taking the breakup bad," Diron said. "He would've got over that, though—if he ever got the chance."

"I'm sure he would've," I told Diron, but I was actually thinking maybe Hector *was* over it. Because maybe he'd already moved on—to Ashton Browning.

I was definitely on to something, but Audrey didn't back me up. She said I didn't have one single fact that tied Ashton and Hector together. Just because I happened to run across Hector's Hispanic cousin in a Hispanic neighborhood didn't mean anything. No, her money was all on Rowan Adams.

"It has to be the ex-boyfriend," she said.

"Hey, it still could be. Maybe Rowan hired this Beto guy to

put out a hit on Hector, and then they had to get rid of Ashton because she knew about it."

"A hit? Are you serious? You really do need to lay off the TV shows."

Okay, that was deflating, but I wasn't ready to give up on my theory. I just had to do some more research. I didn't really know where to start, though. It wasn't like I could walk up to Beto Hernandez and ask him about it. Especially if Oscar Tattoo Head was anywhere around.

But someone else could ask him about it—a cop. As much as I hated the idea of dealing with the police, I decided they needed to know about the Ashton-Hector connection. Of course, no way was I about to go back to Detectives Hair Gel and Forehead, but I figured the police at the main headquarters might be different from the ones at the outpost on my side of town. After all, wasn't I the one who found Ashton's running shoe for them? They were on the news almost every day asking for tips concerning the case; surely they'd listen to one from me.

So I went down to their huge palatial headquarters thinking I'd march right in and talk to the captain in all his starched-white-shirt splendor. Didn't happen.

I waited and waited. Cops came and went. A guy with blood on his sweatshirt and his front teeth knocked out wobbled in and had to wait in a chair next to me.

"I hate my father-in-law," he sputtered without looking at me.

"I'm sorry," I told him.

We waited some more. Then he got called in to talk to somebody before I did. About ten minutes later, a lady cop told me to follow her. She left me in an office with no decorations, not even a family picture or Don't Do Drugs poster. It was like going to the doctor's office—you sit around in the waiting area, and then you go to the examination room and sit around some more.

When the door finally opened, I was disappointed. Instead of the captain, a uniformed officer walked in, the same uniformed officer who tried to take credit for finding Ashton's shoe on the search party.

"I recognize you," he said, sitting behind the desk. "You were at the nature park when we did our sweep—the kid who watches *Andromeda Man,* right?"

I'm like, "Uh, yeah."

"That's a ridiculous show." He leaned back in his chair and looked at me like he was expecting the punch line to a joke. "So you have a tip about the Ashton Browning case, huh?"

I started into how I'd been writing investigative reports about her, trying to establish some credibility, but he wasn't interested in that. All he wanted to hear about was my tip. I'd already decided I wasn't going to name any suspects—that was their job to figure out—so I just explained my theory about how Ashton and Hector might be connected while he jotted notes down on a pad.

When I was done, he set his pen down. "So let me get this straight—you think one of the richest girls in the city was romantically involved with this Hector Almarado, a Mexican drug addict."

"It's *Maldonado.* And he wasn't Mexican—he was American—and he wasn't a drug addict. That's just the point. Someone must have poisoned him with some kind of drug. He didn't take it himself."

"I see. And can anybody confirm that Mr. Almarado and Ms. Browning were connected?"

"You mean like an eyewitness? Not exactly, but it just makes sense."

"And why does it make sense?"

"Because I saw Hector's cousin at a house down on the South Side right next to where the Ockle ladies live, and they were on Ashton's FOKC route."

"Her *what* route?"

"*F-O-K-C.* Feed Oklahoma City. It's this charity thing she volunteered for."

I explained how Ashton wasn't always alone when she delivered meals to the Ockles and that there was a good chance the extra someone was Hector. But the more I described the Ockles, the more his interest faded. Maybe I shouldn't have gone into so much detail about how fond Mrs. Ockle was of Ashton's sandwiches.

He nodded. "Yes, that makes sense all right," he said condescendingly. "A couple of old ladies saw someone they couldn't actually identify, but you're certain it was your deceased buddy Hector. Well, we'll certainly take that into consideration."

"Aren't you going to write it down?"

"Sure, sure. I'll write the whole thing up later." He stared at me for a good thirty seconds. "Is that all?" he said finally.

"Are you going to do anything about what I told you?"

"Definitely. It's all going into the file." He picked up his pen and tapped it on the desktop.

"In the file, huh? Well, I hope someone reads that file because this is something that needs to be investigated."

"I'm sure you do have your hopes up," he said. "But I wouldn't go spending that reward money yet if I were you."

So that was it. He thought I was like the other hundred people who had probably sat in this office before me, making up stories just to get the reward.

128

"Look," I said, "this info is legit."

He gave me the silent stare again, still tapping the desktop with his pen, until finally he's like, "Do you think you can find your way out?"

That was my cue to leave. "I'm just trying to help," I told him.

"I appreciate that," he said as I headed to the door. "In fact, I think this tip is so good I'll probably turn it right over to the FBI—or the Andromeda Man."

What a jerk. By the time I got home, I was more determined than ever to keep up my own investigation—forget the cops. But I didn't have the slightest idea what my next move should be.

Then, after school the next day, as I was walking upstairs to my room, I got a phone call. I didn't recognize the voice, but I did recognize this might just be the opportunity I'd been waiting for.

CHAPTER 25

The caller's voice was muffled, probably intentionally disguised. It was a male voice, but it didn't sound like a kid. Or maybe it was a kid trying to sound like an old guy. I couldn't be sure—he'd blocked my caller ID. Whoever he was, he asked if I was the one doing research on the Ashton Browning case, and when I said yes, he told me we needed to talk.

"We are talking," I said, but he's like, "No. We need to talk face to face. I have something you need to see."

I tried to find out more about who he was and what he had to show me, but he cut me short. If I wanted any more information, I'd have to meet him the next evening at seven o'clock. He'd even let me choose the place. That made the offer a little more tempting. I could pick a location where I wasn't likely to have someone sneak up behind me and punch me in the back of the head—or worse. I chose Topper's. If something bad ended up happening, at least I could have a good burger first.

"How'd you get this number, anyway?" I asked, but the line went dead.

This was very weird, I thought. It was probably the kind of thing that happened to *New York Times* reporters every day, and now it was happening to me.

Either that or someone was playing a practical joke on me. Immediately, I called Randy, but he swore up and down he didn't have anything to do with it. In fact, he wanted to go along. I told him okay, but the truth was I started having second thoughts about the meeting.

I almost had a good excuse to blow it off too. Audrey couldn't give me a ride to Topper's the next evening. She was going to the movies with Trix.

"Can you believe it?" she gushed. "This is like the greatest thing ever."

"Yeah, it's great," I said. "But could you put it off until another night? I think this could be a really important case breaker."

And she's like, "Are you kidding me? Going out with Trix is what I've been waiting for my whole life. I'm not postponing it."

"But is it really a real date? I mean, did you ask her out on a date or did you just ask her to go to a movie?"

Her smile faded. "Just to go to a movie. But that doesn't mean it can't turn out to be like a real date."

"Well, okay," I said. "I guess I'll skip the meeting, even though it could solve the whole case." But truthfully I wasn't that disappointed. It was like this was a sign warning me I'd be better off not taking a chance. Unfortunately, Audrey had to go and come up with a solution—I could take my parents' car.

Now this might seem simple, but you don't know my parents. For one thing, they only have one car. Can you believe that? Whose parents only have one car? They say they want to cut down on their carbon footprint, and also they only need one car because they both basically work the same schedule, but I think it's mainly because they're cheap.

So I'm like, "Yeah, right. You know how my parents are about letting me drive their car. Half the time my mom's on call at the hospital, and when she's not, they're like, 'What if we need it while you're out driving around all over the place? We'll be stuck.' Like they ever go anywhere."

"So, tell them it's important. Make something up. And take Randy with you so you won't be alone. Everything will be all right."

I wasn't so sure about that.

All the way to dinnertime I rolled the idea over in my mind. Should I go or not? Finally, I decided I had to. I quit the grocery-sacking job, I quit FOKC, I even quit football in middle school. I couldn't quit on this case.

I had to come up with a good story about why I needed my parents' car, though. I mean, they weren't about to go along with the idea that I needed a ride to go talk to some shadowy anonymous informant about Ashton Browning. So, after running through several options, I came up with a lie about needing the car for a movie date. Seeing as how I'd never had a date before, this was pretty far-fetched, but when I ran it by them, they didn't call me a liar. No, it was worse than that. They were proud of me.

"That's great," Mom said, beaming like a headlight. She looked at Dad. "Did you hear that? He has a date."

"Fantastic," said Dad, grinning. You would've thought I'd just won a scholarship to Harvard.

Then they launched into grilling me about who the girl was. Not being too quick on my feet when dealing with a situation like this, the only girl I could think of was Trix Westwood. After all, no way would my parents be acquainted with anyone who even knew Trix or her dad.

They bought that lie too but were worried when I told them I met her on the Ashton Browning search party. My mom got this look on her face like she couldn't stand the idea of her boy getting hurt by a rich girl, but my dad was more worried that I'd have to drive the car so far away from home. It was okay, though. The next night, I still got the keys, but I had to leave the house wearing slacks and a button-up shirt so it looked like I really was going on a date with a rich girl.

I picked up Randy, and he made the inevitable crack about how uncool I was to have to drive my parents' old car. Of course, I reminded him he didn't have anything to drive. Still, I did take the feathery dream hoop off the rearview mirror.

At Topper's, Rockin' Rhonda loitered outside as usual. She gave me the "Mr. Mojo Rising" greeting, and I told her I'd slip her some change on the way out like I always did. We arrived early enough to order our burgers before the mystery man showed up, but still my nerves twanged every time someone walked in.

I didn't like the look of this guy who nabbed a booth across the room. He was around nineteen or twenty, thuggish, with skuzzy long sideburns and brown hair that looked like it hadn't been washed or combed since he got fired last month from his job as a motorcycle thief or whatever he did to keep himself in beer and weed. He kept glancing my way, but he didn't come over, so I figured he wasn't my man.

Then, when I was about halfway done with my burger, the door opened, and I knew I didn't have to wait any longer. In walked the same basket-bellied middle-aged dude with the swooping cowboy mustache who'd hassled us outside Gangland.

Randy coughed as a chunk of cheeseburger went down the wrong way. "You didn't tell me we were meeting that guy," he said when he recovered.

"That's because I didn't know it was going to be that guy, genius."

Mr. Mustache pulled a chair up to the side of our booth, eyed Randy, then turned to me and said, "I thought you were coming here alone."

I told him I never said anything about coming alone, and he looked at me like, *Yeah, but you should've known.* Like I was supposed to be some kind of professional at this crap and had broken the rules.

"I've seen you before," Randy told him, and he's like, "And I've seen both of you before too."

I explained how Randy was there as my backup in case anything went funny, and Mr. Mustache goes, "Well, well, well, you two think you're a couple of real detectives, don't you?"

"More like an investigative journalist," I said. "I'm on the school paper."

"Oh, excuse me—*investigative journalist.*" He let out a nasty chuckle, and the wings of his mustache flapped.

"So exactly who are you?" I asked. "I don't think we ever got that figured out last time we met."

He pulled out his wallet and showed me a card that identified him as Franklin Smiley, Private Investigator.

"You can call me Smiley," he said, taking the card back. The mustache cocked up, probably the closest thing to an actual smile you were going to get out of this character.

So I'm like, "Okay, Mr. Smiley—"

"Just Smiley. No need to be formal."

"Uh, okay, Smiley, on the phone you said you had something to show me."

"I do," he said, leaning back in his chair. "But not here. You'll have to come with me."

"I don't know about that," I said.

"Yeah," Randy chimed in. "How do we know you're not some crazy psychopath or something?"

"Now, do I really look like a psychopath?" Smiley said, holding out his hands as if to give us a fuller view of his wholesomeness.

"I don't know," I said. "If you could tell a psychopath just by their appearance, they'd pretty much be out of business."

"Well, maybe you'll trust my employer."

"And who's that?"

He pulled his phone from his coat pocket, brought up his list of phone numbers, then showed me the screen. Among the other numbers, one was highlighted—the number of Eliot Browning, Ashton's dad.

Smiley goes, "Should I call him right now and bother him with everything he has going on, or do you just want to drive over and talk to him?"

"That's okay," I said. "We'll go talk to him."

Smiley tucked his phone back in his pocket. "Good. I don't know what you were worried about anyway." He waved a hand toward Randy. "After all, you have your *backup*."

And there was that nasty chuckle again. I didn't like it one bit.

CHAPTER 26

Smiley wasn't too crazy about the idea of Randy and me packing what was left of our burgers along in his shiny black sedan, but what were we going to do—just leave them on the table unfinished? Wastefulness is supposed to be a sin, isn't it?

Between bites, I questioned Smiley on what he knew about Ashton, but he didn't come forth with any info he couldn't have read in the newspaper. I started to worry that I should've gone through with that call to Mr. Browning after all. I mean, anyone can have a guy's number listed in their phone. That doesn't mean they actually know the guy.

I put my worries aside, though, as it became clear we were heading straight into the maw of the Richie Rich side of town. At first the houses were BIG, then they swelled into full-blown mansions, and finally they turned into these humongous castles where probably about fifty people could live together without ever having to see each other. Smiley pulled up to the gate of the biggest castle on the block. Or at least I guessed it was the biggest—with all the trees you never could get a look at the whole thing at once.

Randy was all excited about touring the house, but we

weren't that lucky. After winding down the driveway, Smiley parked and led us around back to a guesthouse by the pool. The Brownings had made themselves a regular paradise back there: stone paths, flower beds and sculpted trees lit by garden lights, a little waterfall that fed into the perfect blue pool—still filled to the brim even though it was autumn—and an ivy-covered wall around it all to keep the riffraff out. No doubt Mr. Browning had something pretty serious to talk about if he was letting a couple of scurvy dudes like me and Randy into a sanctuary like this.

The guesthouse was equally cool. The ceiling was so high it was like we just walked into a church or something. The furniture looked like it had never been used. A fireplace with gold candlesticks on the mantel, huge glass vases with fresh flowers, wood floors with Persian rugs. At least I guessed they were Persian. Isn't that where all the fancy rugs come from? Golden knobs on the woodwork, chandeliers hanging like clusters of fake diamonds, statues of horses on tables, and six-foot-tall gold-framed paintings of more horses on the walls—as if Mr. Browning wanted you to think he was some kind of gentleman rancher instead of a bank honcho.

Smiley led us through the front room and down this hallway with an arched ceiling of rough stone that made you feel like you were walking into an especially fancy cave. At the end of it, we emerged into the guesthouse media room. That's right—they had a media room in the *guesthouse,* complete with a huge wide-screen plasma TV on the wall, wood paneling, leather furniture, and a wet bar. The only way I can describe the odor of the place is *rich.*

"Have a seat," Smiley told us. "I'll be back in a couple of minutes with Mr. Browning. Don't touch anything."

He left and I sat in a leather chair that felt like it was trying to swallow me whole. Randy immediately walked over to this deluxe armoire and opened the doors.

"Hey," I said. "Weren't you listening? We're not supposed to touch anything."

And Randy is like, "Wow, check this out. It's full of movies."

I started to get up from the chair, but it wasn't letting me go so easily, so I settled back down and said, "Anything good?"

"Mainly a bunch of crap," Randy said. He closed the armoire doors and went over to the TV. "How much you think something like this costs?"

"I don't know. Ten thousand dollars?"

"Damn," Randy said, letting out a whistle. "And he's only offering a hundred grand to get his daughter back? You'd think she'd be worth more than just ten times as much as the guest-house TV."

"Do me a favor," I said. "When he comes in? Don't mention that."

"I'm just saying—he's kind of a tightwad when it comes to rewards. Or maybe he doesn't really want her back all that bad."

"Yeah, maybe. But don't mention that either."

Randy was seated at the bar, fiddling with a metal figurine of a hunting dog, when Smiley came back with Mr. Browning. Immediately, the room charged with electricity. There was something about Mr. Browning. He didn't look as tall as the first time I saw him in person, but his presence could really fill a room.

"I told you not to touch anything," Smiley said to Randy.

"That's all right," Mr. Browning said. "That's what it's there for—to admire."

After introducing himself to Randy and me and shaking

138

our hands with his vise grip, he walked around to the other side of the bar. "Can I get you something to drink?"

"I'll take a beer," Randy said, but Mr. Browning wasn't going for that.

"I was thinking of something more along the lines of a soft drink," he said.

I struggled out of the leather chair and sat by Randy at the bar while Mr. Browning fixed our drinks. Smiley took a seat in the corner of the room. Once the drinks were ready, Mr. Browning pulled up a stool on the other side of the bar and studied us for a second before launching into some small-talk questions about how we liked school and what we wanted to do when we graduated. Randy mentioned that for right now he had a position at a grocery store, but he wouldn't mind going into banking.

"I hear that pays pretty good," he said. "So if you're hiring out, I'm your man."

"I'll keep that in mind," Mr. Browning said, then focused on me. "So, I understand you are quite the journalist."

"Trying to be."

"I see." From a drawer behind the bar, he pulled a stack of papers and spread them out between us. They were copies of my articles about Ashton, not the actual school-paper versions but computer copies.

"Where did you get those?" I asked.

"Your articles seem to be popular among some of my daughter's friends."

Nash, I thought. He probably showed the articles I sent him to Tres, and Tres handed them over to the old man.

Just then my phone rang, and Mr. Browning looked at me like I'd farted or something. I couldn't help feeling embarrassed, especially since my ring tone was the theme song to *Walker, Texas Ranger*. I didn't take the time to see who was calling, but I figured it was Audrey.

After I turned off the ringer and put the phone away, Mr. Browning continued. "For someone who never met Ashton, you seem to have a lot of interest in her."

"It's a big story."

"Is that all?"

"What else would there be?" I glanced at Randy, hoping he wouldn't bring up anything about the reward money. No worries, though. His attention had turned to the thin gold stripe around the lip of his glass. He chipped at it with his thumbnail, probably trying to see if the gold was real.

"I can think of a pretty good reason," Smiley said from his chair in the corner, but Mr. Browning cut him off before he could go into what that reason was.

"Actually, these articles are impressive. I was especially struck by the one about my daughter's charity work. I appreciate you shedding light on that so people can get an understanding of what a caring girl she is." He paused for a moment, looked down, and pinched the bridge of his nose, apparently trying to put a check on his emotions before he started bawling or something.

"Yeah, she seemed pretty caring," I said.

He looked up, his focus returned, though his eyes were a touch watery. "One person in the article, I believe, even mentioned how much the children in the neighborhood adored her."

"That's right. She was sure popular with the kids."

He asked if I remembered the neighborhood where she knew these kids from. I told him about the Ockle ladies, but I couldn't remember the street name.

Smiley spoke up from the corner. "These Ockle ladies—did

140

they say anything about any older kids, like about the same age as Ashton?"

This line of questioning I didn't like. Sure, I thought the cops should know about Hector, but Mr. Browning was still a suspect. Maybe he was fishing for how much I knew that might incriminate him. If he'd hired Beto or Tattoo Head Oscar to put a hit on Hector, he wouldn't think twice about getting rid of anyone who knew about the connection—namely me.

So I'm like, "No, I don't remember any older kids. All I know is she delivered meals and everyone liked her."

At that point, Mr. Browning glanced at Smiley. He seemed surprised about something. Or maybe he suspected I wasn't telling everything. Then it hit me—he knew about my trip to police headquarters and my Hector Maldonado theory. He probably knew everything that'd happened in that police station since Ashton disappeared. The actual cops didn't care about what I had to say, but my theory, coupled with my articles about Ashton, were enough to get me dragged down to the Brownings' guesthouse.

"Well, there was this one guy," I said, figuring I might as well come clean. "Hector Maldonado." I went on to tell pretty much the same thing I told the cops, this time going light on how much Mrs. Ockle liked Ashton's sandwiches. Still, I didn't mention Beto and Oscar. If Mr. Browning wanted to know about those two, he'd have ask about them by name, which would prove he was involved with them somehow.

He didn't, though. All he said was, "So you never saw this Hector person with my daughter. And these Ockle women never said they actually saw him with her. In fact, it might have been her brother they saw."

I had to admit that was true.

He leaned his elbows on the bar top and shot me the stern

authority-guy stare. "Then I suggest you refrain from spreading rumors that Ashton was involved romantically with someone of that nature."

I wanted to ask what he meant by *someone of that nature,* but Smiley cut in with a question.

"What about the rec hall? We know you were there, but you didn't write anything about it in your articles."

I'm like, "The rec hall?"

And Mr. Browning's like, "I believe the kids call it Gangland."

Just to convince them I wasn't holding back information, I told them pretty much all I remembered about Gangland. I figured they already knew most of it, and there didn't seem to be anything that could get me into trouble—with these two, at least. I especially played up the Rowan Adams angle, but they weren't as interested in him as they were in the likes of the Rat Finks and Colonoscopy—as if only non-Hollister kids were worthy of suspicion. Smiley even wanted to know more about the two Vietnamese dudes—Tommy and Huy—I saw walking into Gangland after we had to leave. I told him he was wasting his time thinking about them, but he jotted their names down in his notebook anyway.

"I'll tell you something about that place," Randy chimed in. "The girls there are stuck-up. They don't know what they're missing. If one of them called me right now, I wouldn't give her the time of day. Except maybe that blonde in the tuxedo. If you know her, I wouldn't mind getting her phone number."

Mr. Browning pretty much disregarded that. "So," he said to me, "I don't believe you ever said why you didn't write about any of this in one of your articles."

"I couldn't," I told him. "Nash asked me not to. He said they wanted to keep the place private."

"Nash asked you not to?" Mr. Browning said.

"That's right. He's been a good friend and a good source. I couldn't mess that up by writing about things he asked me not to."

"A journalist's ethics?" Mr. Browning asked.

"Yeah, a journalist's ethics. Some of us still have them."

"Let's hear about the shoe," Smiley said. He sounded exasperated by any kind of talk about ethics. "Ashton's running shoe in the field—it's a pretty big coincidence you were the one who found it, don't you think?"

"That was no coincidence," Randy said. "Dylan's a master at that kind of thing."

Mr. Browning's eyebrows raised. "Oh, really? How so?"

I didn't want to go into how I was actually the one who discovered Hector in the Dumpster and make myself look even more suspicious, so before Randy could crank it up, I said, "It's my job. As an investigative journalist, I have to be observant."

But Smiley's like, "I've heard about enough of this investigative-journalist manure. What we want to know is, did you find that shoe like you pretended or did you bring it with you and plant it there?"

All of a sudden it seemed about ten degrees hotter in that media room. "What are you talking about?" I said. "How could I bring a shoe out there? They didn't allow you to carry any bags or anything with you."

"Yeah," Smiley said, "but you know what? There's plenty of spare room in those baggy pants of yours—you could've tucked a shoe up there and shook it out of your pant leg right where you wanted it."

In my mind, I'm like, *Really? You're making a crack about my baggy pants? Take a look at yourself, why don't you?* But what

143

I said out loud was, "That's ridiculous. Why would I do something like that?"

"Well, there is the reward," Mr. Browning said.

"I didn't even know about that until I got out there."

"About that reward—" Randy started, but I cut him off.

"Not now, Randy. Not now."

Smiley goes, "Let's get down to it—maybe you had her shoe because you had *her*."

No joke. That's what he said. Now I felt like I was back in the cop shop with Detectives Hair Gel and Forehead. Nothing about who I was counted. It was all about how they saw me—a nobody with no mojo.

I'm like, "Come on, that doesn't make any sense. Why would I write all these articles about Ashton if I had anything to do with her disappearance?"

"Maybe because you want to throw the spotlight off yourself," Smiley said.

"How is that throwing the spotlight off myself? If I hadn't written the articles or tried to pass along some solid info to the police, you would never know who I was."

And Mr. Browning goes, "But you want people to know who you are, don't you, Dylan? You want everyone talking about Dylan Jones, the *investigative reporter* who solved the case and got the reward."

Suddenly, I felt naked. Fat and naked. Because he was right. He saw straight through me. I did want that. But he was wrong about what I would do to get it. After all, I was me, not him.

"Listen," I said. "I only came over here to help you out. I didn't come over to have people start throwing accusations at me."

"That's right," Randy added. "Dylan's a good dude. What

144

you should be doing is looking at the Wiccan population in this city."

Smiley's like, "Wiccan? What's he talking about?"

"Nothing," I said. "Forget that. I found that shoe because I just happened to step on it. If I hadn't been there, you might have never found it, and you wouldn't have any clues. And that's all I'm going to say. I'm done."

"We'll tell you when you're done," Smiley said, but Mr. Browning's like, "No, he's right." He leaned back and let out this big breath like he was trying to get rid of all the tension of the past month. "I'm sorry if it looked like we were accusing you of anything, but you have to understand how important this is to me."

"I never said it wasn't."

"We have to cover all our bases."

"Well, I'm not one of your bases."

Mr. Browning looked at Smiley. "I think we've taken up enough of these boys' evening. Would you be kind enough to drive them home?"

Smiley said all right, and Mr. Browning shook my hand, then Randy's. "I think we had a productive talk, all things considered," he said. "And I'll trust you and your journalistic integrity not to mention it in one of your articles."

"That definitely wouldn't be a good idea," Smiley added as he clamped his hand on my shoulder. "Let's go." And then to Mr. Browning: "You want me to call you later?"

"That would be fine," Mr. Browning confirmed.

Outside, the air was cool, but that didn't stop Randy from asking if we could take a dip in the pool.

"Get back to the car," Smiley said.

CHAPTER 27

Except for Smiley's complaints about how the inside of his car now smelled like hamburgers, the drive back to Topper's was pretty quiet. After the way he talked to me in the guesthouse, I wasn't in a hurry to strike up any further conversation with him. The whole experience left me feeling like I'd gotten myself into something that was over my head. With one call from the likes of Mr. Browning, Detectives Hair Gel and Forehead would be only too glad to haul me down for some more grilling.

It was good to get back to my own side of town, and when we pulled into Topper's parking lot, I was more than eager to hop out of that black sedan and get gone. Smiley wasn't in such a hurry to let me escape, though.

"Wait a second, kid," he said as I opened the door. "Let me see your phone."

I'm like, "What for?"

And he goes, "I want to enter my number in there so you can call me if you come across anything new we need to know about."

I told him I'd enter the number myself, and when I finished putting it in, he grabbed hold of my arm and stared into my eyes. "Son, if there's anything you haven't told us or if

146

you find out anything, you'd better call my number. You need to understand that if you don't, you're going to be in a lot of trouble."

"Sure," I said. "No problem."

Once I had my feet firmly planted on Topper's parking lot and the black sedan had disappeared around the corner, I tried to muster up as much of a sense of relief as I could, but something told me I wasn't completely free of Smiley and Mr. Browning quite yet.

"How about that mansion?" Randy said. "I'm going to get one like that someday, only I'm going to decorate it all in NASCAR stuff."

"Go for it," I said as I pulled my phone out, this time to check on who called while I was in the media room with Mr. Browning. The call didn't come from Audrey. No, it was from Beto Hernandez.

He'd left a message asking me to call him back. He didn't say what it was about, but the first thing that came to mind was that somehow he knew where I was and wanted to find out whether I suspected him of working for Mr. Browning. Or maybe whether Mr. Browning was ratting him out.

I wasn't so sure I wanted to call him back right then, but it didn't matter—I never got the chance. Just as Randy and I walked up to my parents' car, who came walking out of the shadows but the scruffy sideburns dude who'd been sitting across the room in Topper's earlier that evening.

He's like, "Hey, losers, what's up?"

And Randy's like, "I don't know, loser. Why don't you tell me?"

Sideburns grinned a sly TV-serial-killer-type grin. "Well, look at you," he said to Randy. "The ant with the almost-mustache can talk."

And Randy goes, "You know what? We can't all be were-wolves like you."

That's just the way it was with Randy—always begging for a punch in the mouth.

Sideburns waved him off and walked up to me, stopping about two feet away. "You Dylan Jones?"

Randy told him it was none of his business, but I figured I might as well admit it since somehow the guy clearly knew who I was.

He leaned toward me. "I got a message for you, fat boy."

He paused and stared at me.

"Okay," I said. "Since obviously you want me to, I'll ask the question—what message might that be?"

"There's some people don't like the way you been poking your nose into places it don't belong."

He stopped again.

"And?" I said to prod him on.

"And you're gonna stop it."

"Wait a minute," Randy cut in. "What places are you talking about? Me and Dylan go a lot of places, and we don't like people telling us we can't go there."

In a whirl, Sideburns turned and shoved Randy to the pavement. Then the next thing I knew he grabbed my throat, pressed me against the car, and flashed a switchblade in front of my eyes.

"You like your nose the way it is?" I could hear that serial-killer grin in his voice, but I couldn't look at anything except the knife blade.

"Yes?" I said.

"Well, you're gonna be breathing out of a hole in your face instead of your nose if you don't stop sticking it in this Ashton Browning business. How would you like that?"

"Not so much."

"And you just stop thinking about collecting any reward money. That ain't for you. Got it?"

Before I could answer, there was a loud crash, and Sideburns lurched forward, almost slicing off my ear. He let go of me and spun around. There stood Rockin' Rhonda, holding up her now-busted stringless guitar like a battle-ax.

"What the hell?" said Sideburns. "You didn't just hit me with that piece of crap, did you?"

Rhonda laughed. "Just like ringing a bell."

"You must want your belly slit," Sideburns told her. The only problem was he'd dropped the switchblade, and it was obvious that if he stooped down to grab it, we could all three jump him and that guitar might just crack his face open this time.

"Go for it," Rhonda said cheerfully. "I'm gonna come at you like a cross-fire hurricane."

Sideburns glanced at the knife, then back at Rhonda, his fingers twitching at his side as if they were arguing the case for making a play for the knife.

"Come on, Mr. Cool," Rhonda invited. "Let's rock and roll."

Finally, Sideburns backed off. "Forget it. Kicking a homeless freak's ass isn't worth my time." Then he turned to me. "But it is worth my time to kick your ass." He jabbed a forefinger at my chest. "It's plenty worth my time."

"Hold on, I'm coming," Rhonda sang, and shuffled closer.

"You better watch your back, freak," Sideburns said as he eased away into the shadows. Then he was gone down the alley behind Topper's.

"Crap," I said. "Thanks, Rhonda. You couldn't have showed up at a better time."

"It's all right now," sang Rhonda. "In fact, it's a gas, gas, gas."

On the way home, Randy talked about how he would've stomped the crap out of Sideburns if he hadn't pulled that switchblade. I didn't mention that Sideburns had about a thirteen-inch and hundred-pound advantage. I was more interested in how he knew who I was and where to find me.

"He probably just wants the reward for himself," Randy guessed.

"But how would he know about me?"

"Hey, it's not like you aren't writing about the case in the school paper, you know. Maybe he's buddies with someone at our high school or something."

"Yeah, maybe." I doubted it was that simple, though.

At home, I didn't have a chance to creep up the stairs to the privacy of my bedroom. My parents were all about wanting to interrogate me over how the first big date went.

"Not good," I told them, trying to head off any further barrage of questions.

"Aw, what happened?" Mom asked, her voice changing to a syrupy sympathetic tone like I was a five-year-old coming home with a bee sting.

"Nothing," I said. "I just don't think we're compatible."

"You can't always tell on a first date," Dad said. He was going for the buck-up-there-little-fellow strategy he probably used on his grade school students. "Sometimes things can turn out a lot different on a second date."

"I don't think so," I said, heading for the stairs. "There won't be any more dates like the one I had tonight."

CHAPTER 28

Here's the weird thing—with that knife blade shining about an inch from my face, I was scared, sure, but I didn't really think Sideburns could actually kill me. After all, I can't count the times the Andromeda Man had knives or guns or even, one time, a medieval sword flashed at him, and he'd always get out of it. I mean, he's the Andromeda Man. The whole show was named after him. He couldn't get killed. But later that night it hit me hard—*I'm not the Andromeda Man.*

It would've been pretty easy to give up on Ashton, but curiosity is a weird thing—it's hard to just turn off, especially feeling the way I did about her. A bunch of ideas whirled in my head, but mainly I kept coming back to the question of why Sideburns wanted me to give up. Maybe Randy was right. Maybe Sideburns was after the reward for himself. A hundred thousand dollars could make a guy itchy with a switchblade all right. But, to me, he seemed more likely to be a thug for hire. But who would hire him?

Mr. Browning?

Rowan Adams?

Or maybe even Beto Hernandez. That could've been why he'd tried to call me. Maybe he was trying to find out when

I'd be back in Topper's parking lot so he could make sure Sideburns would be there waiting.

I couldn't exactly call Beto back and ask him about it, though. That would be a dead giveaway that I was still digging into the Ashton thing, and I sure didn't want to give Sideburns an excuse to come back around to make sure I started breathing through a hole in my face.

I still hadn't figured out what I was going to do, when I got a text message from Audrey. Apparently, her date with Trix was finally over. She said I'd never believe what happened. I texted her back and told her she'd never believe what happened to me more.

We didn't fill each other in on the details until the next day, when we could get together and talk face to face. We sat on the patio at McDonald's, where a lot of us from our high school hung out at lunch. I got two Quarter Pounders. I never, ever get a Big Mac. I don't know what's in that special sauce, but I suspect it's mayonnaise-based. Audrey offered to let me tell my story first, but I told her to go ahead. I was pretty sure whatever her story was it couldn't beat mine.

She's like, "Okay, so we go to the movie—*Georgia's Roses*—which is like this cool indie film about these two women who go into hiding from one of them's despicable husband."

"Who drove?"

"She did."

"That's interesting."

"Why is that interesting?"

"I don't know. I'm just interested in how the lesbian thing works."

"What? Are you trying to figure out who is supposed to be the girl in the relationship and who is supposed to be the boy?"

"Something like that."

"That's just like a guy. You have to think one of us is trying to be like you. But we're not. There's no *one's the girl and the other's the boy*. We're both girls. No boys involved at all. None."

"Okay, okay—I got it. You don't have to act like it's such a stupid question."

"Anyway," she says, all exasperated, "the movie is like so good, and we're sharing popcorn out of the same bucket, and then I put my arm on the armrest, only hers is already there—and neither one of us moves our arms. We're just sitting there watching this amazing movie with our arms touching the whole time."

"Congratulations," I said, though I couldn't see what the big deal was. Plenty of times I'd shared an armrest with Audrey at the movies over the years.

So then she started going on about how they went for coffee after the movie and talked and talked and were finishing each other's sentences because they thought so much alike. At this point, I didn't think it was that big a deal, but I kept listening and nodding because that's what you have to do when you have a friend who's a girl.

"And then when we got back to my driveway, it's like neither one of us wanted the night to end, so we just stood around by her car talking and laughing until finally, she had to get going. And what do you think happened then?"

I'm like, "Uh, I don't know—she went home?"

"She leaned in and kissed me."

"She kissed you, like with tongue and everything?"

"No, it wasn't like that. It was just a sweet little soft kiss."

"On the lips?"

"Yes, on the lips."

"Hmm. So what does that mean? Is she like your girlfriend now or what?"

"Maybe. I don't know. It was like *bang!*—she kissed me, and then she walks around to get in the car and smiles and says she'll call me."

"And has she?"

"No, not yet. But we only went out last night."

So I'm like, "Well, that's pretty cool."

And she goes, "*Pretty cool?* It's like the most awesome thing ever."

"Okay. I'm happy for you." I went back to eating my burger. I have to admit the *most awesome thing ever* line bugged me. After all, Audrey and I had had some pretty awesome times together. Didn't those count for anything anymore?

After a couple of minutes of eating in silence, she finally goes, "So what's your big news?"

I finished chewing, and then I go, "Oh, nothing much. I just had my life threatened, that's all."

"You're kidding. By who?"

I set my burger down and told the whole story of last night, ending with my list of the top three candidates—besides Sideburns himself—for who was behind the threat.

Of course, Audrey liked Rowan the most as a suspect, but she didn't have much evidence besides the fact that she despised him.

"What did the police have to say about it?" she asked.

"Are you serious? I didn't get the police involved. I'm not their favorite guy, you know. I'm not sitting through another one of those interrogations."

She cocked her head to the side. "I still think you should've called them. It's probably too late now."

I popped a French fry into my mouth. "The dude could've cut my nose off and the police would still blame it on me."

"So how did Mr. Browning even know about your articles?"

"I sent copies of them to Nash. I figure he's been spreading them around."

"Nash, huh?" she said, like there was something suspicious about that.

I'm like, "What?"

And she goes, "Have you ever thought Nash might be behind it all?"

"No way. Nash's a cool guy. He's my buddy."

"Yeah, right."

"You think I can't be buddies with a Hollister guy? You're going around like you have this great Hollister girlfriend, but you think I can't have a friend from there?"

"Trix is different. She's not a snob."

"Yeah, well, I think Nash's different."

We finished our burgers in silence. Then Audrey's like, "So what are you going to do? Are you going to quit on the Ashton Browning thing?"

"I don't know. I'm still trying to figure that out."

At that point, who walked by but Corman Rogers from high school. He's like, "Hey, Body Bag, think fast," and threw a wet paper sack smack into my chest. It slid down into my lap, and when I picked it up to toss it aside, a dead toad fell out on the table.

"Real cool, idiot," I said, but Corman and his buddies just laughed.

When they walked off, I shook my head. "Jesus, I don't know which is worse, having my nose cut off or living like this."

CHAPTER 29

Despite Audrey's opinion of Nash, I figured he'd be a good person to call for advice. He'd always been cool to me. Sure, he did put the squeeze on us to do what could've been some pretty humiliating karaoke, but even that turned out all right. I could see us hanging out, doing cool Hollister things. Besides, he owed me. Hadn't I done him a favor and left Gangland out of my articles about Ashton? Now that I needed some deeper scoop on Mr. Browning and Rowan, it was his turn to keep quiet.

First, I messaged him online about meeting in person, said I wanted to write an article on the Hollister football team and that he would be the perfect person to interview. I didn't mention Ashton. No need to leave a written trail showing that I might still be investigating her case. And actually that whole deal was on the back burner anyway. Right now I was more focused on figuring out how to keep my nose on my face.

His reply to my message confirmed just how wrong Audrey was about him. He had nothing but enthusiasm about the idea. One problem—he wanted me to meet him on the Hollister campus so I could actually watch the team practice, and I wasn't so sure I wanted to show my face around there.

Besides, Audrey was no longer a dependable chauffeur. In fact, she claimed she and Trix were hanging out together that afternoon. That was no big deal for Nash, though. He said he'd send Brett out to pick me up. Black-haired, blue-eyed, beautiful Brett. This was going to call for some cologne. And maybe even the porkpie hat.

She agreed to pick me up outside of school after I got done with my journalism stuff, which I admit was my idea. How could I resist showing the nonbelievers that Dylan Jones was more than just some Body Bag fool?

As I waited on her, it was perfect—about twenty kids milled around in front of school, stupid Corman Rogers among them. I couldn't think of a better audience. Unfortunately, Randy showed up and wanted to come along. I'm like, "I don't think so, dude. They're just expecting me."

"Come on," he said. "You can't cut your buddy out of some possible rich-girl action."

That was exactly the attitude that made me not want to bring him. "Forget it. This isn't about trying to pick up chicks."

"What are you talking about? Everything is about trying to pick up chicks."

"Forget it," I told him. "You'll just screw things up."

He didn't like that. "Really, *I'll* screw things up? What—do you think you're some kind of high-class act now?"

"No. It's just that I'm friends with these people, and they hardly know you."

"That's a load of crap. You've hung out with them, what, one more time than I have?"

At point Brett glided up to the curb in a sweet Mercedes SUV, the same deep blue color as her eyes.

"Look," I told Randy. "I'll talk to them. Maybe you can come along next time."

The window of the Mercedes rolled down, and Brett goes, "Hey, stranger, you need a ride?"

I turned away from Randy and tipped the porkpie. "Don't mind if I do."

As I headed to the car, he goes, "You suck, Dylan."

I didn't respond to that, but as Brett and I drove away, Randy slunk toward the building, his head bowed and his hands in pockets. The other kids, though, stood there checking out me and the fabulous Mercedes. Even Corman Rogers, in his usual all-black getup, stared after us, his tongue practically hanging from his mouth.

Of course, the interior of the Mercedes was luxurious, but it still didn't look as classy as Brett. She was the type that would look rich even in jeans and a T-shirt, not that she was wearing that. No, she had on this stylish swirly-patterned mid-thigh-length dress and little ankle-high boots. Needless to say, I immediately forgot all about Randy.

As for my attire, I'd picked out my Beatles Let It Be T-shirt. Brett glanced at it and goes, "So, you like the Beatles?"

And I'm like, "They're just the greatest band ever, probably."

She smiled. "Yeah, that's what I think too. Either them or Death Cab for Cutie."

Comparing Death Cab for Cutie with the Beatles was sacrilegious in my book, but I let it go.

Otherwise, she was pretty easy to talk to and actually seemed interested in my high school and the kids who went there. So I guess my guard was down when she came around to asking me if I'd found out anything new about Ashton. Up to now I'd intended on only discussing the latest developments with Nash, but suddenly here I was telling Brett all about Sideburns and his switchblade and more than a little bit building up my role in chasing him off.

"Wow," she said, flashing me an admiring look. "You're brave."

"I don't know about that," I said modestly.

"Sure you are, going through something so horrible, and you're still not giving up on Ashton."

"I wouldn't be much of an investigative journalist if I let myself get scared off too easily," I told her. What else are you going to say to a girl like Brett? I couldn't let on that I was seriously considering chickening out of the whole deal.

It took about a half hour to get to Hollister. I'd never been on the campus, and let me tell you—it was something. You had to go through a checkpoint to even get on the premises, but that was nothing for Brett. She just gave the guard a wave, and he waved back, and we were in.

The rest of the place looked like how I'd imagine an Ivy League college campus would look. My high school pretty much packed everyone into one big box, but Hollister had a whole assortment of buildings, and they must've used the same landscaper as Mr. Browning. Everything was completely spruce.

I'm like, "How much does it cost to go here?"

Brett laughed. "Enough," she said.

Then, as we passed the auditorium, the very thing happened that I was afraid of—a Rowan Adams sighting. He was hanging around in the parking lot with Tres Browning and the blond and gorgeous Aisling Collins. I'm like, *Don't let him see us, don't let him see us, don't let him see us.* My thinking being that if he, in fact, did have anything to do with Sideburns, he would now figure I didn't sufficiently heed the switchblade warning.

But of course, he did see us, and on top of that, he had to wave us over. Brett pulled up next to the group and not only rolled down the window to chat but made sure they all remembered who I was.

Rowan's like, "Ahhh, Dylan, the master of rap karaoke," and fired an index-finger-pistol-style greeting at me. "You should start a band so you can come back for another appearance at Gangland."

"Oh, he'll be back," Brett said.

"I'm sure he will be," he said. "So, Dylan, am I still the number-one public enemy on your suspect list?"

This, I figured, could be his way of seeing if I was still on the case, so I played it cagey. "I wouldn't say that. Even though you never did tell me where you were the day Ashton went missing. But that's okay. I'm not worried about that anymore."

"Hey," he said. "I can tell you where I was—I was out doing a million things just like I always am."

"Oh, sure," Brett said. "You're such a big shot. At least you used to be."

He put on a wounded expression. "*Used to be?* Really, Brett, you are a big bully."

"Don't worry about me," she told him. "Dylan's the one you need to be worried about. He has your number."

He laughed. "I'm shaking in my boots."

"You should be," she said.

And he's like, "No, you two are the ones who should be shaking."

I didn't like this exchange one bit—Rowan looked like he might be taking it a little too seriously.

They traded a few more semi-nasty quips, and then Brett and I were back on the road to the stadium to watch Nash finish practice. Which was a relief. I could've gone all day without a Rowan Adams run-in.

A handful of students and a smaller handful of parents had collected in the stands, and Brett and I sat about midway up on the fifty-yard line. The team was in the middle of passing drills, and Nash was amazing. The quarterback could throw the ball way too long or way too short, but every time, Nash snatched it out of the air. The guy was a prime athlete. It was almost enough to make me want to cut back on the burgers and get into halfway decent shape.

"So what's the deal with you and Nash?" I asked Brett. "Are you guys just friends or what?"

She flipped her silky black hair back over her shoulder. "I guess you could say we're friends—with benefits."

Friends with benefits. I'd heard of such a thing, but it always sounded so far-fetched, like ghosts or vegan burgers that didn't taste like cardboard.

Finally practice wrapped up, and we waited in the Mercedes while Nash showered. When he came out and hopped in the backseat, he looked as fresh as if he'd been lounging around all afternoon in his air-conditioned bedroom playing Madden NFL on PlayStation instead of digging out actual pass patterns over and over in the sun.

He shook my hand and said he was glad to see me, then leaned back in the seat and goes, "Wow, I'm so hungry I could eat a woolly mammoth without a fork. Let's do this interview thing over a bite to eat. It's on me, Dylan."

Of course, I'm like, "Great, just let me call my parents and let them know." And at the same time I was thinking it was too bad Audrey wasn't here to see what a totally cool guy Nash really was.

We weren't a half mile away from campus, though, when the weirdness set in.

Brett glanced in the rearview mirror and goes, "Uh-oh, looks like we have company."

Nash turned and looked out the back window. "It's on," he said.

"Definitely," Brett said, and punched the gas.

I'm like, "What's on? Who's back there?"

"Just hold tight," Nash told me. "Everything's fine."

I wasn't so sure about that. About a hundred yards behind us, a black car hit the gas just after Brett did. The street was a four-laner and not that heavy with traffic, but that didn't lower my panic level much as Brett zipped from lane to lane, around cars and trucks, and through a yellow light. It didn't matter that the light turned red either. The black car flew right through the intersection.

Brett cut off a car to hit the entrance ramp of the interstate, and a steady torrent of traffic bore down as we merged from the ramp all the way to the far lane. She passed semis and oil tankers, Corvettes and Mustangs, but the black car still wove from lane to lane behind us.

On a steep hill, with semis in front of us trying to cough their way to the summit, she finally had to slow down. In a matter of seconds the black car would swoop vulture-like right down on our tail. But why? I couldn't figure it out. What were Nash and Brett mixed up in?

"Come on, do something!" Nash demanded, and Brett's like, "I'm doing everything I can!"

Zeroing in, the black car jockeyed into the next lane over. It was close enough now I could see the driver—Rowan Adams.

I'm like, "Hey, it's only Rowan! It's only Rowan!"

And Brett goes, "We know! We know!"

This didn't make sense. She'd just been talking to Rowan a little while ago, and now she was running from him? Then I saw the rear window of his car roll down, and the black barrel of a pistol jabbed out—pointing straight at me.

"They have a gun!" I screamed, and Nash goes, "Get us the hell out of here!"

"You got it," Brett said, jamming down on the gas pedal.

I'm going, "Holy crap!" as we roared toward the rear of the semi in front of us, but at the last moment, Brett swerved and took to the shoulder of the road.

"Yes!" Nash hollered. "Yes!"

Blazing down the shoulder, we passed the semi and at least four other vehicles before Brett steered us back into a legal lane. Looking back, I couldn't see Rowan anywhere, and at first I thought that was good. Then I realized it only meant he'd hit the shoulder of the road himself, and if he didn't get killed on the way, he'd be right back on our tail.

Nash told Brett to take the next exit, which she did by veering in front of two lanes of traffic, drawing the blare of honking horns. But it was a relief to get off the interstate. By now we were well beyond the city limits, and the little two-lane country roads didn't have near as much traffic to crash into.

"Do you think they saw where we got off?" Brett asked, and Nash's like, "I don't know. I couldn't tell."

"That's okay," she said. "I have an idea."

She slowed down and pulled onto a narrow side road, one encrusted with trees on either side. Then she turned around so that we had a perfect view of the road we just left.

"Genius," Nash told her. "Now all we have to do is wait for them to pass, and we'll be the ones on their butts."

I'm like, "What's happening? Why was he chasing us?"

"Probably because he knows you're with us, Dylan," Brett said.

"Me? What did I do?"

And Nash goes, "I afraid he knows you're on to him."

"On to him?" I said, trying to sound innocent. "On to him about what?"

"About Ashton Browning," Brett said. "What else?"

And then Nash's like, "But don't worry. We're on your side." He lifted up his shirt and pulled a black pistol of his own out of his waistband.

I'm like, "What the hell? You carry a firearm around with you?"

He winked at me. "You never know when it might come in handy."

At this point, I felt like I'd dropped down the rabbit hole into a nightmare version of Wonderland where everyone but me was a Mad Hatter with a gun. I didn't have a chance to ask any more questions, though. Just then, Rowan's car whooshed past our hideaway.

"Got you, little boy," Brett said, and stomped the gas pedal.

The road stretched long and straight. The black car raced ahead, but Brett scorched after it. Within a matter of seconds, Rowan caught on to our ploy. But instead of trying to outrun us, he jammed on the brakes, fishtailed a one-eighty, and, after sitting still for a moment, his engine breathing heavy, he barreled straight toward us, aiming his shiny chrome grille at ours.

It was a game of chicken that neither side seemed willing to lose. I let out a long, loud *"Craaaaaaaaaaaaaaaaap!"* that only ended when both cars screeched to a standstill about twenty yards away from each other. I was wrong to think it was over, though.

Rowan's passenger-side door swung open, and here came

none other than Aisling Collins striding down the blacktop, packing a big black assault rifle, her blond hair flying back in the wind. *This cannot be happening,* I thought as I scrunched down in the seat. *I escaped Sideburns and his switchblade only to be gunned down by a beautiful rich girl?*

Before she was halfway to us, Nash jumped out of the car, ready to face her down with his pistol. She said something, and I guess he said something back, but obviously neither was asking for mercy. I slumped lower in the seat.

Then it happened—Aisling pulled her trigger and Nash pulled his, and the next thing I knew red splattered everywhere. Aisling staggered back, her finger still clenched to the trigger, and Nash didn't let up either. But they weren't covered in blood. Their guns were nothing but squirt guns filled with strawberry Kool-Aid.

That's when it hit me—the whole thing was just another Gangland goof.

CHAPTER 30

Brett laughed so hard you would have thought it was a terminal disease, and I'm like, "What the hell? Why didn't you tell me what was going on?"

"Oh, come on," she said. "You didn't think those were real guns, did you?"

And I'm like, "No. Of course not."

"Oh my God," she said. "You did. You thought they were real guns. That's hilarious."

By now Rowan was out of his car and Tres Browning had climbed out of the backseat, all of them with their own squirt guns, spraying Kool-Aid everywhere. Only after the guns emptied did Brett and I get out of the Mercedes. She held up her hands. "I'm unarmed," she said.

Everyone was laughing pretty hard—except me. I did try to force a smile like I'd been in on the joke the whole time, but of course, they didn't buy it and flipped me crap about freaking out. Well, Tres didn't, but I figured he probably would have if he could've thought of something clever to say. Actually, I could see how it would be funny—if it happened to somebody else. But since it was me, I was a little bit pissed off.

I guess Nash noticed my mood because he put his arm

around my shoulders and said, "You're a hell of a sport, Dylan. If it was me, I probably would've screamed like a little girl, but you hung right in there. I'll tell you what I'm going to do. I'm going to buy you a thick, juicy steak. How about that?"

"A burger would be fine by me," I said, but he's like, "No way. We're going to get you the best steak you've ever tasted."

After everyone told me a few more times how hilarious I was, Rowan's gang climbed back into his car and we got into the Mercedes. Brett made Nash sit on a towel so he wouldn't drip Kool-Aid on the plush interior. As Rowan drove by, Aisling pointed her gun at me, and I pretended to get shot.

"That's the spirit, Dylan," Nash said.

Heading back to the socialite side of the city, he and Brett filled me in on the rules of squirt-gun gang warfare. I could see how it would be fun, but it also kind of made me wonder if maybe rich kids had a little too much time on their hands to think up weird things to do.

"Poor Rowan," Brett said. "He's still trying so hard."

"I know," Nash said. "It's really kind of pathetic."

I asked why Rowan was so pathetic, and Nash's like, "Financial problems. His dad's not doing so well. The real estate market, you know."

"Uh, yeah," I said as if I knew anything about real estate.

"You don't think his dad's going to have to sell Gangland, do you?" Brett asked.

And Nash's like, "Doesn't matter—as long as the right person takes it off his hands."

They seemed pretty unconcerned about Rowan's family problems, which I thought was a little cold. Sure, Rowan was a creep, but he was still their friend.

Instead of dwelling on the topic, Brett suggested a couple

places we could go for dinner. I repeated how a good burger would suit me perfectly, but Nash insisted that nothing would do but a steak from some place called Geoffrey Mercer's. The odd thing, though, was Brett pulled up in front of what looked to me like a house—a very modern cool-looking house maybe—but there was no restaurant sign or even a parking lot that I could see.

"What's this?" I asked.

"This is it," Nash said. "This is Geoffrey Mercer's."

I looked the house over again. If it was really a restaurant, I figured it had to be pretty exclusive. Apparently, customers had to just *know* about it somehow because there certainly wasn't any advertising going on.

"Do you think we're dressed right for this place?" I asked Nash. "I mean, I'm just wearing a T-shirt, and you have Kool-Aid stains all over you."

And real nonchalant he's like, "No, it's cool. They know me here."

Inside, there was a cramped foyer decked out with fancy vases and flowers and a couple of paintings with gold frames. I kind of liked the one of this pretty lady in a white bonnet, but the one that was nothing but haystacks didn't do much for me.

An incredibly hot waitress or hostess, or whatever you call her, greeted Nash with a wide cheery smile. Here he was, covered in Kool-Aid, and she didn't seem to notice. It was the same as she led us through the small dining room to our table. Several parental types waved at Nash, and he even stopped to talk to a couple, never bothering to apologize for how he looked. He might as well have been wearing a thousand-dollar suit. He just had this incredible cool about him, like everywhere he went he not only belonged but *ruled*.

Me, on the other hand, I felt like every customer in the place was giving me the evil eye. I didn't think it could be my Beatles T-shirt. Who doesn't love the Beatles? So I guessed it must be the porkpie. I took it off as we walked to the table, but then I didn't really know what to do with it, so I ended up stuffing it under my chair when we sat down.

I could describe the upscale décor, but here's all you really need to know about Geoffrey Mercer's: the menus didn't tell the prices. That didn't matter since Nash was paying, but still, it's kind of creepy—you keep looking for the prices, but they just kept not being there—it's like you're an amputee trying to scratch your missing leg. On top of that, they didn't have any burgers either, so I had to go with some kind of steak that was supposed to have wine sauce on it.

After we ordered, Nash leaned back in his chair and told me that, in addition to the steak, he and Brett had another little surprise for me. "How would you like to come back to Gangland?" he asked, smiling his big ultra-whitened half-moon smile. "And this time you can stay after ten o'clock with the rest of us members."

"Uh, wow," I said. "That would be cool." Of course, I was honored, except for one thing—someone could very easily think I was still on the Ashton Browning case if I went back there.

"What's the matter?" Nash said. "You don't sound so sure."

"You're not worried about that guy who threatened you, are you?" Brett added.

And Nash's like, "Threatened? Who threatened you?"

"To tell you the truth, that's what I really wanted to talk to you about."

"You mean you aren't really writing an article about the

football team?" He clasped his hands to his chest like he was wounded.

"Uh, no, sure, I'd like to write that sometime, but right now I'm kind of more worried about who wants me off the Ashton Browning case, and I thought maybe you could help me figure out who it is."

He smiled. "Sure. We can talk about football any old time."

So I laid out the Mr. Browning–Smiley–Sideburns story again, and Nash congratulated me for dealing with the switchblade situation like a regular action hero. This time, unlike when I told the story to Brett, I listed the people who were most likely to be behind the threat. Not wanting to get ridiculed again, I left out Rowan, but I did include Beto. This was the first time I told anyone about meeting up with him on Ashton's FOKC route. What I didn't tell, though, was that there could be a connection with Hector Maldonado.

"Very interesting," Nash said. "Yes, I think it would have to be someone else who wanted to get the reward before you could get it."

And I'm like, "Yeah, I thought of that. But I also wondered how Mr. Browning got hold of my newspaper articles."

Before Nash could respond to that, the waiter arrived with our food. Everything was very artistically arranged on the plate, but the portions were way small.

When the waiter left, Nash admitted he'd made copies of my articles and handed them out to a lot of Hollister kids, mainly Ganglanders, as a way to keep Ashton's story alive. But he was certain none of them would be involved in making a threat to cut off my nose. That included Mr. Browning. Maybe it was because Ashton's dad was one of their own kind, but he and Brett both insisted Mr. Browning was only after one thing—finding his daughter.

"Besides," Nash said. "None of them are worried about beating you to the reward. No, I'll bet it's the Mexican guy—what was his name?"

"Beto."

"Right. I'll bet Beto is working on his own way to score the reward and, since you know who he is, he hired this Sideburns character to scare you away. Why else would he specifically tell you that the reward money was not for you?"

"So you don't think they really have anything to do with kidnapping Ashton?"

"No. For one thing, I don't see those guys hanging around the nature park waiting to kidnap Ashton without someone noticing them and thinking they looked suspicious."

"Yeah, you may be right," I said between bites of meat. Although the steak was great, I would have preferred it on a bun with lettuce, tomato, onion, and mustard—no mayonnaise. However, I was pretty sure asking for that would amount to some kind of social blunder.

"And besides," Brett said, "if these two were actually involved in taking Ashton, I'm sure the police would've released something about it to the press by now."

I'm like, "The police?"

"Of course. After you reported what happened, they probably checked those guys out."

"Oh yeah," I said. No reason to mention how I didn't inform the authorities. Nash and Brett probably wouldn't be able to relate to my fear of the police.

"There have to be hundreds of people after that reward," Nash said. "From what I hear, the police are getting so many tips they can't keep up with them all. Everyone wants a piece of the action. It's like they think finding Ashton is the same as hitting the lottery. They'll collect that sad little hundred-thousand-dollar check and it'll change their lives. They're not like you, Dylan. They don't really care about Ashton. They just want the money. But I know you do care about her."

"I do," I said. "I really do." And I did, but also that reward didn't seem so sad or little to me. Plus, I'd done a lot of pondering on how a hundred thousand bucks could change my life.

"But what those people don't know," Nash said, "is that the police already have a pretty solid suspect. They just haven't released anything about it to the media yet."

I'm like, "What?"

"You haven't heard about that?" Brett asked. "I thought Mr. Browning might have said something to you about it."

"He didn't tell me anything about a new suspect."

"Yeah," Brett said. "Tres told me and Nash about it. The story came straight from his dad, so you know it's reliable information."

"I can't say I'm really surprised," Nash said. "I always thought she was weird, so it's no shocker to find out her dad's a pervert."

I'm like, "Whose dad?"

"Trix," Brett said. "Trix Westwood."

"What?" I couldn't believe what I was hearing.

"That's right," Nash said. "The word is her father has a thing for young girls. Apparently, he sent out a bunch of nude photos of himself to girls' cell phones. And I'm talking about girls seventeen and under. A couple of them have admitted to having sex with him."

"And not only that," Brett said, "but where he and Trix

172

used to live in California? One of her friends was murdered, and the police are looking into that to see if he had anything to do with it."

"But she told me about that murder. The pool guy got arrested for it."

"That's her version," Brett said. "But you know what I think? I think Trix is in on it with her dad. I'll bet she lures girls over to her house so he can pick his favorites."

"Isn't that creepy?" Nash said, and I go, "I can't believe it. I've hung out with Trix, and she seemed pretty cool. Except for the murder-in-California connection."

"Well, I'd stay away from her if I were you," Brett said.

"Yeah," I said. "I guess I should." But I wasn't worried about myself. I was thinking about Audrey. She was probably with Trix right now. Maybe at her house meeting her father.

CHAPTER 31

I excused myself to go to the bathroom, where I immediately dialed Audrey's number. "Come on, pick up, pick up," I muttered into the phone, but she didn't. She was probably afraid I'd spoil her "romantic evening." So I called her mom and found out she was at an outdoor jazz concert in a little park not far away. *Jazz.* Audrey didn't even like jazz.

There was nothing to do but go back to the table and explain to Nash and Brett that Audrey was with Trix and that we had to head to the park right now. They didn't even argue. They could see how upset I was. And here is another thing that struck me about how cool Nash was—he didn't worry about all the expensive food we left on our plates. He just paid the bill, and we were on the road in five minutes.

"Can't you go faster?" I asked Brett, and she's like, "Faster? You were way freaked over the way I was driving before, and now you want me to go faster?"

"But this is important."

"Calm down," Nash said. "If she's at a public park, I'm sure she's safe."

I dug my fingers into the edge of my seat. "I just hope she really is there."

At the park, the good parking spaces were all taken, so Brett let me out while she went to look for one. By now the sun was down, but there were plenty of lights shining on the small stage and the crowd of maybe a hundred and fifty people. It wasn't hard to spot Audrey and Trix perched in lawn chairs about two rows back from the stage. They were snuggled pretty close together, but at least they weren't holding hands or anything.

I squeezed down the third row until I came to Audrey from behind. I tapped her shoulder and she jumped.

"What are you doing here?" She didn't sound happy to see me, but Trix looked up and cheerfully goes, "Oh, hi, Dylan. How's it going?"

To Trix, I'm like, "Not great," and then to Audrey, "I need to talk to you."

"You can talk to me later." Now Audrey was mega-irritated.

"No, I can't." I pulled her arm, but she yanked it away.

"Go ahead," Trix told her, and then with a flirty smile, "Don't worry. I'll save your seat."

"Oh, all right," Audrey said. "But this better be important, Dylan."

I led her to the back of the park where no one could listen in. It wasn't so easy to get started with what I had to say, so I opened with a simple question: "Has Trix introduced you to her father?"

"What kind of question is that?"

"Just bear with me here," I said, and Audrey's like, "You know what? Unless you just found out some really big news like you're dying or something, I'm going to kill you."

"I'm getting to it, but first I want to know if you've met Mr. Westwood."

175

"Okay, yes, I've met him. She introduced me to him tonight. So what?"

"Did he seem kind of weird to you?"

"Weird? No, he didn't seem weird. He was nice."

"Nice, huh?" That didn't sound good. "How nice? Was he like *dad* nice, or was he more like, uh, um—"

"What?"

"Or was he like *I-want-to-get-in-your-pants* nice?"

Her mouth dropped open. "It finally happened," she said. "You lost your mind. What kind of question is that?"

"Look," I said. "Don't get defensive. It's just that I have pretty good reason to believe Mr. Westwood has a thing for young girls."

"Where did you get a stupid idea like that?"

I hated to say because I knew she didn't think so highly of Nash and Brett, but since the word came from Mr. Browning himself, I figured I had credibility on my side. Still, when I told her the details, she wouldn't believe it.

"You know what?" she said. "If you actually believe Trix would ever do anything like hooking up her dad with girls, you're the biggest fool in the universe. She's like the best person I've ever met in my life, and you want to come along and ruin it. What's the matter with you?"

"Oh, really?" I said. "You don't even know her."

"Yes, I do. When someone's your soul mate, you know them like you do your own self, and I know she'd never do anything like what you're talking about."

Just then, Trix stepped up behind Audrey. "Who wouldn't do what?" she asked.

"Nothing," Audrey said. "Dylan just has a stupid new theory about Ashton Browning."

Trix is like, "A new theory? I'd like to hear it."

"No," Audrey said, stepping back next to her. "Believe me, you wouldn't."

But Trix goes, "Sure I would. After all, haven't I been helping you with the investigation? I'm practically one of your partners."

"Yeah," I said. "I was wondering why you were so anxious to help."

And she's like, "What's that supposed to mean?"

I stared her straight in the eyes. "It means I think you had your own motive for getting involved, and it wasn't exactly something unselfish."

"Motive?" Trix looked at Audrey, and Audrey goes, "Don't listen to him."

But I wasn't about to let it drop now. "Yes. A motive. As in you wanted to cover up your dad's involvement with Ashton."

"That's like a joke, right?" Trix said. "That's the most ridiculous thing I've ever heard." But what else was she going to say?

I kept going. "I always thought it was suspicious how you just happened to be at Ashton's search party after you were also at one for that girl in California. That was just too big a coincidence. But it wasn't a coincidence at all, was it? Because the truth is your dad has a thing for young girls, and you know it. You knew it in California and you knew it here, and you didn't say anything about it because you were daddy's little helper all along. And now you're trying to pull a fast one on Audrey just because she's desperate to feel like somebody loves her."

I would've gone on, but at that point, Audrey hauled off and punched me right in the gut. And let me tell you—that girl has some muscles. It doubled me over. I thought I might puke up my high-dollar half a steak.

Between coughs I'm like, "Crap. What the hell?"

But Audrey wasn't listening because she was too busy apologizing to Trix. And then Nash and Brett showed up. Nash looped an arm around my shoulders and goes, "What happened, buddy?"

But Trix is like, "I should've known you two would be involved in this."

"Oh, don't try to act like you're some kind of wronged woman," Brett said. "We heard all about you and your sick father."

"You'd better shut up about those lies," Trix said. "My dad's the best lawyer in this state, and he'll have you in court for slander so fast you—"

She couldn't figure out how fast that would be before Nash cut in: "Your dad's not going to do anything. People like us don't get sued by people like him."

"Just get out of here," Audrey barked. "We don't have anything else to say to any of you. And that includes you, Dylan."

I'm like, "Wait. Just listen," but she and Trix turned and walked away.

Nash patted me on the back. "Well, you tried."

On the drive home, he and Brett laughed about Trix's reaction and how her face had turned nearly as red as her hair. I guessed they were just trying to cheer me up, but I couldn't laugh. Sure, Audrey and I had had our spats over the years, but nothing like this.

When we pulled up in my driveway, Nash goes, "Hey, don't forget, next Saturday you're coming to Gangland."

"And this time you're staying till closing time," Brett added.

"I don't know," I said. "If Audrey's still mad at me, I may not have a ride."

"Don't worry about that," Nash said. "We'll give you a ride. And believe me, you'll be riding in style."

"Okay," I said. "But no more karaoke or car chases or anything, right?"

Nash laughed. "I don't know if I can promise you that."

CHAPTER 32

I thought having a best friend was a good thing. You always had someone to hang out with, to talk to, and to just, in general, back you up on things. But what if you happen to lose that best friend? Then what do you have? Nothing.

That's how I felt when Audrey wouldn't return my calls or even talk to me at school. I couldn't believe she was that mad at me, but I figured when a person thinks they're in love, they can get pretty unreasonable.

Journalism class was the worst. She wouldn't even look at me, much less give me a chance to explain that I was just trying to look out for her own good. When the bell rang, I tried chasing her into the hall, but I accidentally bumped into Jared Hess, who as a senior, a giant, and an idiot felt it was his duty to pin me against a locker and fling a spit-soaked lecture in my face about how, if I wanted to keep up my health, I should stay out of the way of my betters. At least he didn't call me Body Bag.

And there wasn't anyone to confide in about my Audrey problem either because she was the one I always confided in about everything. I didn't want to talk to my parents—they were likely to go all Oprah on me—and I was never the type to cultivate some kind of huge network of friends. I never needed that. I had Audrey. I figured I always would.

So that left Randy. He was still a little pissed at me for not taking him along with Brett, but he had even fewer friends than I did, so it wasn't like he could hold a grudge against me for very long. Still, I didn't mention that Nash and Brett had invited me back to Gangland. Obviously, Randy would want to go, and I didn't see any reason to get into that argument again.

Without a ride, we were stuck meeting for lunch in the lowly school cafeteria. At least they were serving cheeseburgers— if you want to call those things cheeseburgers. I swear they painted stripes on the patties to make them look like they were actually grilled.

As I should have predicted, Randy had no interest in counseling me about best-friend issues. Instead, he totally wanted to focus on Mr. Westwood's sex scam. How many girls had he run it on? Who were they? What did they look like? What kind of things did he do with them? These were questions I didn't have the answers to, which was probably for the best. Randy's interest seemed a little unhealthy.

"Well, let me ask you this," he said. "What if Trix isn't covering up for him? What if he's covering up for her?"

I'm like, "You mean maybe Trix is the one luring in the girls like for a lesbian thing, and her dad knows about it?"

"Why not?" he said around a mouthful of French fries. "Trix probably killed that girl in California to keep her quiet, and now she's doing the same thing here."

For the first time ever in my life, I didn't feel like finishing off my second cheeseburger. "I didn't think about that," I said. "But maybe the whole story is false. After all, there hasn't

181

been anything on the news about it. Not that I think Nash would lie to me, but what about Mr. Browning? Maybe he made it up."

"I doubt that," Randy said. "He seemed pretty determined to get to the truth."

"Yeah. Damn, we have to do something."

Randy nonchalantly poked another fry into his mouth. "What for? The cops are already on to the deal, right?"

"Not exactly," I said. "Apparently, the cops only suspect Mr. Westwood. For all they know, Trix is just his innocent little girl."

"But I thought you'd quit this investigating crap after the switchblade thing."

"I don't care about that," I said. "I'm not dropping anything if Audrey's involved."

After school, I cracked the laptop and did some more snooping, checking over all of Trix's social sites and Googling her dad. There was quite a bit on him, mostly about legal cases he'd worked on for one corporation or another. It was all very boring and, aside from proving that he was pretty great at his job, didn't give me anything to go on.

As for Trix, of course I'd looked her up before, but now I went over every photo and post as if I was an archeologist trying to decipher the meaning of a foreign culture. She had a bunch of photos of herself with girls I'd never seen, probably California girls from the looks of them, so I checked the captions for names and then Googled them to see if there was any news about them getting kidnapped or murdered. Nothing—until I took a closer look at one of the photos of Trix and a friend.

Behind them a poster hung in a store window. When I zoomed in, I saw that it bore the picture and the name of the missing California girl Trix told us about. With that I was able to search for news articles about the case, and sure enough, it was true—the pool guy was convicted. That info could've confirmed Trix's story, but then again, this poor guy wouldn't have been the first to get thrown in jail for something he didn't do. After all, Trix's dad was a lawyer. Maybe he knew just how to frame someone.

Checking one of the earlier articles about the case—one written before the pool guy's arrest—I found something intriguing. Where was that little California girl last seen? That's right—a *park*. It was a city park and not a nature park like in Ashton's case, but still that was too much of a coincidence.

I knew I couldn't sit around on my fat butt poring over the Internet any longer. I had to get out and do something. Even though that might mean drawing Sideburns and his switchblade out of the shadows to de-nose-ify me. But what could I do? Where could I go? Who could I talk to? The answer to that last question was obvious, but it wouldn't be easy. I had to talk to Trix—in person.

I called her, pretty much expecting her not to answer, but she did. Obviously, she wasn't thrilled to hear from me, but I convinced her I wanted to get together and talk things over, not for my benefit but for Audrey's. Finally, she's like, "Okay, I'll meet you at the coffee shop we went to last time. But I'm only doing it because you've been Audrey's friend for so long."

Now my problem was how to get there. Obviously, Audrey wouldn't drive me, and Nash had football practice. Besides, he and Brett probably would think I was crazy for even wanting to talk to Trix. And then there were a couple of other halfway good friends at school who had cars, but this might end up being a dangerous trip—it wouldn't be fair to drag halfway friends into it. What choice did I have? A taxicab was the only option left. You know you have to make a change in your life when you're reduced to paying somebody to drive you around.

On top of that my anxiety level rose with every mile the cab traveled. All sorts of scenarios played in my head, the main one being that Trix was the one who hired Sideburns in the first place and now she was just luring me in for a quick knifing. Thinking about it, I actually felt a little queasy, and the cabdriver's gas problem didn't help. I'm not talking about fuel for the car either. I'm talking the guy couldn't control his rotten-egg farts. It was brutal.

When we got to the coffee shop, I didn't ask him to wait. I didn't know how long I'd be, and besides, I figured I could get a more fragrant ride home from a different driver. Trix, in her usual black-and-white outfit, was already at a table inside, so I ordered a large café mocha and joined her. The place was filled with the usual professional types, who, I was pretty sure, weren't packing knives.

I'm like, "Hey, thanks for meeting me."

And she goes, "To tell you the truth, I thought about backing out. Those things you said about my dad were pretty unforgivable."

"Yeah, well, it's not like I made any of it up. I was just trying to protect my best friend, you know."

"So do you still believe it?"

"I don't know. That's why I'm here."

"You should be at the police station. They'll tell you how stupid it is."

I shook my head. "The police and I don't get along too well."

"Then what do you want from me?" she asked. "I've already

told you it wasn't true. Are you waiting for me to swear on a stack of Bibles or something?"

"But why would Nash and Brett make up a story like that?"

"Why?" She sounded like the question exhausted her. "Because I'm different? Because I don't fit into their stereotype of what a Hollister kid should be? People like they are can always find reasons. Kind of like how the kids at your school found a reason to call you Body Bag."

I guess she caught the surprise on my face because she's like, "That's right, Audrey told me all about the Body Bag thing."

"My school ranks pretty high on the vicious scale."

"Yeah, but kids at my school know how to be vicious on a whole different level." She paused to take a drink of her coffee. "You know, what I don't get is why you puppy-dog around after the likes of Nash and Brett. That doesn't make you a rich kid too, you know."

"They're my friends."

"You really believe that, don't you?"

"I don't see why I shouldn't. You never hear them calling me Body Bag. Actually, we're pretty close."

"Right," she said sarcastically. "But you don't think I could be good for Audrey?"

"That's different."

She looked up from her drink. "Why is that different? I mean, why are you so ready to believe bad things about me but not the others? Is it because you think I might just be gay?"

"What? No."

"It seems pretty homophobic to me."

I felt my face suddenly flush. "Are you kidding? You can't even play that card on me. I've been best friends with a lesbian practically my entire life."

Trix leaned forward and rested her elbows on the table. "But she never went out with a girl that whole time. Not in any kind of romantic way. Now she might actually start dating someone, and you can't take it."

Personally, I don't like getting pissed off—it can make me lose control of my tear ducts—but this was pissing me off. "You're wrong," I told her. "You couldn't be more wrong. It wouldn't be any different if you were a dude. I still wouldn't trust you. I mean, we don't really know each other."

"Okay," she said. "Don't pop a blood vessel. It just seems weird that you're able to trust someone like Nash but not me. All of that aside, though, how about Audrey? How about putting some trust in her? Like you say, she's your best friend. I'd think you would have more faith in her judgment."

"I do, but—"

"But what? You don't trust her when it comes to dating a girl? Forget about me. If you really want to smooth things out with her, you need to trust her to know what she wants from life."

"How am I going to do that? She won't even talk to me."

"Well, she's really mad at you right now. But what do you expect? Not only did you call her desperate, but you also made it sound like there was no way I could really love her. Getting past that is going to take time, so just try this—give her some space for a week or so. Then, when you see the police haven't arrested my dad—or me—for anything and there's nothing in the news about us, you can apologize."

"I don't see what I have to apologize for."

She leaned back in her chair. "All I can say is if you don't see that, then you're probably going to lose the best friend you ever had."

"I'd rather lose her that way than lose her to something worse."

"And I'm worse—is that it?"

"I guess I'm just wondering why you never mentioned how that girl in California went missing from a park—just like Ashton Browning."

Trix stared at me for a moment. "So you didn't want to talk to me about Audrey at all, did you? You're still playing detective. Well, if that's how it is, then I don't have anything else to say to you." She unlooped her purse strap from the back of her chair and stood. "Except one last thing—that girl in California? My dad put up the reward to find her."

Watching her walk away, I didn't know what to think. None of the articles I'd read mentioned anything about who put up the money for the reward, but if what Trix said was true, I had to admit it made a good case for her father's innocence. Unless he knew all along no one would ever find her alive.

After finishing my drink, I called the taxi service and went outside to wait for my ride. Nobody popped out of the shadows to stab me. I was pretty confused and not just about the deal with Trix's father but also about how I'd handled things with Audrey. It was true—I had called her desperate. That was just the kind of thing that would really piss her off. Plus, she usually was a good judge of character, so there was a chance that maybe I should go ahead and trust her on this. But if she was wrong, I hated to think what might happen.

Saturday night was right around the corner. Then I'd have a chance to dig into the story about Trix and her dad a little deeper. I figured I could at least hold off on bugging Audrey about it anymore until I did that.

It took about twenty minutes for the cab to show up, and

when it did, who was behind the wheel? Mr. Fartmaster, of course. He's like, "Hey, buddy, we meet again. Need a ride?"

What could I do, tell him thanks but no thanks, you stink too much? No. So I climbed into the backseat and rode home with bad thoughts in my head and the fragrance of rotten eggs in my nose.

CHAPTER 33

The whole homophobe accusation boiled in my stomach for most of the evening, but when the anger cooled off, I started to wonder if maybe there was something to what Trix said after all. True, I never cared when Audrey just *said* she was gay, but now that she had a chance to do something about it, did it really bother me? Was I prejudiced against Trix because of it?

No way. Not a chance. Maybe that's how other kids Trix knew thought, but not me. Period. On the other hand, I had to admit it did rankle me that Audrey actually got a girlfriend before I did. If she and Trix started getting all romantic, hanging out, going to movies, showing up at stupid jazz concerts, where would that leave me? So, yes, maybe I was a little jealous. No one wants to get squeezed out. But that didn't necessarily mean my judgment got all clouded when it came to Trix, did it?

So Saturday rolled around, and I must have tried on about six different T-shirts before I settled on my new Notorious B.I.G. shirt. I checked my look with the porkpie and without and finally decided to go without. Sure, I was a little anxious about my night at Gangland, but, as with most things these days, I didn't let on to my parents.

I didn't even tell them about Gangland, only that I was hanging out with my Hollister people. And I assured them this was not a date with the same imaginary girl I pretended to go out with before. They were happy I had some new friends, but that didn't keep them from being suspicious. That's how it was—my own parents acting like I wasn't good enough to hang out with the Hollister crowd. I figured they'd see the truth one day, though. Everybody would.

About eight o'clock the doorbell rang, and unfortunately I couldn't just slip out. I had to ask Nash and Brett in for the parental inspection. They were both real cool with my parents, making small talk and doling out compliments. Brett told my mom she really liked our house, and Mom giggled and goes, "Oh, it's not much, but we call it home." Pretty lame.

My parents were impressed, though. They told us to have a good time, and let us squeeze out the door without too much damage. It was a cool, clear night, a little too cool for just the Notorious B.I.G. T-shirt, but I wasn't about to go back for a jacket now. And let me tell you, Nash wasn't kidding when he said we'd be riding in style. Was it Brett's Mercedes parked out front? Nash's Lexus? No, a glimmering white limo sat idling next to the curb, as out of place as a diamond in a sparrow's nest.

I'm like, "Are you kidding me? You rented a limo?"

"Sure," Nash said. "We do it all the time. It adds fluidity to the night."

I didn't know what he meant by *fluidity,* but it sure added something.

We got into the back of the limo, and Nash rattled off an address to the driver—not the address of Gangland—and then pushed a button that raised a window partitioning off the back from the front. I didn't really see why that was necessary. It wasn't like this driver was likely to gas us out with an unrelenting fart attack.

"I thought we were going to Gangland," I said, and Nash goes, "We are, but we need to make a couple of stops first. Just sit back and enjoy."

As soon as we cruised out of my neighborhood, he opened the cover on this little bar and pulled out a bottle of champagne. "You have to try this, Dylan," he said. Apparently, it was supposed to be excellent as far as champagnes go. He even pronounced the name with a French accent, which I thought was pretty cool.

"I'm not much of a drinker," I told him. This was a bit of an exaggeration because actually I wasn't any kind of a drinker.

"Don't worry," Brett assured me. "It tickles a little going down, but it's all good from there."

Nash filled a glass for each of us. Not plastic cups like kids from my school would drink liquor from, but actual champagne glasses.

"Here's to a winning night for the O-Town Elites," he said, and we all clinked our glasses. They both took healthy drinks, but I barely wet my tongue. It wasn't bad, though, so I downed a little more.

"You like?" Brett asked.

"Excellent," I said.

So we rode and chatted with the hip-hop pounding from the speakers. For a while we got on the subject of crappy teachers at our schools. It's funny—kids from any kind of background all have their teacher war stories. Except Nash and Brett tended to sound more like they were talking about the incompetent hired help than some enemy commander. Me, I didn't lock into interrogation mode. Not yet.

The first place we stopped was even further from being

limo-worthy than my neighborhood. I mean, this place could've been on the cover of *Better Crack Homes and Gardens.* Our driver pumped the horn a couple times, and a minute later there was a tap on the roof of the car. The window glided down next to Nash, and in looks this enormous face that more than a little bit resembled the face on my T-shirt.

"Nash, my man, you riding slick tonight."

"You know it, D-Stack," Nash said.

"When you gonna invite me to cruise with you and the lady?"

"Right now, if you want."

D-Stack laughed. "I would, but me and my lady's got our own party happening tonight." He nodded toward the porch, where his big-boned girlfriend lounged on the steps, flicking her awesome hair extensions away from her cigarette smoke.

"Another time, then," Nash said. "You have anything for me?"

"You know I do." D-Stack lifted up his shirttail, revealing two items tucked in his waistband, a small brown paper bag and a shiny, pearl-handled pistol. Luckily, he only pulled out the bag.

Nash traded it for a little package of his own, which I assumed contained a wad of bills.

D-Stack grinned warmly. "Always nice doing business with you, man."

"You too," Nash said, and the window glided silently up.

As we pulled away, I'm like, "What the hell?"

"Just a little pre-party purchase," Nash said.

"Let me guess—something to help make the night more fluid?"

"Something like that."

"But did you have to come here?"

"Hey." Nash knocked back his champagne. "If you're going to run with Gangland, you have to live the part."

From there the stops didn't get any classier. Next we hit the Vietnamese pool hall, but this time not to play. Nash went in alone and was back in five minutes. After that we pulled into the parking lot of the Virgo Club, which I judged from the neon dancing girls on the sign was obviously a strip joint, and not an upscale one either.

"Are you kidding?" I said as Nash opened the door. "We can't get in there."

"You're right," Nash said. "You can't. But I can. You should know by now I can get in anywhere."

And it was true—he walked right in the front door. I asked Brett how he was able to work it, and she explained he'd visited the Virgo earlier in the week with his big brother and a hearty helping of cash to look over some prospects.

I'm like, "Prospects?"

She tossed me a flirty smile. "Just some of our after-ten-o'clock entertainment."

"Let me guess. He's hiring the ugliest stripper he can find."

"You're catching on," she said.

I'm like, "Really? You mean I'm right?"

She just laughed.

When Nash stepped out of the dark entrance into the neon glow outside, I swore he had a child with him, but then I realized that his stripper of choice was actually a little person—as in dwarf. The bowlegged walk gave her away.

As they settled into the limo with us, he made introductions, giving fake names to Brett and me—I was Nitro and Brett was Belladonna—which was only fair since the stripper gave her name as Tangerine, no doubt a stage name.

"Wow," Tangerine said as she stuffed her bag onto the floorboard. "Cool wheels, T-Bone." I guessed *T-Bone* was Nash's pseudonym.

It's hard to tell with a little person, but I figured she was somewhere in her middle twenties. She wore a shoulder-length pink wig and a pink tracksuit—for now. When Nash offered her some champagne, her big blue eyes sparkled, and she threw off a wide smile, revealing braces on her teeth. That almost made me revise my estimate of her age, but I decided she probably hadn't been able to afford braces until hooking up with the Virgo Club.

But no way was this girl ugly. Actually, she was cute in an Anna Paquin sort of way. You know—the girl who plays Sookie on *True Blood*? This irked me. Not that she was cute but that Nash only chose her for ugly-stripper night at Gangland because she was a little person. I thought he was cooler than that.

She polished off her champagne in a couple of gulps. "This is the life," she said, holding her glass out for a refill. "You know what would go great with this? A fried-bologna sandwich."

At that, Brett laughed, and with a squinty stare, Tangerine's like, "What? Have you ever had one?"

Brett admitted she hadn't, and Tangerine goes, "Well, don't laugh, then. Fried-bologna sandwiches are delicious."

"I bet they are," Nash said as the limo rolled out of the parking lot. There were no more pre-party visits to make now. It was back to the expressway—next stop, Gangland.

CHAPTER 34

This time we didn't enter the same way as before. I suspected this was because Nash didn't want anyone to catch an early glimpse of his pick in the ugly-stripper contest. Instead, we went in through what was originally the front door of the warehouse and directly to an office that was outfitted with all sorts of dark, polished furniture, probably castoffs from one of Rowan's dad's swanky offices.

This place also had framed posters of gangsters on the walls along with a glass case exhibiting what might have been an authentic old-fashioned tommy-gun-style machine gun. Or maybe it was just a squirt gun that looked real—I didn't ask. Nash sat behind the big desk and broke out the sack he'd scored from D-Stack. Inside was a very large plastic bag of weed. He poked his nose inside and goes, "Mmmm—that's the stuff."

Surveying the room, Tangerine's like, "You guys have more money than you know what to do with, don't you?"

And Brett goes, "That's not true. We know what to do with it."

Nash loaded a pipe with weed and offered it to me. I declined—I already felt queasy from my one glass of champagne—but Tangerine took a hit, inhaling so deeply her face turned a darker shade of pink than her wig.

"You got anything around here to eat?" she said after exhaling a plume of smoke.

"We'll get you something to eat later," Nash told her. "Here, have some more champagne." He handed the nearly empty bottle to her. Then he and Brett traded hits off the pipe.

After they were all good and loaded, Nash said he had a little business to transact, and he and Brett headed for the door. "You two stay here for right now," he said. Then he walked back to me. "Here, I want you to hold on to something for me." He pulled out his wallet and handed me a hundred-dollar bill.

I'm like, "What's this for?"

And he goes, "I might need your help with something."

"Like what?" I asked, staring at the money. I'd never held a hundred dollars all in one bill before.

"Don't worry. We'll be right back," he said, and he and Brett left.

Tangerine wrestled her way up into a chair, which was no easy feat considering the champagne bottle tucked under one of her arms. She took a swig and goes, "So what are you in for?" Like we were in jail or something.

"What are you talking about?"

"I mean, what did they hire you to do tonight?"

"They didn't hire me. We're friends. We're just hanging out."

"*Right*," she said. "Then what did he give you the money for?"

"I don't know." I looked at the bill again. "Probably part of some game they have going on tonight."

"Yeah, rich uppity-ups and their games." She pulled a pack of cigarettes from her bag and lit one. "What's your real name? I know it's not Nitro."

I told her, and she's like, "My real name's Melody. You

know how I knew you weren't rich like the other two? Because in the limo they were just kind of melting into the seats, just as comfortable as could be, but you looked like you were sitting on a block of ice. It was obvious you'd never been in a limo before."

"Have you?"

"Once." She blew out a cloud of smoke. "But don't get me started on that. Uppity-ups are crazy. That's all I'm going to say. They're warped. I'll work with them if I have to, but I'd rather hang out with the girls at the V anytime. I liked you right off, though."

The *V,* I guessed, was the Virgo Club.

"Thanks," I said. "I liked you too."

"You just need to quit trying so hard to get them others to like you, that's all. You know my friend Tanya had her baby tooken away? Well, she did. Little Serenity Ann. The Human Services people got her. Now there's this old uppity-up couple wants her. They think they can just pluck her away like she's a berry growing on a bush."

"That's terrible," I said. "Is Tanya one of the strippers you work with?"

Her face puckered at that. "We're not strippers," she said. "We're exotic dancers. It's an art form, you know."

"Oh, sorry. I'm sure it is."

"Anyway," she said, "I don't like games. I like things straightforward. Like tonight—I told that T-Bone character how much I'd charge and how long I'd stay and what I'd do. I dance, and that's that. Nothing more. Rick up at the V knows where I am. All the girls know where I am. There better not be any funny business. Uppity-ups like games, though. That's all they know."

"But I guess sometimes you have to figure out how to play the game," I suggested.

"I ain't into those games," she said. "Give me the girls at the V."

At that point, Nash showed back up and asked us to come with him. We ended up in the same dark corridor I'd investigated my first time at Gangland, and he told Melody to wait in the dressing room. She wasn't too happy about having to wait there instead of the plush office, but Nash assured her it wouldn't be for long. To me he goes, "Come on, Dylan, let's roll. The real show is almost ready to start."

The warehouse was full of the same crowd as last time, but now the musical act was, of all things, a guy with an acoustic guitar, a guy on accordion, and a girl on trombone. Playing emo. Actually, they could really play, but who wants to listen to that combination?

"Did you line up this act?" I asked Nash.

"Not a chance. They have too much talent."

Brett was hanging toward the back of the room with Aisling and Holt and a couple others I didn't know. We joined them, and I figured this was as good a time as any to bring up Trix and her dad.

"So," I said, "I noticed there hasn't been anything in the news about Trix Westwood's dad getting arrested or even being a person of interest."

Brett's like, "Wow, Dylan, do you always have to talk about that?"

"What do you mean?" I said. "I figured you'd want to talk about it. Ashton was your friend."

"All the more reason for us to just want to get away from it sometimes," Aisling said.

"Yeah, Dylan," Nash said. "Loosen up. We can talk about that stuff later. Anyway, you know how the police work—they have to have a mountain of evidence before they can arrest someone like Mr. Westwood."

I'm like, *That's fine for you to say, but your best friend isn't hanging around with a potential serial killer.* I didn't say it out loud, though. Pressing things wasn't likely to do any good with these people.

Ten o'clock came, and the band kept playing. That was strange. I figured at ten something big would happen—maybe Lady Gaga would burst onto the stage, or the floor would roll back and underneath there'd be a swimming pool filled with champagne. Instead, the only difference was that a crowd began to gather around a table on the west side of the room. I asked Nash what was up, and he told me to come with him and he'd show me.

On the fringe of the crowd, I couldn't really tell what was going on, but I caught a glimpse of Tres sitting behind the table with his laptop open in front of him. Someone handed him some cash, and he stowed it in a metal box next to the laptop.

"You have that hundred I gave you?" Nash asked me.

I patted my pants pocket. "Right here."

"Excellent. This is your chance to parlay a little extra cash for yourself. Sound good?"

"Uh, sure. I can always use some extra cash. But how?"

"Simple. You use the hundred I slipped you to make a bet, and if you win, you roll that over on the next bet. After that, you give me back my hundred and you leave here with a nice little wad."

"Yeah, but what am I betting on?"

"What are you betting on? You're betting on the midget, of course."

"You mean Melody?"

"Who?"

"Tangerine—her real name's Melody."

"Whatever. She's a sure thing. I mean, I haven't seen the other dancer, but how could she possibly beat a midget?"

"Little person," I said. "They don't like to be called midgets."

He laughed. "All right. Have it your way—*little person.* So are you betting?"

"Sure," I said. "What do I have to lose?"

"That's the spirit."

He pushed his way through the crowd, dragging me with him, and when we reached the table, Tres looked up at me and goes, "Ah, look who it is—the guy who's afraid of squirt guns." It probably took him all day to make that one up. "Do you have a bet?" he asked.

"Of course he does," Nash said. "A hundred on Tangerine."

I forked over the bill, and he stashed it in the metal box and made an entry in the computer. "How about you, Nash?" he asked, and Nash is like, "You know what my bet is—same as usual."

After that we nabbed a spot near the stage, and it wasn't much later that the band knocked off, only to be replaced by Rowan in a lemon-yellow blazer. He cranked up one of his long smarmy spiels—even using the term *feminine pulchritude* at one point—before finally cueing the music and announcing, "Let's hear a loud round of applause for the lovely, the talented Tangerine!"

One of those interchangeable dance anthems blasted from the speakers, and soon after, Melody strutted out in a hot-pink bikini. The crowd erupted in laughter, but that didn't faze her. She had a bit of a problem with the steps leading to the stage, but after that she really put on a show. The girl wasn't lying when she said she was an artist—she could really dance.

A lot of people kept laughing, but she still didn't give a crap. She didn't even look at the crowd—she stared over them. Then she march-danced to the edge of the stage and looked me straight in the eyes—I was the only one she ever looked at directly—and I gave her the thumbs-up. She smiled back, a cunning little smile that said, *You see the kind of people I'm dealing with here, don't you.* Then she whirled around and marched back to the middle of the stage.

As the song soared toward its big overblown ending, she dropped to her knees and whipped her head like wild. I half expected the pink wig to fly off, but luckily it never did. As the last notes crashed down, she popped up to her feet, threw back her head, and jammed a fist into the air. The crowd hooted and laughed, but that didn't matter. She knew she was good, and that's all she cared about.

After she left the stage, Rowan came back out, and I had to hand it to him—he didn't make any wisecracks about her. In fact, he seemed authentically impressed. "Now, that was something," he said into the mike. "I don't even think you asses can appreciate what you just saw. Nash, you screwed up your pick for this contest—she's way too good."

"Don't be bitter, Rowan," Nash called. "Just because your day is over doesn't mean it is for the rest of us."

"Ouch," Rowan said, holding one hand over his heart like Nash had just shot him. "It's funny how your friends will treat you at the first sign of a little trouble." He seemed different from usual. Maybe his dad's financial problems had knocked a little humility into him. But then the master-of-ceremonies smile came back, and he rattled off another long introduction, this time ending with, "Let's hear it for the sexy, the stylish, one-of-a-kind Miss Chastity!"

The thump of another dance song cranked, and out pranced this extremely bony and pale redhead with heavy eye shadow, a blue-and-red bikini, and—wait for it—a very obvious baby bump. There was no doubt about it—this girl was way pregnant. She looked like a drinking straw with a cherry caught in the middle.

Her reanimated-skeleton dancing style was nowhere in the same league with Melody's, but I'm sure it wasn't easy packing that belly around. The crowd didn't laugh at her the way they did Melody, though. They booed. Especially when she sort of creakily scrunched to the floor to do a spin on her back. I thought for a second she'd never be able to get back up. At the end, she grabbed at her lower back in pain and gasped for breath so hard you would've thought she was ready to have the baby right then. There was definitely no sense of triumph.

The crowd was still booing when Rowan took the stage. "Calm down, calm down," he said. "Just remember, this time I didn't have anything to do with either of these acts, so don't kill me over it."

Miss Chastity remained onstage, still trying to catch her breath, and Melody came back for the final vote. I hated this part. I just hoped the girls didn't know the vote was for *worst* dancer instead of best. Rowan singled out Miss Chastity first, and the crowd howled their opinions. Next came Melody, and the howls cranked to a whole new level. Sure, I bet on her and everything, but I still hated to see her win a contest like this. It didn't faze her, though. She just stared over the crowd like she could see the girls of the V in the distance giving her all their support.

Nash slapped me on the back. "See there, Dylan. You're already raking in the cash. Now let's go roll that over on the next wager."

"Uh, okay," I said, but I couldn't help looking back to see Melody struggling down the stairs and then making her way to the hall. *Whatever I made on this bet,* I thought, *I ought to give half of it to her.*

CHAPTER 35

I didn't even know what the next bet was about, so I just put my money on Nash's pick and waited to see what new weirdness came up. The lights brightened a little, and Rowan leaped off the stage and waved his hands to move the crowd away. Everyone knew exactly what to do—they huddled back into a large ring and started chanting, "Rumble, rumble, rumble!"

"That's right," Rowan said into the mike. "It's that time. We're gonna rock. We're gonna roll. We're gonna throw down a showdown. May the mighty survive and the weak slink back into the slime. Right here and right now we're gonna go for the glory. Don't you cry, little babies. It is time for the—fifteen-minute ruuuuuuummmmmmmble!"

The crowd cheered, and I leaned toward Nash and asked him what a fifteen-minute rumble was, but he just goes, "You'll see."

Rowan waved his hands to quiet the audience. "Okay, okay. All bets are closed. Let's do it to it." He glanced at a card he held in his hand. "First, from east Oklahoma City, the bad, banging brawler Markelle Thomas!"

Out of the darkened corridor jogged this wiry little African American dude with his hair knitted into cornrows and lightweight orange boxing gloves on his hands. When he got to the center of our human ring, he raised his hands and hopped around the way you see boxers do in the real ring, soaking in the cheers and the jeers. I was never a fan of watching fights. Who wants to pay to see someone get hurt? It seemed even more stupid to want to be one of the fighters. I figured, for Markelle, it was all about the money.

"Is this the guy I bet on?" I asked Nash, and he's like, "No way. You bet on the next guy."

"And our second fighter of the night," announced Rowan, "is that fiendish phenom, the Lilliputian powerhouse who has never lost a rumble at Gangland, the incredible Huy 'The Mangler' Pham!"

And sure enough, out of the hallway danced the very same Huy I'd met at the Vietnamese pool hall. That's why I'd seen him and his buddy Tommy walking into Gangland the first time I went there—Nash probably won so much money off them at pool they had to enter the rumble just to pay it back. But Tommy must have lost somewhere along the line because he was nowhere to be seen this time.

The two fighters settled into different sides of the ring while Rowan explained the rules: there would be one nonstop fifteen-minute round; fighters could use hands, feet, knees, elbows, and anything else on their bodies but no weapons; and barring a knockout, the winner would be chosen by the members of Gangland, which was pretty much the whole audience, except for me.

"Now, boys," Rowan continued, "come to the center of the ring and shake hands." They did it, and Rowan asked if they were ready. They nodded and stripped off their shirts. For little guys, they both had some pretty serious muscle definition. On

Rowan's signal, the audience started the backward countdown from ten. At zero, the fight was on.

Since Huy was Asian, I figured he'd come out with some flying karate kicks, but that didn't happen. Instead, both guys circled each other, looking for an opening to throw a punch. Markelle launched the first fist, but Huy dodged it easily. Speed was the key to his fighting style. Every time Markelle threw a punch, Huy practically seemed to vanish, then reappear on one side or the other and pepper Markelle with sharp blows to the cheek. Markelle had a hard head, though, and never got hurt so much as frustrated with Huy's elusiveness. The crowd booed. Apparently, they wanted to see more damage.

Finally, Markelle got tired of missing punches and tried to wrestle Huy down. Mistake. Huy dodged him again and Markelle crashed to the floor. Huy jumped on his back and jacked a few punches into the back of his head. I thought it was probably time to stop the fight, but the crowd had a different opinion. They cheered.

But Markelle wasn't done. He bucked Huy off, and they continued the match on their knees, punching and slapping and spitting. It was ridiculous. At this point, even I had to laugh. The crowd yelled, "Get up! Get up! Fight like men!" but it was too late. Rowan blew the whistle to end the rumble.

Since nobody got knocked out, Rowan called for a vote from the audience while both fighters stood there sweating and huffing for breath. It wasn't even close—Huy won again.

"Perfect," said Nash. "Let's go roll your money over on the next fight."

I wasn't so sure about that. I figured I should quit while I was ahead, but he argued that it would be bad manners to cash in early. That was a manners rule I'd never heard, but like I say,

I never was much of a gambler, so I went along to put down my bet.

"Dylan's going to double down on my man," Nash told Tres, and Tres goes, "That's what I'm talking about."

But I'm like, "Double down? I don't have any money to double down with."

"That's all right," Nash said. "Trust me. I haven't steered you wrong yet."

"Well, okay," I said. "But this is my last bet."

Rowan announced the next two fighters as Dancin' Dan and Robo-Troy. I'm like, *Dancin' Dan? Maybe I should introduce him to Rockin' Rhonda*. He was too young for her, though—a white dude with long stringy brown hair—while Robo-Troy was black and sported an Afro that could have housed several weapons if they'd been allowed. Both fighters were several inches taller than the last two but just as wiry. Stripped of their shirts, they looked like they could inflict some serious damage.

Like Markelle and Huy, they circled each other at first, but Robo-Troy was pretty quick to jump in and show how he got his nickname—his machine-like arms pumped quick, sharp punches past Dan's defenses, landing with loud thumps and drawing red splotches on Dan's face and shoulders.

On the other hand, Dan imagined he knew karate, but all his spinning kicks and roundhouses came off like magic tricks that didn't work. He was definitely no Walker, Texas Ranger. And his head didn't have the cinder-block quality of Markelle's. After ten minutes, blood flowed from his lips and nose. My stomach didn't feel so good. It must have been the combination of the blood, the champagne, and a bet that looked more and more lost with every blow.

Finally, Dan tried one too many flying kicks and ended up on his back with Robo-Troy on his chest cranking one robo-punch after another into what was left of his face. The crowd cheered. Not a single person showed pity on Dan. Robo-Troy had to do that himself. Before the finishing whistle blew, he stood, looked at Dan for a second, then stared into the crowd, disgusted. "I hope you got your money's worth," he said.

Dancin' Dan tried to get up but couldn't quite make it until Robo-Troy and Rowan helped him. His bloody face had the look of melted wax, his features smeared all over the place. "Woooo-hoooo!" he hollered. "Dancin' Dan is a bad, bad man. He stings like a butterfly—" He paused to spit a gob of blood on the floor. "And floats like a bee."

As Rowan and Robo-Troy helped him to the dressing room, I turned to Nash and go, "Someone needs to get that dude to a hospital."

"He'll be all right," Nash assured me. "Guys like that, you can't really hurt them."

"What do you mean?" I said. "Guys like what?"

"You know—the Dancin' Dans of the world." He shook his head. "It is too bad he lost, though. I could've sworn he'd be the one to finally beat Robo-Troy. But I guess you can't win all your bets, can you, Dylan?"

"Are you kidding me?" I said. "Robo-Troy's never been defeated, and you told me to double down on the other guy?"

Nash shrugged. "I thought he was a sure thing. But that's okay. I'm sure you'll be able to pay me back."

"Pay you back? I've got like seventeen dollars."

"Well, you're going to have to pay it back somehow. I mean, that's just the honorable thing to do, and I know you're an honorable guy. That's why I let you in on the after-ten-o'clock action."

"But you told me who to bet for. I wouldn't have bet on anything if it was just me."

"Wait a minute now. I didn't make you bet. I just advised you. If you didn't want to, you should've just said so. But now you owe me."

"That's not fair."

"Really? But it's fair that I'm out all that money? I don't see it that way."

I looked toward the door, thinking maybe I should make a run for it, but I knew I'd never get there. "How about this? Maybe I could pay you back a little at a time like a loan at a bank."

"But the thing is, I'm not a bank. I need to get paid back tonight."

"I told you I don't have that kind of money on me."

"Right. But there's something else you can do." He cocked an eyebrow and smiled. "There's one more fight tonight, the heavyweight bout, and let's face it, you're pretty much a heavyweight."

"Yeah, sure," I said, but I could see he wasn't joking.

"Look, the problem is, I don't have a heavyweight tonight, and I can't afford to forfeit. The competition is too close. So I figure you owe me this favor."

"But I can't fight anybody. I've never been in a fight." This was true. I'd never had any interest in fighting. Part of why I quit football in middle school was because I didn't like to hit people—that and all the exercising.

But Nash's like, "What do you mean? You got in a fight with that guy with the switchblade, and you came out of that all right."

Okay, maybe when I told Nash about Sideburns and his switchblade, I exaggerated my role in chasing him off, but that was no reason to get my butt pummeled tonight. So I'm like, "That was different. I didn't have a choice that night."

Nash's eyes narrowed. "I don't see that you have a choice tonight—except to pay me my money or do me this favor. Besides, it's only for fifteen minutes. What can happen in fifteen minutes?"

"What can happen in fifteen minutes? Did you just see Dancin' Dan's face?"

Nash smiled as if recalling a fond memory. "Okay, I'll make this deal with you. If things start getting out of control, I'll stop the fight. How about that?"

I glanced around the room. "Can I see who I'm supposed to fight first?"

"Sorry, that's against the rules. But think of it this way—all these pretty girls around here are going to see you standing up like a man. Even if you don't win, can you imagine how much sympathy you're going to get? You'll be a bigger part of Gangland than ever. Hey, Aisling Collins, I guarantee, is going to love you for it."

Aisling was standing next to the betting table. She caught me looking at her and smiled.

"I don't guess there's any way out of it," I said.

"That's my boy," Nash said. "I knew you'd come through."

CHAPTER 36

When Rowan returned from stowing Dancin' Dan in the dressing room, an oblong smear of blood decorated the front of his yellow blazer. Taking his place in the center of the warehouse, he pawed at the stain nervously like he was afraid it would crawl up and attack his jugular. The crowd gathered back into a ring, and he started his spiel, though his confidence seemed shaken by the disaster of Dancin' Dan's face.

"I'm glad to report that Dancin' Dan is fine," he offered. "We cleaned him up and gave him a six-pack of beer, so he's in good spirits."

The audience responded with the sort of lame applause you hear at golf tournaments.

"And now for what you've all been waiting for—the heavyweight match." Rowan pulled his note cards from his blazer pocket. "First, we have the big, the bruising, the large-and-in-charge man-beast from the Lower East—Nitro the Annihilator!"

At that, Nash shoved me forward into the ring. Rowan's eyes inflated with genuine surprise. "Wait, Nash, you can't be serious. This is your heavyweight?"

"The one and the only," said Nash happily.

"And you're okay with this?" Rowan asked me.

Of course, I wasn't okay with it. Far from it. If Rowan was worried about me fighting, I figured I should be about ten times more worried. And on top of that, I realized Nash had been setting me up all along. The note card with my name on it was the giveaway. Obviously, he gave the card to Rowan earlier in the evening—before I lost any money on bets. But what could I do? Whine about the unfairness of the situation? Everyone was staring at me, including a heavy dose of perfect girls. Quitting football had been easy. All I had to do was not show up for practice. But quitting this was impossible.

I nodded. "Let's get it over with."

The crowd cheered.

For a second, Rowan looked like he wanted to throw down his note cards and resign his membership in Gangland. But he didn't. Fumbling with the next card, he started the introduction. "Second up in the heavyweight bout, we have the dapper scrapper of the South Side, El Tigre Grande, El Matador, El Conquistador—Beto Hernandez!"

No, I told myself. *It can't be. It can't be the same guy.* But it was. Out of the dark corridor strode Hector Maldonado's cousin. The audience booed, and he lifted his black fedora and waved it at them. The image of Robo-Troy on top of Dancin' Dan flashed into my head. This wasn't going to be good.

Then Beto did something strange. He smiled at me and winked.

Nash led me to my side of the ring, and Rowan brought my boxing gloves. Rowan's like, "I don't know what you're up to, Nash, but this isn't funny. Bad karaoke is one thing, but this is out of hand."

"Hey," Nash said. "You're not giving my boy, Dylan,

212

enough credit. He's a hero." Then he turned to me and told me to take my shirt off.

Of course, I'm like, "No way." Taking my shirt off in public was pretty much at the top of my things-to-never-do list. I mean, I always cringed when I had to do it in gym class, and that was with just a bunch of sweaty guys around.

Nash wouldn't take no for an answer, though. It was part of the rules—you had to take your shirt off before they put the gloves on you. If I didn't take my shirt off, then both of us would have to fight bare-knuckle style, he said. I glanced at Beto. Suddenly, getting hit in the face with one of his naked fists knocked my anti-shirtless policy down to second place on the list of things to never do.

So I peeled off the Notorious B.I.G. T-shirt, and Nash and Rowan stuffed my hands into the boxing gloves. Nash took my glasses for safekeeping. Then they moved away and left me standing there in the harsh light with not even a hint of a tan and my belly sagging over the waist of my jeans. Somebody yelled, "Look at that sexy, sexy jelly belly!" And the laughter that followed didn't exactly bolster my confidence.

Rowan went over the rules again, and the whole time Beto stared at me. He seemed to be trying to communicate something through his eyes, but I couldn't figure out what it was. Then came the countdown, and at zero he stalked into the middle of the ring. I wasn't so eager to go there, but Nash gave me a shove to get me started. Keeping a wide distance between me and Beto, I circled to the right the way I saw the other fighters do, and he did the same.

The crowd booed. "Quit stalling!" somebody yelled, and Beto moved in closer.

His first punch came at me almost in slow motion, but I

still wasn't able to block it. His aim wasn't good, though, and his fist whooshed by my face, catching nothing but air. The same thing happened with the next two jabs, and I started to wonder if maybe he was missing on purpose.

"Come on, Nitro!" This time I recognized Brett's voice. "Show him what you can do!"

I had absolutely no idea what I could do, but I figured I ought to try something, so the next time Beto lunged at me, I took a wild swing. He blocked it easily and countered with a smack to my chest. It stung but not that bad. It reminded me of my short football career. Sure, I didn't like hitting people, but getting hit never hurt that much. *Maybe I have tough skin,* I thought. *Maybe I can actually get through this fight okay.*

Then Beto faked a high punch, and when I threw up my arms, he ducked and tackled me to the floor. My head hit pretty hard, and I was so stunned I couldn't keep him from wrestling me over onto my stomach and grinding my face into the concrete.

Expecting punches to start slamming into the back of my head, I gritted my teeth, but the punches didn't come. Instead, Beto pressed his mouth close to my ear and goes, "Don't worry. I won't hurt you. When I let you up, I'm going to cock back my right arm so you can see the punch coming, but I'll pull up short. You just act like I hit you and go down and don't get up. You got that?"

I nodded as much as I could considering the circumstances.

"Okay, I'm going to hit the floor next to your head two times, and then you act like you're throwing me off."

His fist pounded the floor next to my nose, and I lurched upward. He pretended to spill off to the side, and then we jumped to our feet and started circling each other again. My head was a little woozy from bouncing off the floor, but I concentrated on his right fist, preparing for the phony knockout blow. I didn't know why Beto would want to help me like this, but I was glad he did. I just hoped Nash and the rest of the audience would buy it.

Beto came at me, but his right fist never cocked, and instead he peppered my shoulders with a volley of lefts. The crowd wasn't happy. They kept calling out for more action. I threw a couple of punches, but again Beto blocked them easily. Unlike Huy, I didn't have speed on my side. Then Beto motioned with his head for me to come in closer. I did, and he started to set his right for the big punch. One problem—the floor was slick from my own sweat, and I slipped just as his fist launched, so instead of jerking back before he could hit me, I fell right into the punch. His fist crunched into my nose, and the next thing I knew I was lying facedown on the floor again, no faking to it.

I wasn't exactly knocked out. I could hear everything around me—jeers and laughter and boos—but it all sounded as if it came from far away. Nash's voice finally reached me, yelling at me to get up, and then other voices joined in the chant: "Get up! Get up! Get up!"

My brain heard the chant, but my arms and legs didn't. It was like they belonged to someone else, someone who was pissed at me for getting them into this situation. Then a collection of anonymous hands grabbed me around the biceps and rolled me over onto my back. Rowan and Beto leaned over me.

"Are you okay?" Rowan asked.

My mouth moved, but I'm pretty sure no real words came out.

They helped me to my feet, and my legs started to solidify under me while, at the same time, cursing me for weighing so much. A few people applauded, but more jeered as Rowan and Beto half dragged me back to the dressing room. Aisling Collins did *not* run up, throw her arms around me, and kiss me on the cheek for my bravery.

In the locker room, I sat on a bench while Rowan went for paper towels for my bloody nose, which felt like it weighed about sixty pounds all by itself.

"I'm sorry about that, man," Beto said. "You were supposed to pull back."

"Is it broken?" I asked, gingerly touching the bridge of my nose.

"I don't think so," he said. "You'll be okay."

"What happened?" It was Melody. She and Miss Chastity stared at me. The other fighters, including a puffy-faced Dancin' Dan, stood behind them.

"An accident," Beto told her.

"Some accident," she said.

Rowan came back with the paper towels and dabbed the blood away from my face. "Here," he said, giving me a towel. "Keep your head tilted back."

My mind was clear now, but my whole face hurt. Melody stood on the bench next to me and brushed my hair back from my forehead. "Stupid uppity-ups," she said. "You're better than them any day."

The bleeding had slowed to a trickle by the time Nash showed up and handed over my shirt and glasses. Brett and Aisling came with him. "I guess we're even," he said. "Let me get you a bottle of beer. That should help."

I took the towel away from my face. "I don't need anything from you."

And he goes, "What's the matter with you?"

216

"What's the matter with me? Are you kidding? You set me up. You had this whole thing planned all along."

And he's like, "How could I know it would end up like this? I thought you were supposed to be some kind of hard-boiled investigator guy, fighting off thugs with switchblades and everything. I didn't know you'd turn out to be such a wimp."

I looked at Brett. "And you—I'll bet you knew about this too. Both of you going around acting like you're my friends, but you're just a couple of phonies."

"Oh, come on," she said. "Are you telling me you didn't enjoy the steak and the limo ride?"

"Maybe I did, but that's when I thought we were friends. But we never were, not even for a second. All you are is a user. You might think that makes you better than us, but you're wrong."

"That's right," said Chastity. "You aren't any better than us."

"Oh, shut up," Nash told her. "You got paid."

"Don't tell her to shut up," said Dancin' Dan from over my shoulder. "She can talk anytime she wants to."

"Yeah," confirmed Robo-Troy. "Anytime she wants to."

"You suck," added Melody.

Nash backed up, obviously uncomfortable with the bristling attitude in the room. "Wow, talk about ingratitude," he said. "We didn't do anything but hire you out of the kindness of our hearts. And on top of that, do you know where this city would be without my dad and his business and all the jobs it provides? Right in the toilet."

"You know what?" Beto said. "We don't care who your dad is because he's probably a *pendejo* just like you."

"Just like you," Dancin' Dan agreed.

"Anyway," Beto went on. "I don't care about your daddy's

money. What'd you ever do but sit back and sponge off him? All you had to do was get born. That's no kind of accomplishment to brag about."

And Nash's like, "That's big talk coming from an illegal. You better make sure your papers are in order."

Beto didn't respond to him, though. "Put your shirt on, Dylan," he told me. "Let's get out of here."

"Wait for me," Melody said. "I've had enough of this scene for the night."

Dancin' Dan and Robo-Troy chimed in that they were ready to go too.

As we started out of the room, Nash is like, "Go on, slink out, Dylan. Go pretend you're somebody because you're nobody to any of us."

The words had barely dropped out of his mouth when Beto's fist launched. This time it didn't fly in slow motion either. It landed square against Nash's jaw, dropping him to the floor on his butt. The look on his face told me he'd never imagined a world where something like this could happen to someone like him.

"See you later, douche bag," said Melody as we walked around him.

In the main room, everyone stared at us. They didn't look the same as they had before. They were much smaller.

CHAPTER 37

Beto drove a sleek green lowrider with awesome chrome rims, which I decided was way cooler than any limo or Lexus or Mercedes. Melody rode up front with Beto, and I squeezed into the back with Robo-Troy and Dancin' Dan, who had already become the best of buddies despite their fifteen-minute rumble. In fact, we all became instant friends. When we got tired of talking about how funny it was to see Nash land on his butt, the conversation switched to how each of us ended up at Gangland in the first place.

Dancin' Dan's story was loaded with a bombshell. Originally, Nash hadn't wanted to hire him as a fighter at all. The two met through one of Dan's buddies, a guy named Dickie, who had rumbled for Nash before, also losing to Robo-Troy.

"That's kind of why I wanted to get in there and try to kick your ass," Dan told Troy, and Troy's like, "That's all right. I would've felt the same way."

"But the thing was," Dan continued, "at first he wasn't about fighting. He wanted me to do some burglaries for him."

I'm like, "Burglaries? No kidding?"

"That's right. He had him some floor plans and all kinds

of other information on these mansions he'd been to. He knew how to get in without setting off the alarm and where all the good stuff was to steal and everything. The deal was supposed to be he'd pay me, and I'd also get to keep everything I stole except for a few items he could use to prove to his friends he was in on it."

"That must've been one of his games," I said. "He figured he'd pull off a real crime instead of just this fake-gangster stuff."

"I don't know about that," Dan said. "It seemed real important to him. But I wasn't about to get involved in all that. Sure, me and Dickie done a couple burglaries when I was a kid, but I'm through with that kind of stuff."

And Troy goes, "How do you like that? Same thing happened to me."

It turned out Troy had been hired by Rowan toward the end of summer, but after the first two fights, Rowan approached him about robbing a pharmacy.

"Can you believe that?" Troy asked. "Like just because I'm black, I'm gonna knock over some pharmacy for his punk ass. He don't even know I'm only doing these fights so I can get some extra money and get back in the community college. But I pretended like I was all for doing a holdup if he'd drive, just to see how far he'd go. He kept putting it off until one night I tell him, 'Hey, bro, tonight's the night. We gotta hit that pharmacy, man.' It was just like I thought—he couldn't go through with it. I thought he was gonna start crying. Nothing but big talk, that's all he was."

Things started to come clear. The Gangland boys wanted to pull something big—an authentic crime they could brag about on Saturday night after ten o'clock, something that would push them into the all-time winner's circle of their pathetic competition. Sure, Rowan was too chicken to drive the getaway car, but maybe he thought he could still find someone who'd pull the deal off without him anywhere near it.

I asked Beto if Rowan wanted him to do a crime too, and he said no. "I never seen that dude before tonight," he said. "It was the little skinny one who hired me."

"Tres?" I asked.

"That's right—Tres. From what he told me, he just took over half that club. He didn't ask me to do no crime, though. He just wanted a fighter."

More ideas started clicking. Tres had a deeper stake in Gangland than I thought. Now somehow he'd managed to take over Rowan's half interest in the club. At least he hadn't tried to recruit Beto to do any dirty work besides fighting for him. Not yet anyway. That didn't mean he wasn't a creep. After all, he never tried to stop the fight between Beto and me. Only Rowan had that to his credit. Maybe Tres had his sights set on making himself the one and only godfather of Gangland, and Nash knew it all along. Now that I knew what a lying dog Nash was, I could see him snatching Ashton as a way to gain an advantage on Tres in the Gangland wars, and maybe Hector got in the way.

It sounded plausible, but who could I get to believe me?

Since I lived the furthest away, Beto dropped everyone else off first, and I told them all to Facebook me. In the Virgo Club parking lot, I opened the car door for Melody, and she told me to bend down. When I did, she said I looked great for having just been punched in the face, and then she gave me a kiss on the cheek.

"When you get old enough," she said, "come by the V. You can buy me a drink."

"You bet," I told her, but I hoped when I got old enough, she wouldn't be working at the V anymore.

As Beto and I cruised to my house, the streetlights shimmering on the green hood of the lowrider, I figured I ought to try to dig a little deeper into what he knew about things. There were just too many coincidences concerning him and Hector, Ashton Browning and Gangland.

"So," I said, "how did Tres happen to get in touch with you about fighting for him?"

Beto kept his eyes on the road. "He didn't get in touch with me. I got in touch with him."

"You got in touch with him?"

"Yeah, only he didn't know it. He thought he was doing it all."

"But why? What interest did you have in it?"

"I been wanting to get in that place for a while. That's why I called you that time. I heard you was involved. But you never called me back, so I had to go about it like this."

This was getting more interesting all the time, so I'm like, "Yeah, sorry I didn't call, but how did you know anything about me ever going to Gangland?"

Still staring at the road, he goes, "I got a friend who used to have something to do with that place—until things got too weird."

"Yeah? Who was it? One of the other fighters?"

"Nah. You don't know 'em."

"But you thought Gangland might have something to do with Hector's death, right?"

Now he looked at me. "What makes you say that?"

"Because the first time we met, you said something about the North Side Monarchs. And anyway, why else would you

222

want to go there? I don't peg you for someone who wants to make money by pummeling a guy."

"I don't know," he said. "You can never tell what people will do for money, man. But you're right. Hector went to that place at least once that I know of. I can't say which one hired him, but I think it was someone on the Monarchs' side. He didn't fight nobody, though. Hector never was much of a fighter, and besides, I talked to that Troy dude in the dressing room, and he said he never saw Hector do a rumble."

"But you think someone there was responsible for what happened to him?"

"Like I say, he wasn't no fighter, but he wasn't no druggie either."

"Did he need money for something?"

"He didn't need it, but he wanted it."

"Yeah," I said. "I can understand that. So what do you think happened?"

He scratched his chin. "I haven't figured that out yet, but I'm going to."

"So that's what you're interested in?" I asked. "Not the reward for finding Ashton Browning?"

"Hector was family. I don't let nobody mess with my family." He looked at me. "Or my friends."

"Thanks, Beto," I said. "That means a lot to me."

"That's okay. You're a good dude. I like how you never thought Hector OD'd himself. And it's cool how you been sticking with trying to find that rich girl. You and me got a lot in common—we don't let nothing get in our way when it comes to someone important to us. I gotta really give you props for coming out to fight like that. You got a lot of guts and a lot of loyalty. You're the kind of dude wants to help people. I like that."

223

"Yeah," I said. "I guess." I didn't let on that the reward was also pretty important.

When we finally reached my house, we shook hands before I got out of the car, and he goes, "You know you can call me if you need to. You still got my number?"

"Yeah, I still have it. Thanks. And thanks for not kicking my butt too bad tonight."

He smiled. "Anytime, man."

Since I'd blown the hell out of my curfew, I let myself into the house as quietly as I could. A monster flick played on the TV in the living room, where my dad snored away in the recliner. Mom must have gone to bed and left him on duty to wait up for me. If I was lucky, he'd fallen asleep early and would never know what time I got home.

First thing I did was go to the bathroom to check my battle scars. Besides my nose shining like a tomato, there wasn't a mark on me. I decided I did have a pretty hard head after all. If I could get my speed up, I might even make a decent fighter.

For appearances, I went back to the living room and scrunched down on the couch, where I could pretend I'd been since before curfew in case Dad or Mom woke up. It was weird how they hadn't seemed to notice how I'd grown up. That's why I couldn't tell them about all this Gangland stuff. They'd never understand in a million years.

Back when I was a kid, I pretty much told them everything, and they always came up with some way to try to fix things. What parents don't understand is that there comes a time when you don't want them to fix everything for you. You want to do it yourself. Otherwise, you don't have any mojo at all.

But as I sat looking at my dad in the TV glow, this warm

wave surged up inside me. I was glad he waited up for me—or tried to. I was glad he had his job teaching second grade and my mom had hers as a nurse. They didn't go around worrying about what anyone thought of how much money they had. They were the ones who really helped people. That's what they did with their lives. And that was another weird thing—for too long I'd forgotten how proud I was of them.

CHAPTER 38

When I woke up Sunday morning, the main thought that burned in my head was that I owed a big fat apology to Audrey and Trix. Obviously, the story about Trix and her dad was just another one of Nash's lies. I should have seen that before. If he'd been telling the truth, the newspapers would have been all over the story days ago. Trix was right—I'd been kidding myself that I could be a real friend of someone like Nash.

Now, as far as I was concerned, the lying scumbag topped my list of suspects in the Ashton Browning case.

That afternoon, I tried Audrey's cell phone but got no answer. Then I tried her mom and she told me Audrey went to see a movie with Trix. So I got my mom to drop me off at the theater. It was a gamble. If they didn't forgive me, I'd be stuck without a ride home until either my mom or dad could come get me.

The theater had a little juice and coffee shop inside, so I waited there for about thirty minutes until the movie let out. With probably about twenty different movies playing at different times, the theater's lobby always had a crowd, but Audrey and Trix weren't exactly ones to blend in. I spotted them right where I expected—at the rear of the latest pack to stroll into view. Audrey always liked to watch a movie until the last credit rolled.

I bushwhacked them before they got to the front door. Audrey's smile instantly drooped, and Trix's eyes popped so wide you would've thought I'd pulled a gun on her.

I'm like, "Hey, don't freak out. I'm here to apologize if you just give me a chance."

They traded looks and Trix goes, "Okay, I guess we can at least listen to what you have to say."

And Audrey's like, "But it better be good."

I led them to my table in the juice and coffee place, where the girl behind the counter looked at me like I was a loser for coming back instead of going to a movie. Audrey and Trix sat down and waited for me to start. I felt like I was on the witness stand and they were expecting a confession. This was no time for small talk or jokes, so I just launched into the apology.

"First of all, I'm sorry. You were right all along about Nash. I'm sorry for not trusting both of you. I was an idiot."

"Yes, you were," said Audrey. "But I guess I probably shouldn't have punched you in the stomach."

"Yeah, you shouldn't have." I shifted uncomfortably in my seat. "I didn't really deserve that because even though I was kind of an idiot, I wasn't a mean idiot. I didn't do anything out of hate or prejudice or anything. Sure, maybe I was a little jealous of you, Trix. After all, Audrey and I have been like the two musketeers for almost as long as I can remember. But that's not why I showed up at the park that night throwing those stupid accusations around."

"Then why did you do it, Dylan?" Trix asked.

"Because I was scared out of my head. I mean, someone just

told me my best friend was hanging out with a girl whose dad might be some kind of hideous serial killer. Do you know what will run through your mind at a time like that? I was flipping out. I had to do something. Okay, yes, I should've thought it over more first, but it was hard to stay cool."

Tears started to burn in my eyes, and I thought, *Oh, great, now I look like a big wimp,* but I was on a roll, so I kept going.

"Audrey, believe me, I want you to be happy. Never doubt that, okay? But if anything happened to you, like something bad—well, I don't know what I'd do."

Now we were all tearing up, Trix included, and Audrey's like, "I'm sorry too, Dylan. I know you were just trying to look out for me, and you hadn't even been around Trix enough to know what she's really like. And the truth is, I don't know what I'd do if anything happened to you either."

"You two can't let anything get between you." Trix patted us on the arms. "Your friendship's too important."

I guess we looked pretty pathetic, but I didn't care.

"It was so stupid of me to believe Nash," I said. "That guy's such a dick. He makes Rowan Adams look like the Dalai Lama."

"Well, at least you saw through him," Audrey said. "I should've known you'd get around to it."

"I don't deserve much credit for that," I admitted. "A sledgehammer pretty much had to pound it into me." I went on to explain the whole ugly Gangland night, including all the humiliating details.

When I was done, Audrey's like, "There was a dwarf stripper?"

And Trix goes, "Yeah, that's the part I was wondering about too."

228

"You're missing the point," I told them. "These Gangland idiots aren't just creeps. They're like real live criminals, and they'll use anybody to get what they want. I should've known Nash was lying about Tres saying your dad was some kind of molester serial killer. I mean, that's too far-fetched even for an episode of *Andromeda Man*."

"Wait a minute," Trix said. "Nash told you it was *Tres* who said that?"

"Yeah, I guess it sounded more believable that way."

Trix leaned forward. "Maybe Nash wasn't lying after all," she said. "Maybe Tres is the one who made that story up."

I'm like, "Tres? Why would he lie about something like that? I mean, it's his own sister who's missing. He wouldn't have any reason to invent a story that would probably just make it harder to find her."

"I'll tell you why he'd lie," Trix said. "Because he's a little pimple. And because, when I first got to Hollister, he was always bugging me to go out with him, probably because every girl who already knew him had turned him down. But when I wasn't interested, suddenly this rumor started going around school that I was having an affair with my English teacher, Mrs. Simpson."

Audrey looked at her. "You never told me about that."

Trix shrugged. "It's not something that's fun to talk about."

But I'm like, "You know what? This shines a whole new light on things. I just assumed Nash made that story up because he's such a phony liar—plus I never figured Tres would have enough imagination for something like that—but I'm starting to get a whole new picture of him, and it's a twisted one."

"Uh-oh," Audrey said. "I don't like that look on your face.

You're not thinking Tres was involved in his own sister's disappearance, are you?"

"Maybe," I said. "At least I've narrowed it down to two suspects. Of course, Nash is number one, but coming up hard on the outside is Tres Browning at number two."

CHAPTER 39

That evening after dinner, I hopped onto my bed with my laptop to see what research I could do on Nash and Tres, only to find they and pretty much the rest of the Ganglanders had unfriended me on Facebook. About the only one who hadn't was Rowan Adams.

Of course, I'd checked all his photos and posts plenty before, but now I was going over them to see if I could learn anything, not about him, but about my two top suspects. He still didn't have any pictures of himself with Ashton, but Nash showed up in a handful of older photos with her and quite a few without her. Before last Saturday, I would've admired the confidence Nash put on display in every scene. Now, though, I couldn't help wondering what scheme he had going on behind that big white smile.

Tres also appeared in a few pictures. The one that interested me most showed him and Rowan dressed up possibly for a night at Gangland. Rowan wore one of his gaudy blazers, and Tres wore a suede sport coat. The intriguing thing about it was—from the furniture, curtains, and wall hangings—I could tell they were in a girl's room. Most likely Ashton's. And most likely Ashton had taken the photo.

I studied the picture to see if I could get any new insights into her relationship with her brother. Her room was pretty orderly for a teenager's, but I wasn't sure that meant she was a neat freak or if she just had a maid. The more telling detail in the picture was Tres's phony smile. He didn't look happy at all. He looked more like a guy who was trying to pretend he hadn't just crapped his pants.

But what did that mean? Did he have issues with his sister? Or did he just hate having his picture taken with a guy like Rowan who outshone him in every way except for how much money their daddies had? To get an answer, I'd have to do something I really didn't feel comfortable with—I had to talk to Rowan personally.

I didn't have his phone number, so I sent him a message online giving him mine. Just to make sure he contacted me, I also thanked him for helping me Saturday night. It meant a lot to me, I said, made me see that he was probably the only one who had enough of a conscience to really care about whether Ashton came back or not. I didn't mention another thing I learned about him—that his smarmy vanity routine was more than likely just the act of a desperate character trying to save his place among all his using-user Hollister friends.

Still, the chances of him calling me seemed slim at best, and by the next afternoon when I got home from school, I was about to give up on it. That's when the phone rang. Rowan sounded different. The master-of-ceremonies shtick was gone. I told him I wanted to talk about Ashton, and he said he was out doing some errands and could swing by my house in thirty minutes. This wasn't what I expected. I really just wanted to talk to him on the phone—a face-to-face visit seemed like a serious infringement on whatever mojo I had—but since he made the offer, I said okay and gave him the directions to where I lived.

I didn't want to encourage him to hang around till my parents got home from work, but at the same time I didn't want to be a bad host, so I broke out the Dr Peppers and Chex Mix and laid them out on the kitchen table. Almost exactly thirty minutes after our phone call, the doorbell rang. No ironic blazer for Rowan this time. Instead, he wore a sweatshirt, jeans, and sneakers. He looked almost like a regular guy. Although I'll bet that sweatshirt cost three times as much as my Pink Floyd sweatshirt.

"Well," he said with a smile, "it seems like everything worked out after all."

"I guess," I said, assuming he meant that at least my nose wasn't broken.

In the kitchen we sat at opposite sides of the table. He looked around and goes, "So this is it—the abode of the master karaoke rapper."

"This is it," I said. "I'm sure it looks pretty small to you."

"No," he said, helping himself to a handful of Chex Mix. "I like it. It looks happy."

"I'm surprised you didn't unfriend me on Facebook like Nash and the others."

"They did that?" He shook his head. "Wow. They probably felt guilty about that fifteen-minute-rumble thing. Hey, I feel guilty about it, and I didn't even know Nash set you up for it. I promise—I didn't know a thing about that."

"Yeah," I said. "I doubt they felt guilty. It's more like they didn't have anything else to use me for."

Rowan leaned back in his chair. "You must have a pretty dim view of us. I can't say that I blame you. I'm not so happy with how things have turned out either."

He went on to talk about how Gangland had started as a lark, a way to make their senior year more interesting and fun.

Then the competition set in. "Don't get me wrong," he said. "I believe competition is a healthy thing, but it gets corrupt when people on top don't think they have anything to fear if they lose."

"It's not so great for the people they trick into doing their losing for them either."

"You're right, of course. It took me longer to see that. Or maybe it just took a little misfortune of my own to start caring about it."

"Yeah, I heard your dad's been having financial problems."

He smiled sadly. His Draco Malfoy qualities had lost their edge. "How news does get around. I suppose you also heard that I lost my stake in Gangland."

"There was some talk going around about that."

"It's the bitter truth." He took a sip of Dr Pepper. "You don't know how it is to walk down the hall at school and know people are looking at you thinking, *There's the guy whose dad's probably going to be filing for bankruptcy any day now.* That'll make you feel like a bottom-feeder very quickly."

"You might be surprised," I said. "I know the feeling all too well—in my own way."

He looked at me and nodded. "But that's also why I didn't know anything about Nash's plot to squeeze you into the rumble. No one tells me anything anymore. I've been relegated to master-of-ceremonies duties only. And I might not even have that if Tres wasn't such a boring inept speaker without an ounce of charisma."

"Yeah, I can't picture Tres trying to announce the rumbles."

"Hey, I wouldn't have thought he could do much of anything, but it turns out he's quite the little schemer. His dad's bank gobbled up several of my dad's properties for a song. You might think Tres would talk to him about at least letting us hang on to Gangland, but no. He's always wanted it. I guess he thought it might garner him some respect for a change. But the funny thing is everyone still thinks he's a little prick."

"Better than being a big prick like Nash," I said.

"I'm not sure about that. Nash, he doesn't know any better. I'm sure he thinks everyone just naturally wants to do fifteen-minute rumbles for him—or dance ridiculously or sing bad karaoke. In his mind, using people is his birthright. I should know—I thought the same way. Funny how getting hit in the face with a couple of disasters, like Ashton disappearing and this stupid financial situation my family's in, can change your mind."

He stared solemnly at the Dr Pepper can for a moment before going on. "But Tres? He never had any self-confidence. He's always been eclipsed by his sister. She was always such a supernova. I really did love her, I suppose. But you would think Tres was adopted from the way his parents treated him compared to her. It really has turned him into a snake. And snakes might be little, but they can be very poisonous."

"So," I said, "you think he might've manipulated his dad into taking over Gangland so he could grab a little of the spotlight?"

"Oh, I have no doubt of that. He probably played like he was all broken up over his sister and got his dad to give him Gangland out of guilt. But to tell you the truth, for a little while there, I wouldn't have been surprised if he hadn't done something to get her out of the way himself."

"You're kidding."

"No. But maybe it was just bitterness over losing Gangland. After all, Tres doesn't really have the intelligence to pull off something like that. Anyway, it doesn't matter now with the way things have turned out."

"What do you mean—the way what things have turned out?"

He cocked an eyebrow. "The fact that Ashton's been found, of course. What did you think I meant?"

At that, I almost swallowed a whole mouthful of Chex Mix. "They found Ashton? Are you for real? When did this happen?"

Now it was his turn to be surprised. "You mean you haven't heard this? It's been all over the news this afternoon. That's why I came over here. I thought you had something to tell me about it."

"No." I coughed a couple of times to clear my throat. "I called you last night. Nothing was on the news about it then."

"I know," he said. "But you being an investigative reporter, I thought you might've received a tip or something."

He went on to explain that the police had located her around noon today, and she was safe back at home with her family.

"Do they have any suspects?" I asked.

"Sure. They already made an arrest—the same guy who nearly broke your nose Saturday night—Alberto Hernandez."

CHAPTER 40

Rowan was right—the story was everywhere. The local and even the national news couldn't get enough of it, and over the next couple of days, I read and watched everything I could. Apparently, someone called the cops with an anonymous tip that led straight to Beto's South Side apartment, where they found Ashton handcuffed to the plumbing in the bathroom. She had a black eye, but otherwise she was okay. After a trip to the hospital for a checkup, she was now home recovering with her family.

So far the media hadn't been able to score even a half second's worth of video of Ashton. The Brownings and their lawyer kept her under wraps, but apparently she had identified Beto as her abductor.

As for Beto, he didn't have anyone to shield him from the press. His face looked out from the front pages of newspapers and websites from all over. TV news opened with his photo morning, noon, and evening. The cops arrested him at the body shop where he worked, and every TV station in town had a video of him in the police car and then as the cops dragged him from the car to the jailhouse.

On the way, reporters called out stupid questions like "Why

did you do it?" and "Are you guilty?" and "Why didn't you ask for a ransom?" He didn't try to cover his face the way so many sleazebags do on their way to jail. Instead, he stared straight ahead and kept his mouth zipped.

Ashton's parents didn't have much to say either, except for a brief quote from Mr. Browning: "We're glad to have our daughter back and hope that we will be left to heal in private as much as possible. We fully trust law enforcement to seek justice against the insidious criminal who could not conquer Ashton's spirit."

In all of this, nobody bothered to mention Hector Maldonado.

Sitting on Trix's fancy patio Thursday afternoon, I told her and Audrey and Randy how that bugged me. "Beto was all about finding out who killed Hector," I said. "He didn't care about kidnapping anyone."

Trix set her glass of Thai iced tea on the patio table. "Maybe he kidnapped Ashton as a way of getting revenge—or at least some information about what happened to Hector. Did you ever think of that?"

"Yeah, I thought of that," I said. "But it just doesn't go with what I know about Beto. It's not in his character. I mean, the dude didn't even want to hit me, and now he supposedly chained Ashton to a pipe and gave her a black eye? It doesn't make sense."

"Maybe not," Trix said. "But Ashton did give a statement to the police accusing him."

"I know. And that's weird. That makes things look bad. But maybe her parents forced her to say that to keep the cops from finding out what actually happened. What if Tres really was the one who nabbed her? They'd do anything to protect him. Or what if it was Nash? I'll bet his parents are tight with the Brownings. They probably figured Beto didn't matter.

They'd easily sacrifice him to save their golden boy's shining future."

"Well, it's in the hands of the police now," Audrey said. "Looks like you can turn in your private detective license, Dylan."

"No hundred grand either," added Randy.

But I'm like, "That's okay, I don't care. I owe Beto."

"But what can you do?" Audrey asked.

"I don't know. I'm still thinking."

We all picked up our glasses and took sips. That Thai iced tea was delicious.

"So," Randy said, looking at Audrey. "On a different topic—have you and Trix done the nasty yet?"

Audrey's mouth dropped open, but Trix just calmly goes, "Wouldn't you like to know."

"Yeah," Randy said. "As a matter of fact, I would. It's just natural curiosity."

Then Audrey's like, "You're such an ass, Randy. I ought to punch you right in the mouth."

In response, Randy ripped a fart worthy of a crosstown cabdriver.

"Wait a minute," I said. "I have an idea. We could pay a visit to Beto's grandma, maybe see if she knows of an alibi for him. After all, wouldn't it be more fun to see Tres or Nash go down for this thing than a guy like Beto?"

Audrey's like, "Give it a break, Andromeda Man."

But I wasn't about to let it go. "Think about it. I can't buy it that Beto had any kind of motive to kidnap Ashton—there wasn't even a ransom—but like Rowan said, Tres had plenty of reasons to get rid of his sister, mainly that she got all the attention."

"There's one problem with that," Trix said. "He didn't really get rid of her, and now she's getting more attention than ever."

"Okay, then," I said. "Let's look at Nash. He used to date her, and maybe their breakup didn't go as friendly as he makes out. He's probably had a grudge against her this whole time. Taking her would've given him all sorts of leverage at Gangland. And he definitely has a motive for setting up Beto to take the blame after Beto knocked him on his butt. Maybe he took her and said he'd kill her whole family if she tried to get away or rat him out."

"I don't see it," Trix said. "Sure, Nash is evil, but he's not cartoon-villain evil. Besides, where would your friend Hector Maldonado come into this?"

"He just got in the way. And if Nash knew she started dating Hector—this Hispanic dude whose dad's just a tile layer instead of a millionaire—that might've been too much for such an egomaniac."

"Come on," Audrey said. "Face it. The case is over. I know you wanted to solve it and get the reward and be a big deal and everything, but really there never was much of a chance of that happening. Just be happy with what you got—some good articles for the school paper. Now it's time to move on."

"Yeah," Randy said. "I don't see the point if there's not going to be any reward."

"But Beto didn't do this," I insisted. "I know him. He couldn't have done it."

"Do you?" Trix asked. "Do you really know him? You thought you knew Nash too, but look how that turned out."

I couldn't argue with that. Maybe you couldn't ever really know anyone, not deep down. Not what they were truly capable of.

"So that's it, huh?" I said. "It's all over?"

Audrey patted my arm. "Sorry," she said.

CHAPTER 41

The case wasn't the only thing that was over. It looked like my series of articles on Ashton was finished too. With all the news coverage everywhere you looked, what did I have to add? That is, unless I took a whole new direction and wrote about how Beto couldn't have really had anything to do with the kidnapping.

That idea excited me. I could go on a crusade. Save an innocent man. Up to now my motives for doing all this investigating weren't so stellar. Audrey was right—I wanted the reward, the fame, the mojo. I wanted to stop being Body Bag. I wanted a future where I wouldn't be just a speck of plankton whirling in the ocean. I never would've done anything to find out what really happened to Hector Maldonado because there wasn't anything like that in it for me. I could change that now, though.

The problem was, sitting in front of the computer, I knew I didn't have any real proof. I met Beto at Hector's funeral, then again at their grandmother's house, then again at Gangland, where he could've beat the hell out of me but didn't. None of that would get him off. In fact, the cops might even use it against him. No, I'd have to find out more about Beto before I could write anything that would help him.

Tattoo-head Oscar might be a good candidate to talk to, but I didn't know how to get hold of him or even what his and Beto's exact relationship was. Were they friends? Cousins? Brothers? I decided to call Beto's phone in case maybe his family had possession of it now, but nobody picked up. The phone was probably ringing and ringing somewhere in the police station where the cops stashed it along with everything else they had Beto empty from his pockets before throwing him in a cell.

All stalled out, I was sitting aimlessly looking over the different numbers I had stored in my phone when one jumped out at me—the number for Franklin Smiley. As Mr. Browning's private detective, he would no doubt want to make sure the police had the right guy—unless, of course, he was part of the conspiracy to put the blame on Beto. Even then, I might find out something useful by talking to him. Or I could also get myself into a whole lot of hot water.

I probably debated the issue for ten minutes before making my decision. There was nothing to do but jump in headfirst. I made the call, and he picked up on the third ring. I almost hung up, but of course, my name had already shown up on his caller ID.

"Well, well, Dylan Jones," he said. "To what do I owe this pleasure?"

At first, I couldn't get any words out, so he's like, "Come on, son, what's on your mind?"

"Um, you know how you told me to call you about anything I knew about Ashton Browning?"

"Yeah, I remember that. But you know that case has been solved, don't you? I believe there's been a story or two about it on the news."

After a couple of false starts, I finally got to the point that

242

I thought the cops made a mistake and arrested the wrong guy. Smiley reminded me that they'd found Ashton handcuffed in their suspect's bathroom and that she had identified Beto in her statement to the police, but I'm like, "I know, but that has to be some kind of frame-up."

"Oh, a *frame-up,* is it?" Smiley sounded amused. "I can tell you've been watching your detective shows on TV."

I disregarded that dig. "This isn't a joke," I said. "Beto's not the kind of guy who'd ever hit a girl, much less kidnap her and chain her up."

But Smiley's like, "So you call him *Beto,* do you? I didn't know you two were on such close terms. Maybe we should get together and talk about this."

"Look," I said. "I don't have a whole lot to go on. It's just a hunch. But I thought you and Mr. Browning would want to find out the truth."

"We do, we do. Mr. Browning would be very interested in that. That's why it'd be best for you to come over to his place, just like last time, for a chat." And then he sarcastically added, "You can even bring your *backup.*"

Of course, that was not what I wanted to do. "I don't really think it's necessary to get together, you know? I just wanted to give you a heads-up over the phone, maybe so you could investigate Beto—I mean *Alberto's*—background more. The cops aren't going to do it. All they see is a Mexican from the wrong side of town."

Smiley was quiet for a moment, then said, "Would it be easier for you if Mr. Browning and I came over to your place? Or just to keep things on the up-and-up, we could talk at the police station."

Now it was my turn to pause.

"Uh, no," I said. "That wouldn't be easier."

"Good, good," Smiley said. "How about this evening around seven? You know the way to the house. I'll meet you at the front gate. We'll have a nice chat. I'm sure I can help you get your friend off if he's really innocent."

He had me. No way did I want him coming to my house or, worse, getting the cops involved.

"Okay," I said. "But I can't stay long."

CHAPTER 42

My backup this time would have to be Audrey. Randy was working at the grocery store, and besides, I needed Audrey to drive. She wasn't exactly eager to go, but I explained how I just wanted to make my case in defense of Beto to someone who might actually be able to do something about it, and she decided if that's what I needed to get this whole ordeal out of my system, then she couldn't say no.

So there we were that evening right in the middle of Richville again. It's kind of weird riding in a Ford Focus through a neighborhood like that. You feel paranoid, as if the cops might pull you over for driving a car that isn't expensive enough.

"Wow," Audrey said. "Why does anyone need a house as big as these? I mean, like, what are all the extra rooms for? Just to prove you can have extra rooms?"

"Maybe they don't like to use the same bathroom twice in the same month," I suggested.

And she's like, "This is ridiculous. Twenty minutes south of here there are homeless missions with every bed full so they have to turn people away, and there must be a hundred empty rooms on this block alone. If this was France during the revolution, the guillotines would be pretty busy around here."

"Hey," I said. "Don't forget Trix doesn't live too far away."

"She's different."

"Why? Because you like her?"

"She doesn't care about this kind of stuff." Audrey sounded pissed at me for bringing Trix into the picture. "And besides, her house isn't near the size of these."

"Right," I said. "Her house could only fit three families in it."

Audrey glared at me. "I didn't have to take you out here, you know."

And I'm like, "I'm just saying—cutting people's heads off might be a little drastic."

"Maybe," Audrey said. "Just a little."

Finally, we made it to the Brownings' mansion gate, and Smiley was waiting there just as he said he'd be. He climbed into the backseat, and I introduced him to Audrey, and he's like, "Well, I see you made an improvement to your backup muscle."

We pulled back to the same place as last time, but when Smiley and I got out, Audrey stayed in the car. That was our plan—she'd wait outside with her cell phone ready in case I didn't come back safe and sound.

In the guesthouse, Mr. Browning was already waiting for us. Instead of sitting behind the bar like before, he sat, legs crossed, in a chair that, in a pinch, could've made do for a throne in one of those French palaces just before the heads started to roll.

He stood up to shake my hand and motioned for me to sit on the hard-cushioned sofa. Smiley sat in a chair across from me.

"First," Mr. Browning said, "I'd like to thank you again, Dylan, for the interest you've taken in helping to get my daughter back and, of course, for the positive articles you wrote about her in your school paper."

"That's okay," I said.

"But"—he brushed some invisible something from the knee of his expensive slacks—"I hear you're not completely satisfied with the outcome."

"He thinks it was a *frame-up*," Smiley said, but Mr. Browning's like, "Let's let Dylan do the talking for the moment, shall we?"

I shifted in my seat, but those sofa cushions were too hard to find any comfort on. There were a couple of things I still didn't want to let on about, so I just went with the vague stuff I'd already given to Smiley.

None of this had much of an effect on Mr. Browning. He was more interested in how I got to know Beto in the first place. This gave me a chance to make Beto seem more sympathetic. I explained how I met him at Hector Maldonado's funeral, making it sound like me and Hector were closer than we really were. Beto was really broken up over his cousin's death, I said, but I didn't mention how Hector died.

"And on top of that," I added, "there was this time he saved me from getting the hell beat out of me by this enormous dude with a huge tattoo on his scalp. That's what kind of a good guy Beto Hernandez is." No reason to bring up how this had happened next door to one of the houses on Ashton's FOKC route. Still, I noticed Smiley writing something down about it in a little notebook.

Mr. Browning rubbed his chin and goes, "I appreciate how that might make you feel obligated to Mr. Hernandez, but I'm afraid I'll have to take my daughter's word over your character reference. However, I would like to hear whatever else you might know about him."

His eyes narrowed, and across from me Smiley sat with his pen ready to take down what I might say next. It was clear to me now—they hadn't asked me over to find out how Beto might be innocent. All they wanted was extra evidence they could use to hang him with.

"Hey," I said. "If you want me to say something bad about Beto, you have the wrong guy. I'm on his side. But if you really want to find out what happened to Ashton, you need to take a close look at some of her Hollister friends. I think there's a good chance she's being coerced into accusing Beto. I mean, do you even know what goes on in their so-called rec hall?"

And Mr. Browning's like, "What are you talking about?"

"I'm talking about Gangland—you know, the place you ripped off from Rowan Adams's dad so your kid would have his own playpen? What do you think they're doing there on Saturday nights, drinking ginger ale and playing pin the tail on the donkey?"

You could tell Mr. Browning didn't expect a guy like me to talk to him like that, but he kept his cool. He goes, "I don't see what the social activities of my son and his friends have to do with any of this."

I hadn't meant to talk about Gangland, but I was pissed about how they were trying to trick me into screwing over Beto, so I kept going. "*Social activities?* Is that what you call it when your son and Nash Pierce go around hiring strippers to laugh at or guys to beat each other to bloody messes just for entertainment? They probably enjoy seeing a good guy like Beto thrown in jail for something he didn't do. Who knows—Tres and Nash might even be the ones who made Ashton give him up to the cops."

Mr. Browning stood up. "That's enough," he said. His face had gone red. No more Cool Mr. Rich Man for him. Strangely, though, Smiley seemed to be enjoying himself.

"I won't have you drag my son into this," Mr. Browning said, pacing in front of his chair. "He's been through enough."

Then Smiley goes, "If I could interrupt for a second, sir, I think it might be interesting to find out a little more about these purported fights." He looked at me. "Is it possible Alberto Hernandez was involved in one of them?"

"I don't know anything about that," I said, but I could tell Smiley didn't believe me.

Mr. Browning was too busy being pissed that I brought up his kid's bad behavior, though, so he goes, "Of course he doesn't know anything about it, because he's making it up." He walked over to where I sat and looked down on me. "What you need to tell us is how much you knew about Alberto Hernandez and his involvement with my daughter. When did he start seeing her? And when did you realize he wouldn't let her go?"

And Smiley's like, "Hold on, sir. I don't think we need to get into that."

It was too late, though. Big Daddy Browning had spilled something he didn't mean to—that he thought Ashton and Beto were an item. That seemed like as good a motive as any to railroad Beto off to prison.

I stared up at him, and one side of his mouth twitched with anger. He was so close I couldn't stand without my stomach brushing up against his, but I got up anyway.

"I don't have anything else to say." It was funny—I thought he'd be taller, but we were the same height. "You'd just twist what I said anyway."

Then I squeezed by him and headed for the door.

"You'll have plenty to say," he called after me, "when the police come to interview you about your involvement in this."

Without turning around, I'm like, "Well, you have my

249

address. Send them on. I'm sure they'll want to hear all about Gangland."

Practically my whole body was shaking when I stepped onto the front porch. I'd never been through something like that, and truthfully, if someone had told me I'd talk back to the big banker man the way I did, I wouldn't have believed them. But somewhere along the way you get tired of being bullied.

My mind was so wired as I passed the swimming pool, I didn't notice someone sitting in the dark on the far side, but I nearly jumped out of my shoes when a girl's voice called my name.

I'm like, "Who's there?"

The girl stood and walked into the light. "You are Dylan Jones, aren't you?"

"Yeah, that's me," I said.

She was wearing a white sweater, blue jeans, and sneakers, but what really stood out as she walked toward me was the stunning combination of black hair and blue eyes.

"Brett?" I said. "Brett Seagreaves?"

Then I realized I was wrong. I was staring straight at Ashton Browning. The sight of her made me feel like Chuck Norris just kicked me in the chest.

"Sorry," I said. "I didn't recognize you. You dyed your hair."

"It seemed like a good idea," she said, reaching up to touch her hair. "Too many pictures of me in the news. I thought it might buy a little privacy."

I'm like, "Uh, it looks good." After all the times I'd thought of meeting her face to face, I couldn't think of anything better to say.

Next to the swimming pool, we stood only a couple of feet

250

apart. The pool had finally been covered for the off-season. Ashton smiled shyly. An extra dab of makeup covered what was left of the bruise under her right eye, but none of the photos I'd seen of her had prepared me for how beautiful she was in person. I asked her how she knew who I was, and she explained her brother told her about me and how I tried to find her.

"He even gave me your articles for the school paper," she said. "It means a lot to know that someone cared so much. That's why, when I heard you were coming to visit my father, I had to talk to you."

Looking into those blue eyes, I could almost forget what had just happened inside the guesthouse. Almost.

"I'm glad that's how you feel," I told her. "But I don't think your dad agrees. I was just talking to him. You'd think he suspects me of being involved in what happened to you somehow."

And she goes, "Oh, don't let him scare you. I'm sure he doesn't really think that. He's just upset. We've all been through so much."

"I know. I can't even imagine the stress your family's been under." I looked across the covered swimming pool. "But I'm pretty confused about this whole thing with Beto Hernandez."

"Why? What did my father tell you?"

I looked back into her eyes and thought I caught a trace of worry, like maybe she was afraid of her father. "He didn't say a whole lot at first. But I think he ended up saying more than he wanted to."

"What do you mean?"

"I mean he mentioned something about you seeing Beto."

"Seeing?"

"I'm guessing he meant like romantically."

"And you don't believe that?"

251

"Not really. I was thinking more along the lines that you were actually involved with Hector Maldonado maybe."

I could tell she hadn't expected that name to come up.

"So you did know Hector," I said.

Nervously, she glanced over my shoulder. "I can't talk about that right now. My father might be coming back from the guesthouse soon."

"Just tell me real quick—what was going on?"

She backed away. "I will, but not now. Not here."

"Why not?"

"Too dangerous. You know that place Gangland, right?"

I nodded.

"Okay, meet me there tomorrow afternoon, say at four o'clock. It's closed then, but I can get my brother's key. We can talk without anyone else around."

"I don't know if I want to go there. Can't we meet somewhere else?"

She was getting more nervous. "No, that will be the best place. I can't be seen in public right now. It'll be safe—no one goes there in the daytime. Please, say you'll come."

I told her okay, and she started away but turned back, grabbed the front of my T-shirt, and kissed me on the cheek. "Thanks again for caring so much," she said, and then she dashed down the stone path into the dark.

CHAPTER 43

"You're not going to believe this," I told Audrey as soon as I scrunched down into the front seat of her car.

"Oh no," she said. "You think you have another clue."

And I'm like, "More than that."

As we drove away, I filled her in on what'd happened, starting with the prickly conversation with Mr. Browning. She had to admit she was pretty impressed with how I stood up to him, but she was more impressed by my surprise meeting with Ashton.

"Wow," she said. "You know what? I would never have thought it, but you might actually be on to something this time."

"Yeah, I'm sure I am. You should've seen her. She was definitely worried someone would see her talking to me, someone who is making her keep quiet about what really happened."

"Like her father?"

"Either him or Tres or both. I wouldn't be surprised one bit if Tres was the one who snatched her and her dad's the one who's making her put the finger on Beto. There's only one way to find out. I have to meet her at Gangland."

Audrey thought about that for a moment. "Well," she said finally, "you can't go by yourself. If her brother finds out, he might send Mr. Sideburns after you with his switchblade again."

"You're right," I said. "I hadn't thought of that."

By the time we got back to my house, we had a plan worked out: Randy and I would take Audrey's car to Gangland while Audrey and Trix waited for us down the block in Trix's BMW. As an extra precaution I'd call Audrey's phone just before going inside and leave the line open so she and Trix could hear what was going on. That way if anyone started pulling out switchblades, they could call the cops pronto.

The next afternoon, we got together with Trix and Randy and laid out our idea. Trix's like, "That is the coolest plan ever," but Randy didn't exactly agree.

"Let me get this straight," he said. "You wouldn't take me to Hollister with you in the hot chick's Mercedes. You didn't even bother to tell me you got invited back to Gangland that second time. But now when things might get all hairy, you want me to tag along and maybe take a switchblade in the ass? I don't think so."

He was right, of course. I'd let the glitter of Gangland mix me up. "I'm sorry about that," I said. "I really, truly am, dude. I forgot who my real people were for a second. And I wouldn't blame you if you didn't want to come along, but I need you. No one else but you could help us pull this off. Besides, think of it this way—we'll be like secret agents. Chicks love that."

He stroked his pseudo-mustache for a moment, then goes, "You're right, dude. Chicks *do* love that. I'm in."

"All right," I said. "Let's do it."

It was true—the plan was fabulous. It really was secret-agent-worthy. Still, when the time came to head to Gangland, my nerves twanged like an electric banjo. And not just because

254

of the potential for danger, but also because now I finally had my shot to show Ashton what I was worth.

As we drove, I kept checking the rearview mirror to make sure Audrey and Trix were behind us. Meanwhile Randy rattled on about how, if Sideburns showed up, one of us should hit him high while the other hit him low. This might've been a good idea except, as I remembered it, Randy hadn't been much help the last time Sideburns rolled into the picture.

When we got to Gangland, there was only one car parked by the loading-dock entrance, a white Porsche, which I assumed belonged to Ashton. While I called Audrey, Randy pulled down the sun visor to check his mustache in the mirror. It was no less scraggly than the last time we came to Gangland, but he was proud of it anyway.

On the phone, Audrey's like, "Okay, we're all set. Keep the line open."

"Roger that," I said. It seemed like the situation called for something official.

Figuring out where to stash the phone so she could hear what was going on presented a problem, though. I couldn't carry it, and I was afraid it might accidentally turn off if I put it in my pocket. I'd worn the porkpie, thinking I might lodge it under there, but it jostled around too much, so I ended up tucking it into my sock.

On the loading dock, I knocked on the metal door where we entered Gangland the first time we came. No answer. I tried the knob. It was unlocked, so Randy and I ambled right through. Inside, the place was so movie-theater dark it was hard to see. And without the crowd and lame music, the emptiness and silence of the place gave off more of a graveyard feel than a party atmosphere.

"Is anyone here?" I called, but still didn't get an answer.

We walked further in, and Randy goes, "Come out, come out, wherever you are."

There was actually an echo, it was so hollow in there.

"This is weird," I said. "We got here at almost exactly four o'clock."

We went across to the corridor, which was even darker than the main room, but a thin sliver of light shone from beneath the door at the far end. I bent down so my phone would pick up my whisper. "Okay, Audrey, I think she's in the office. Keep listening."

Just behind me, Randy goes, "All this dark is weirding me out."

"Yeah," I whispered. "I don't like it either."

Somewhere along the way, I knew we'd pass the dressing room where the bands, dancers, and fighters hung out while waiting to entertain the stupid Gangland members. This would be a good place for some paid long-sideburned skulker to lie in wait, ready to jump us from behind as we passed, so I ran my hand along the wall until I felt the opening of the doorway.

When I stopped to check it out, Randy rammed into me from behind, almost knocking me over. My phone fell out of my sock. I picked it up, but now I'd lost my connection to Audrey. I was just about to call her back when the door at the end of the hall opened.

"Is that you, Dylan?" All I could see was a black silhouette in the doorway, but it had to be Ashton.

"Uh, yeah," I said, tucking the phone into my pocket before I could finish dialing Audrey's number.

"What are you doing stumbling around in the dark?" she asked.

"I didn't know where the light switch was."

"Well, come down here so we can talk in the office."

She backed into the light. She was gorgeous in a white sleeveless top and black slacks. It was like those near-death stories you hear where there's a light with an angel in it waiting at the end of a dark tunnel.

As Randy and I walked into the office, she goes, "I thought you were coming alone."

And I'm like, "I would have, but you seemed so nervous last time we talked, I thought maybe you could use some extra help."

She smiled. "That's nice of you, but it really wasn't necessary."

"Don't worry about Randy," I said. "He's okay. He's been helping me search for you, so we're both on your side."

Randy walked over and shook her hand. "I met your dad," he said. "We talked a little bit about the banking business. I'm thinking about going into a career in that line."

She looked past him toward me. "I'm sure if you trust him, Dylan, then I can too. Why don't you have a seat? I'll fix you something to drink. Will diet soda be okay? I think that's the only thing in the fridge."

Of course, I'm not a fan of diet anything, but I said okay just to be sociable, and Randy, well, he'll take anything that's free. She fixed the drinks in whiskey-style glasses and talked about how good a writer she thought I was after reading my articles about her. She thought I really had a future in journalism. She even thought I should start my own blog.

She handed me and Randy our drinks and then sat behind the desk. After one sip, I remembered why I didn't like diet soda—the aftertaste was like liquid rubber.

Randy disagreed. "That hits the spot," he said. "You

wouldn't have a little rum I could splash in here, though, would you?"

"No, sorry," she replied. "I'm not really the partyer like some of my other friends you've met."

Randy's like, "Me either. I just like a little rum now and then. And a good cigar."

This, sadly, was what he thought would impress her.

"Look," I said, "I'm sure you didn't ask me here to talk about rum and cigars."

"No," she said. "Not exactly."

"You want to know what I think?" I asked.

"I'd love to."

"I think you couldn't talk last night because your dad is putting pressure on you to say what he wants you to say."

She shifted uneasily in her seat. "Why would you think that?"

I took another pull of my soda. "For one thing, because you got kind of panicky when I mentioned Hector Maldonado's name, and for another, because I don't think Beto Hernandez really kidnapped you."

"You don't?"

"It's that brother of yours," Randy said. "We think he's kind of a douche."

She's like, "What? Tres? Don't be ridiculous."

And I go, "What Randy's trying to say is that some things don't add up. For example, I got the idea your dad thinks you and Beto were, like, a couple until you wanted to break things off, and then he wouldn't let you go. I know Beto a little bit, and he just doesn't seem like that type. And I don't think he's *your* type either. No, I figure you'd be more likely to go for a guy like Hector."

"You think you know me well enough to say that?"

"I've done my research. You and Hector are both good people. Idealistic. Kind of like me. I can see the two of you hitting it off."

"But why would you think I even knew this Hector person?"

"Well, you obviously recognized his name. You probably met him while you were delivering meals to the Ockle ladies. Hector's grandmother lives right next door. It all fits—you broke up with Rowan right around the time you started at FOKC, and then not too long after that, Hector's dead and you vanished. Seems pretty likely somebody didn't like the idea of you and Hector together. At first, I thought it might be one of your exes—Rowan or Nash—but if it was either of them, you wouldn't have that good a reason to go along with the story about Beto, would you? Rowan's family doesn't have the status anymore to apply any pressure on your dad, and truthfully, your dad's probably not the type who would be pressured by Nash's family either, no matter how much money they have. No, I think your dad's private detective found out Tres had you locked up somewhere and then framed Beto to keep Tres from getting into trouble. Your dad can't have people knowing his own son killed Hector and then tried to get you out of the way because you knew about it."

"Yeah," added Randy for emphasis.

"You're wrong." Ashton shook her head. "Tres didn't have me locked up anywhere. I *was* with Beto. In fact, he took me with him to his grandmother's house the day you came by asking questions. That's why Oscar hit you. They didn't want you to find out I was in there."

That was a stunner. And cut a pretty big hole in my theory. "But what about Hector?" I asked. "Someone killed him, and I know for a fact Beto figured that someone was mixed up in

Gangland. So, yeah, maybe you were with Beto, but not involuntarily. He wouldn't take you to his grandmother's if he kidnapped you. No, he was helping you hide from whoever poisoned Hector."

Just then her phone rang, but she only glanced at it for a second, then muted the ringer. With a sigh, she looked up and goes, "Poor Hector." That was all for a moment, then she went on. "He had the loveliest brown eyes. So sweet. And ambitious in his own way. He really wanted to have a career doing something for his people. And not just Mexican Americans but working-class people everywhere. He loved that I worked with FOKC. You should've heard him talk about our future together. We were going to change the world."

Her voice trailed off, and I thought she might start crying.

"Hey," I said. "It's okay." I felt pretty proud of myself for finally getting to something that resembled the truth. "Whatever you're mixed up in, you can tell me about it. I'm just here to help you and Beto."

"I wish you could." Her voice was almost a whisper.

I started to tell her what I could do, but someone from behind interrupted me. "She doesn't have to tell you a single thing, *Nitro*."

It was Tres. He stood in the doorway wearing a black button-up shirt with a black-leather sport jacket. Like he thought he really was some kind of gang kingpin.

"Look, it's Casper the Friendly Ghost," said Randy.

And Ashton goes, "Tres, what are you doing here?"

"I'm just worried about my big sister." He sauntered into the room. "You know, Ash, you shouldn't really leave the house. The parents wouldn't condone that. Especially when it comes to meeting with these two dregs."

260

"Why's that?" I said. "Oh, wait. Let me tell you. It's because you're afraid your whole story's going to come unraveled, aren't you? Sure, maybe your sister was with Beto, but not because he kidnapped her. No, she stayed with him because she was afraid of you. You couldn't stand that she fell for this guy you saw as some kind of low-class loser, so you overdosed him with something. I don't know how, but you did. And she was afraid to tell Beto. After all, you're still her little brother. How am I doing so far?"

Tres scratched his cheek. He couldn't look me square in the eye, so he stared over my head. "To me, it sounds like something no one's going to believe. I wouldn't have to kill a kid like Hector to keep him from seeing my sister. I'd just pay him off."

"But Hector wouldn't take your money, would he?" I said. "He wasn't that kind of guy."

"Everybody's that kind of guy." Tres leaned against the wall. "In fact, I'll bet you're that kind of guy. Ordinarily, I wouldn't even bother with you and your little guesses about what happened, but I can't have you start throwing around Hector Maldonado's name in connection with this. Not that I had anything to do with him. You think I'd ever believe my sister would fall for a nobody like that? But at the same time I can't have his name out there. It just won't do."

He took out his wallet and started thumbing through the bills. "So let me tell you what kind of bargain I'm prepared to make. I have five hundred dollars here. I was going to let you have it all, but it looks like you'll have to split it with your friend with the pubic mustache."

Randy leaned forward in his seat. "Hey, buddy, don't dis the 'stache."

261

Tres disregarded that. "Two hundred and fifty apiece—that's still a lot of money for guys like you. All you have to do is keep your mouths shut about this Hector business, and you can walk out of here a couple of wealthy individuals, and everything will be all right."

"You have to be kidding," I said. "You think I'd sell Beto out?"

But Randy's like, "Wait a minute, Dylan. I could use two hundred and fifty dollars."

I glared at him. "No, Randy, we're not taking the money."

"Think about it," Tres urged. "You could buy all the stupid retro T-shirts you want. And your buddy—maybe he could get a date for a change."

"I bet I get more tail than you," Randy said.

And I'm like, "Forget it. As far as I'm concerned, your money's no good."

Tres snapped his wallet shut. "Too bad."

Then Ashton jumped into the discussion, pleading, "Dylan, you should really think about taking the money. I know how you feel about Beto. Believe me, I do. And I wish there was another way, but this is bigger than you."

Her blue eyes went watery, and I started to feel a little dizzy looking into them. But I couldn't do what she wanted. "I'm sorry, Ashton. Maybe a few weeks ago I would've just taken the money, but not now."

"That's okay," Tres said. "I have an alternative plan." He walked to the open doorway, leaned out, and called, "Hey, Dickie, get in here, will you?"

Dickie? The name sounded familiar, but with the way my mind was racing, I couldn't slow my thoughts down enough to grab hold of where I'd heard it before.

Then in through the doorway walked Sideburns himself, grinning maliciously. I bolted to my feet so fast my head went light. Randy stood up too. I didn't know if he was scared, but he was sweating so much you would've thought he just took a hot shower.

"You have your switchblade with you, Dickie?" Tres asked, and Dickie's like, "Sure do." He pulled the knife from his pocket and flicked out the blade.

Ashton got up and walked to the side of the desk. "No, Tres, you can't be serious." Then to me, "Dylan, you have to take the money. Please, take it."

"I can't," I said, but the words sounded weird coming out, like someone else was saying them.

Then Randy looked at Dickie and goes, "Are you one of those Wiccans? I heard they had a coven here. Is it true they know magic and stuff? I don't believe in the whole broomstick deal, but I figured maybe they made potions and charms, that kind of thing."

It was Randy's dumb-ass routine all over again.

"Shut up," Dickie told him. "Or I'm gonna work on you first."

Randy backed away, but his routine did buy me just enough time to catch hold of how I knew Dickie's name—Dancin' Dan mentioned it the night we drove home from Gangland. Dickie was the one who fought Robo-Troy before Dan.

Now Dickie stood right in front of me, swishing the knife blade in the air. "Here we are—you and me again. Looks like I'm gonna have to do that nose job on you after all."

"So, you're Dickie," I said.

His eyes narrowed. "Yeah, what of it?"

And I'm like, "Dan told me about you."

The knife stopped swishing. "You know Dan?"

"Do I know Dan? Are you kidding? Dan and I are tight. We fought in the rumbles on the same night. He told me all about you and Robo-Troy, said you came the closest of anyone in the history of the rumbles to beating Troy."

Dickie smiled. "Dan said that?"

"Sure."

"Well, I guess I done pretty good. A lot better than Dan, that's for sure. Old Dan sure got a faceful, didn't he?"

"Not as bad as me," I said. "I almost got my nose broken."

Dickie gave me a playful punch on the shoulder. "Well, how do you like that? You're buddies with Dan."

"Would you shut up," Tres ordered. "Forget whether he knew some stupid guy named Dan. We have a little persuading to do here, remember?"

Dickie glared at him. "Dan's not stupid. He's my main man."

"That's okay," Tres told him. "Marry him if you want to, but I'm the one who's paying you."

Dickie folded his knife shut. "I don't believe I like the way you're talking."

"Look," Tres said. "I have a hundred extra dollars here if you'll just forget about how I'm talking and get back to doing your job."

During this, my heart pounded so hard I thought it might crack a rib. You never know how you'll react in a situation like this, but I was beginning to think there was something more wrong with me than just stress. Randy didn't look so good either.

"I don't know," Dickie said. "If you got an extra hundred, I'll bet you got an extra two hundred."

Tres pulled out his wallet. "Okay, two hundred."

The switchblade flicked open again, and Dickie's like, "Or maybe I'll just take everything you got."

Tres reached into his jacket pocket and pulled out a black pistol. That's Oklahoma for you—even the rich kids are packing. But he wasn't exactly Mr. Cool about it. His hands shook so badly he fumbled the pistol and couldn't catch it before it clattered onto the floor.

Dickie's like, "Ha! Looks like I got the advantage in this deal here."

Tres looked panicked.

"Oh, for Christ's sake." Ashton strode around the desk. "Do I have to do everything?" She had a pistol of her own.

"Drop that knife," she ordered Dickie. "And get over there with those two idiots."

All in a moment her softness had hardened into steel. She pointed the gun with the barrel turned sideways the way gangbangers in movies do, which struck me as a kind of reverse pretentiousness.

As Tres plucked his pistol from the floor, Dickie warily followed Ashton's orders. Now the three of us stood with our backs to the desk, and Tres stood next to Ashton. She had all the beauty of a well-polished missile.

I'm like, "What's going on?"

"It really is too bad you had to know about Hector Maldonado," she said, her hard blue eyes fixed on me. "Things would've been so much easier if you had never found him in that Dumpster."

I tried to speak, but suddenly my mouth wouldn't work. My thoughts had sped to a blur. Then something strange happened—it was like a bottle rocket exploded in my mind. Everything around me glowed, especially Ashton.

My whirling thoughts lined up in order, and it was like I could turn them over one by one in rapid succession and inspect them from all sides. I knew what'd happened—the liquid-rubber aftertaste in my drink hadn't come from some diet sweetener. It came from the drug Ashton added. The same drug she killed Hector with. Of course. There was no doubt. But how long would it take to kill me?

"You expect me to believe you're gonna shoot us?" said Dickie. His voice rang like a gong. I felt like I could hear his whole life in it. "You don't have the guts."

She smiled. "You might ask your two compadres about that. I can see they're starting to feel the effects of the deadly little cocktail I mixed for them."

"I think I'm getting ready to puke," Randy said. "You'd better let me out of here."

"Sorry," she said. "You should know by now I was never going to let you out of here, not even if you took the payoff. I just had to buy enough time until I was sure the drug was working. And you know what the beauty of it is? It's not an illegal drug at all. They call it Dragon Ice. You can order it online. The company pretends it's a type of bath salt, but it gives off a lovely little semi-hallucinogenic buzz if you take the right amount. There's just one tiny problem—if you take too much, you die."

"Just like Hector did," I said. The words came out perfectly now as if my mouth was a mold forming them from silver. "You were just using him all along, weren't you? Making him think he was your boyfriend, making him deliver meals for FOKC with you. He was the one the Ockle ladies saw you with. But that whole charity thing was an act. You only did it so you could dig up some poor guy like Hector to drag to Gangland,

266

just like Nash did to me when he pretended to be my friend. Maybe you even wanted Hector to do some crime for you. Like rob a pharmacy. Rowan chickened out on that, so you dropped him and went looking for someone of your own to do it."

"So you know about Rowan and the pharmacy, do you?" With her free hand, she flicked her hair away from her face, and waves of color wafted from her fingertips. "He was always a bunch of flash and no substance. It was so ridiculous that his father owned Gangland and Rowan and Nash paraded around as godfathers. They thought they were quite the pair of rulers, but they were wrong. If you want to rule, you have to be ready to do anything. And I mean *anything*."

"I'm not kidding." Randy leaned over and clamped his hands to his knees. "I'm going to puke any second now."

I chuckled at that. Somehow, the idea of puking struck me as funny. I wondered if I might have to puke too. At the moment, it seemed like an interesting topic to explore, but I had to squeeze it out of my head and get back to the situation at hand.

I fixed my gaze on Ashton's eyes. The blue in them vibrated to the tinkle of invisible wind chimes. "You were just playing with people's lives, weren't you? Everybody was a chess piece that you moved where you wanted so you could beat Nash and Rowan."

She sneered. "They were small-time."

"Sure," I said. "Small-time. They only wanted to humiliate people and steal from them. They didn't have what it took to actually kill someone."

"Wait a minute," Tres cut in. His little turtle face appeared to be melting into his shirt collar. "We didn't set out to kill anybody. That was just a side effect of the plan. We were just about the pharmacy thing. That's all."

"Right," I said. "But Hector didn't want to go along with it, did he? He thought he was in love, but he was too honest to pull something like that, so you drugged him."

"Hey," said Ashton. "I just thought if I got him a little high, he'd loosen up and see we were just having fun. But he kept insisting he couldn't go through with any kind of robbery, even for me."

"Then you kept on dosing him with that Dragon Ice crap."

"Everything would've been all right if he'd just gone along with the plan," Ashton explained. "But he started freaking out, said he saw the devil in my eyes. It was pretty funny until he started turning blue. They really should include better instructions with that stuff. But when you're playing to win, sometimes you end up with a little collateral damage along the way."

"So this whole thing was just a game," I said.

She shrugged. "Isn't everything?"

"You're one cold bitch," Dickie told her.

Ashton laughed. It came out of her mouth in silver swirls. "Why am I a bitch?" she asked. "You wouldn't say that if I were a guy."

"No," Dickie said. "If you were a guy, I'd say you were a cold bastard."

I pressed my hand to the desktop to steady myself. "But why the phony kidnapping? Why drag Beto into it if you weren't trying to hide from Tres?" I didn't have to wait for the answer—it flashed in my mind like my own personal true-crime-show reenactment. "Oh, wait, I get it. Beto knew you were with Hector that night. He would've given you up to the cops if you didn't come up with some phony story—like that the North Side Monarchs had threatened Hector. And you probably threw in a few other suspects to confuse things. I can see it—you run into Beto's arms, sobbing, telling him he's got to hide you because whoever killed Hector would be after you next, and that's when the kidnapping plan kicked in. If you made people think Beto kidnapped you, you could probably blame him for Hector too."

"You know what?" Ashton smiled. "You're pretty good. You should take Dragon Ice more often. But sadly, you won't get the chance."

"What I don't get is why you stayed with Beto for so long. I would think even you wouldn't want to make your friends and your parents go through something like that."

She laughed. "Friends? Don't you know there's no such thing as real friends? There are only competitors. That was one of the funniest parts of it—fooling my so-called friends into thinking I had suddenly developed some kind of warm, fuzzy social conscience. And as for my parents—it was pure pleasure watching them come on the news and pretend they cared what happened to me. I mean, they don't even know who I am. One of their cars or paintings could've been stolen and they would've cared just as much. It was hilarious watching my father play the suffering parent who lost his golden girl. I figured I would hide out until he raised the reward to a half a million dollars or so. But did he ever do it? Not a chance."

"A half million?" Dickie interrupted. "And you were only gonna cut me in for ten grand?"

"So that's it." It took all my concentration to stay focused on what I needed to say. "Instead of robbing a pharmacy, you were going to rip off your own parents without even having to bother with a phony ransom. You'd just get someone to collect the reward and then pay them off. But you knew you couldn't get Beto to go in on that part. You had to recruit Dickie to pretend he found you, and you knew the cops would never believe Beto's story over yours."

"Beto had a terminal weakness—he wanted to help people." She sneered. "He wouldn't rest until he found out who slipped Hector the overdose. It was Hector this, Hector that. All the while I was in that cramped apartment or over at his ridiculous friend Oscar's or his stupid little grandmother's place. That's really why I dyed my hair black—so I wouldn't stand out too much around that filthy neighborhood. Still, I could've held out a little longer to see if the reward would go up, but you had to come along. You were a real pest. When Tres told me about Nash's plan to trick you into fighting in the rumbles, I thought, *Hey, we'll just get rid of you by having Beto beat your brains out.* Then he got back from Gangland that night and started going on about how you and he were big buddies now, and I knew it was only a matter of time before you found me."

I'm like, "Wow, you must be some kind of actress to fool all those people into thinking you were this fabulous, funny, heart-of-gold chick."

She smiled. "That's easy. People want to believe you're good—all you have to do is throw them a few scraps to confirm it."

Next to me, Randy started sobbing. "Why is the floor covered with water? There's too much water."

I patted him on the back. "There's no water, Randy. It's just your imagination. Hold on, buddy, you'll be all right."

That wasn't easy to believe, though. My body ached all over. My stomach began folding itself into little squares. The hallucinations multiplied. For a second, I could've sworn I glimpsed

Audrey in the hall behind Ashton and Tres, but she disappeared back into the liquid darkness.

"It won't take long now," Ashton guaranteed. "Hector thought he saw water everywhere too."

"What about me?" Dickie asked. "You think you're gonna make me take some of that Dragon whatever stuff you gave them? Because that ain't gonna happen."

"Now, now," Ashton said. "How could we make you take it? You're the one who gave the overdose to them."

"What? I didn't give them nothing."

"Yes, but that's how it's going to look to the police when we get done."

Just then Randy puked on the floor in a rolling brown wave, and Tres is like, "Dammit, can't you at least use the trash can?"

"Okay," I said. "That's it. We're leaving."

Ashton pointed her pistol directly at my face. "I wouldn't try it. That would be inconvenient."

"You can't stop all three of us," Dickie said.

"Oh, you don't think so?" She waved the gun in his direction. "Let me be clear—I'll gladly shoot you first if I have to. The shape these other two are in, even Tres can take care of them. The only problem we'll have then is figuring out which Dumpster to throw you in."

I stared at the black barrel of her pistol. The idea occurred to me that it might be made of licorice. All I had to do was take a bite out of it. But then a better idea hit me.

"You know what?" I said. "I don't even think you have real pistols. I know all about your Gangland squirt-gun wars. You're not fooling me. If Randy and I decide to leave, all you can do is shower us with Kool-Aid."

Ashton smirked. "Really? Do you want to try me?"

"Come on, you can still claim Hector's death was just an accident. You don't want real murders hanging over you." I took a step forward.

She cocked her head to the side. "Last warning."

I took another step, and she pulled the trigger. The gunshot banged so loud I swore I heard it with my kneecaps. A bullet dug into the floor just in front of me.

Her lips moved, but with the ringing in my ears I couldn't hear what she said. Randy crouched next to me, throwing up again. Tres grinned with satisfaction.

Then the image of Audrey flashed in the corridor again. But it was no hallucination. She blazed into the room like a comet with pigtails, crashing straight into Ashton's back. The gun flew into the air and the two of them hit the floor.

Tres's eyes popped wide. His hand trembled as he attempted to train the gun on the three of us in front of the desk. For a split second, I looked straight into the barrel, into that deep black hole, and then I screamed.

I screamed and it filled every inch of Gangland as I charged. The pistol fired, and for all I knew the bullet got me straight between the eyes. It didn't matter. I was on top of Tres, pinning his arms to the floor, looking into his eyes, the sounds of scuffling around us.

"Get off of me, you fat pig," he yelped, but I just kept staring into his eyes.

"You lose," I said.

And then my stomach came unfolded, and I puked and puked, in a dazzling display of yellow and gold, straight into his pale turtle face. Somewhere the Beatles were playing "Here Comes the Sun."

CHAPTER 44

But it wasn't "Here Comes the Sun." It was the wail of sirens. Shouts and the noise of stampeding feet battered the air. Trix's voice sounded like a trumpet. Colors whizzed everywhere. Then I was on my back, the light in the ceiling showering me with warmth. A huge face replaced the light, but I didn't recognize it. Jigsaw pieces of voices whirled around me. Then another strange face appeared. "Can you hear me?" said the face. "Can you hear me?"

Was that another Beatles song? I couldn't be sure.

Hands grabbed hold of me, and I lifted into the air. Everything swirled. Straps snapped across my chest and legs. Wheels whirred underneath whatever I was lying on. Staring up, I rolled into the darkness, and then the ceiling of Gangland's main room gazed at me in awe. Outside—blue sky shimmering. A shake and a clatter, and I lowered down the concrete steps, and people surrounded me.

"Open the ambulance door," someone shouted.

The image of my own funeral popped into my mind. The place was crowded, but it was too late for that to matter.

Then Audrey appeared, tears singing in her eyes. "You're going to be okay," she cried. "You're going to be okay."

273

I closed my eyes, held on to those words, and forgot all about measuring my life by how many people showed up for my death.

I woke up in a hospital bed the next day. Every muscle in my body ached. My stomach felt like a sumo wrestler had used it for a trampoline. For the first time since I had the flu in seventh grade, if someone had set a burger down in front of me I couldn't have taken a single bite, not even if it came from Topper's. There was a tube stuck to my arm dealing out saline solution. Flowers crowded the side of the room where the window let in the afternoon light.

A soft hand touched my forehead. It was my mother's.

"He's awake," she said, and then my dad appeared at her side.

"You had us scared there for a little while, Dylan," he said with a big grin.

My mouth was drier than the sun, but I still managed to form some words. "Did I get shot?"

"No, you didn't get shot," Mom said. "But you had some pretty bad stuff in you."

I remembered the drug—Dragon Ice. "That wasn't my fault," I explained. "I did *not* take any drugs. Not on purpose anyway. I swear. There was something in this diet soda I drank."

Mom patted my shoulder. "We know, Dylan. We know."

Dad goes, "That doesn't mean you're totally off the hook, young man."

But Mom's like, "Not now. We can talk about that later."

"How about Randy?" I asked. "Is he okay?"

Dad nodded. "He's okay. It was a close call for both of you."

"And Ashton Browning?"

Mom and Dad glanced at each other, then Dad goes, "Audrey got her whole confession recorded on her phone. Pretty smart girl."

And Mom's like, "You know what? It looks like you may have your biggest news story yet."

CHAPTER 45

Mom was right—my next article for the school paper was big. You might even say it was a corker. This time Ms. Jansen pretty much ran it as written, except for fixing some spelling and punctuation. But it wasn't the whole story. The district attorney banned me from telling that until the trial.

Of course, by the time the school paper came out, Audrey, Trix, Randy, and I had been all over the real news—photos and/or videos of me at the hospital, the four of us at a press conference, outside our high school, in front of Gangland with our arms looped around each other's shoulders. One photographer even got me to wear the old porkpie for a picture—it had a bullet hole through the crown.

Ashton and Tres were all over the news too. This time it was their turn to star in a video that showed them fighting through the mob of journalists on their way from the cop car to the jail while questions whizzed at them like fastballs. Ashton threw her hands in front of her face. Tres draped his black-leather sport coat over his head like a hood. They weren't in jail long, not with their daddy's money behind them.

But they would be someday. The DA pledged to try them as

adults so they wouldn't get away with nothing but a couple of years in juvie.

By the time my article came out in the school paper, I'll admit I was pretty famous, though that didn't stop us from throwing a celebration at Topper's later that afternoon. On the way to the front door, Audrey, Trix, and Randy walked in front of me so Rockin' Rhonda couldn't see what I was carrying. Ever since she busted her old stringless guitar over Dickie's shoulder blades, she'd had to make do with an imaginary one. But no more.

She was singing "Jailhouse Rock" when I walked around my crew and showed her what I had for her: a brand-new acoustic guitar. Well, it wasn't exactly *brand* new—I bought it at a secondhand store—but it did have all the strings intact and in tune.

"Lord, have mercy," she said as I laid it in her hands.

Then she started crying and I started crying and everybody started crying.

"You deserve a better one for what you did for me," I told her. "But this is all I could afford right now."

She whanged a good loud strum across the strings and started singing the chorus to "With a Little Help from My Friends."

I patted her shoulder. "We'll catch you with some change on the way out."

Inside, we took our regular booth, and Brenda brought the menus over. "You all order as much as you want," she said. "It's on the house."

I'm like, "For real?"

She grinned. "It's not all the time we get people off the news in here."

As she walked away, Randy goes, "Well, it's not a hundred grand, but I'll take it."

"Yeah," I said. "You'd probably drink another dose of Dragon Ice if it was free."

Randy ripped a high-pitched fart, which seeing as how we were in a restaurant was totally uncool.

Looking at the menu wasn't necessary. I knew a Number 11 was in my near future. Sure, I'd made up my mind to cut back on the burgers, get in better shape, but now wasn't the time for that—too much celebrating to be done.

There wasn't time to browse the menu anyway. This man and woman and their little boy recognized us from TV and came over to the table to offer their congratulations. The kid looked up at me and goes, "Is that the hat?" I was wearing the porkpie.

And I'm like, "It sure is."

"Can I touch it?" he asked, all wide-eyed.

"Sure."

I handed it to him, and he put his finger through the bullet hole. "Wow."

"I could get used to this celebrity treatment," Randy said after they left.

"It's okay," I said. "But it'd be better if I wasn't grounded on the weekends."

Trix's like, "You're kidding—you're still grounded?"

"Until next week. Unless your dad can get me off." Her dad was acting as our lawyer. It wasn't exactly his usual line, but I'll say this—the dude was good. He even handled some of the stuff with the press for us.

"Hey," Randy said. "I just hope he can get us some coin for telling our story when the trial's over."

And Audrey's like, "Yeah, Dylan, maybe you can go on one of those true-crime shows you always watch. They can get Jack Black to play you in the reenactments."

"He probably wants to sell the story to *Andromeda Man*," Randy said.

But I'm like, "Forget that. I'm writing my own book about it. And this time I'm going to tell everything just like I want to."

"Okay," said Trix. "But just make sure to describe me as a sultry beauty."

Randy suggested that when the money from my best seller started rolling in, I could finally buy myself that sweet '69 Mustang, while Trix thought I should go for a Jaguar.

"No," I said. "I'm over all that kind of thing. I just need something nice and dependable. Maybe I'll buy my parents' car. It worked well enough for them. Besides, whatever money I make, I'm splitting with you guys. It's only fair. We did it together."

At that Randy made another high-pitched noise, this time with his mouth. That, he explained, was him taking back his earlier fart.

Randy, I had to hand it to him—he definitely had his own kind of mojo. He always told you what he thought, talked back to anyone regardless of how big their muscles or bank accounts were, and wasn't scared to mix it up with every hot rich girl at Gangland. I used to think he was that way because he lacked any understanding of other people's opinions. Now I realized he simply liked what he liked, and if everybody else didn't agree, that was their loss.

"You know what, Randy?" I said. "None of this would've worked without you. I never even would've jumped in that

Dumpster with Hector if it wasn't for your loud mouth. You are a total champion, dude. And you were right—those snooty Gangland girls really missed out on a stellar opportunity with you."

"Oh God," Randy said, looking at Audrey. "He's getting sentimental." He turned back to me. "That still doesn't mean I'll go out on a date with you, Dylan."

Everyone laughed. I thought about coming back with a crack about his pseudo-mustache but decided against it this time.

Brenda came over to take our order, and when she left, we started in on how stupid it was that the lawyer for the Brownings kept coming on TV and blowing off about how Ashton and Tres were innocent and that it was all a mix-up.

"That's just what lawyers have to do," Trix said. "They have to lie. You should meet some of the hotshot creeps my dad deals with. If he told the truth about them, they'd all be in jail."

"Anyway, it doesn't matter what their lawyer says," Audrey reasoned. "I mean, we have the whole thing recorded, everything Ashton said."

Randy's like, "I can't believe you guys were hiding in the hall the whole time I was about to croak."

"Well, not the whole time," Audrey said. "We only went in after we saw Tres and his hired muscle show up."

"You still took your sweet time doing something," Randy told her.

"Yeah, well, I was trying not to get you guys shot. It was the luckiest thing ever that Tres missed Dylan at such close range. You know what? If he'd been aiming at your belly instead of your head, you wouldn't be sitting here getting ready to eat your Number 11 right now."

"But I loved how you threw up on him," Trix added. "That was the pièce de résistance."

"Glad I could oblige," I said.

We'd already talked this stuff over a hundred times, but it never got old.

Trix went over how furious Audrey looked when she first saw Ashton with the gun, and I imitated Randy's Wiccan speech and Randy explained how I got Dickie on our side.

"Yeah," I said. "I hope Dickie doesn't get into too much trouble, but he should've never hooked up with those idiots."

Then, across the restaurant, the front door opened and in walked Beto. He had his straw porkpie working, and I'll admit he pulled his off better than I ever did mine.

I waved him over. "Hey, Beto, glad you could make it."

After shaking hands with everyone, he pulled up a chair to the end of the booth. I'd talked to him on the phone a bunch, but this was the first time we all had a chance to get together at the same time since he got out of jail.

"It's great to have you here," I told him.

And he's like, "Oh, man, you don't know how good it is to be here."

Brenda showed up with a menu for him, and he went into how bad the jail food was, along with some of the other horrors of being locked up. But he didn't linger on that. Instead, he turned to how thankful he was for what we did to spring him.

"Dylan," he said, "I should've trusted you from the first, man. I should've told you about that girl. I can't believe I fell for all her lies."

I'm like, "Hey, she was a good actress. I fell for her crap too."

I already knew a lot of his story, but he explained to the others how he and Hector first met Ashton when they were visiting at their grandmother's place next to the Ockles'. She seemed cool, even knew some Spanish. He could tell Hector was falling for her right away. Then one night she showed up at Beto's door, crying, hysterical, saying someone killed Hector and they were after her too. So Beto told her she could lie low with him until they figured out who did it.

It was Ashton's idea to pull off the fake disappearance from the nature park. Looking back, Beto said, that was when he should've got suspicious. She had the plan all figured out in detail—making sure someone saw her leaving her car, planting the running shoe so searchers would find it, meeting Beto along the side of the road a mile from the park. It was pretty coldly calculated, not like something a girl who just lost her boyfriend would come up with.

Then she fed him phony clues about who killed Hector. Maybe it was someone from Hector's school or some South Side gang. Then she'd change and say she suspected her father or an old boyfriend or one of the Hollister gangs. She even pushed him to meet up with her brother and get himself invited to Gangland.

"She seemed so real," he said, bowing his head. "But now I can look back and see she was just using me, right down to the day she gave herself that black eye and handcuffed herself in my bathroom."

"Damn uppity-ups," I said. "You never can trust them."

When our food came, we let go of Ashton Browning and her wicked ways and turned to what we were going to do now. Beto said he was swearing off women for six months, but after that they better look out because he'd be back on the town. Randy said the women better look out right now because he was already on the town, and Audrey and Trix said they'd let those other women take care of themselves because they'd already found who they wanted. Me, I had my book to write, and if there were any ladies out there who didn't mind a writer who drove around in a used mom-and-dad car, then that'd be all right too.

The Number 11 never tasted better. I didn't leave a crumb on my plate. We kicked back, finished our drinks, told jokes, and laughed about things that wouldn't be funny if they weren't already over. Our group was just herding to the front door when who came in but Corman Rogers and his two black-clad best buddies, their silver chains jingling from their belt loops.

"Well, look who it is," said Corman. "It's Body Bag and the Body Baguettes."

Beto looked at me. "You want me to punch this dude?"

"No," I said. "Don't waste your energy."

"Hey," Corman said. "Do you think you're some kind of hero now? Because we sure don't."

I stopped and looked him in the eyes. "You know what, Corman? I'm not like you. I don't need somebody to tell me what I am."

His eyes darted back and forth as he tried to think of a response, but he came up empty.

"Yeah," I said. "That's what I thought."

Outside, the sky was a perfect blue, but the air was a little chilly for my new Andromeda Man T-shirt. We threw some change into Rockin' Rhonda's cup, and she nodded her appreciation.

"Keep on rockin', Rhonda," I said.

And as we headed toward the parking lot, she cranked up her new guitar and started her mighty wail. "Mr. Mojo risin'. Mr. Mojo risin', risin', risin', risin'."